MALICIOUS INTENT

A Sam Parker Mystery

Maria Pease
Sweet Pea Press 2005
www.sweetpeapress.biz

MALICIOUS INTENT

A Sam Parker Mystery

MARIA PEASE

Dedication

For my husband Scott, and my children,
Steven and Ali,
I love you with all my heart.

Steven, if you hadn't negotiated staying up that extra
half hour longer than Ali so successfully, this book
never would have happened!

Acknowledgements

Thank you to my friend and consultant on this book, James Stice, Director of Investigations for Blackhawk Investigations, located in Temecula, California.
To my editor Mary Linn Roby, you are amazing! Karen Hill, thank you for your final proof. I appreciate your time and commitment. It made all the difference.
I would also like to thank my family for their inspiration and support, but especially my sisters, Andrea Tomes, Lisa Beach and Deborah Brischler for their continued encouragement and unwavering confidence in me.
And Mom & Dad, thanks for everything!

Author's Apology

If things and places in Temecula or Coronado are not as you know them or remember them, I claim literary license. I hope that any liberties I have taken will be forgiven.

CHAPTER 1

Here I am, in a great little town called Temecula, also known as "Wine Country" because of the many fine wineries that are located here. Temecula is somewhere between Orange County and San Diego, California. Yes, I know what you're thinking, you didn't even think there was anything between Orange County and San Diego, and if there were, why would anyone want to live there? Well, I like it here. It is a growing city that still has the feel of a small town. Small towns appeal to me, they are cute and comfortable. Comfort, justice, and fairness are all important to me. My name is Samantha Parker, I like to be called Sam, and I am a paralegal of sorts. No, I never did want to be a lawyer. In fact, I really don't like lawyers, which makes working for them almost impossible, at least for me, since I seem to have a bit of trouble when it comes to holding my tongue.

Although I am technically a paralegal, I specialize in research and do a bit of snooping as well. Somehow, I seem to find myself in trouble on a regular basis, due, perhaps, to my intolerance for unfairness and injustice. Basically though, I just become too engrossed in things I have no business being involved in. In fact, I freely admit that I don't know my boundaries.

Monday morning. February 12. Another beautiful day in my little town, and the last thing I wanted to be doing was sitting inside at my desk, staring at my computer screen. I had received an odd visit late Friday afternoon from a dark haired stranger with a mustache and the most unbelievable crystal blue eyes I have ever seen.

He said his name was Ronald Gregory. Perhaps it was because of the way he had paused before introducing himself, or maybe it was how he looked at me. Whatever it was, I didn't believe him. He also said he was sure someone was after him but he wasn't sure why. I didn't believe that either, but when someone gives you a large envelope with twenty-five thousand dollars in cash in it, in return for vaguely outlined services of finding out who was following him and why, you don't argue, especially when your income, like mine, is less than regular.

After he left my office I put the cash in my safe, so I could take the weekend to sort things through without worrying too much about the money part of it. Now it was Monday and had I sorted things out? No. I couldn't get past the fact that none of this made any sense whatsoever. I'm just an overly curious paralegal for God's sake. Why me?

I wasn't sure where to start but I thought I'd better do something. I needed the money and as I mentioned, I do love to snoop. I sat there as I always do when I get a new file, head in my hands, eyes closed, thinking intently about a plan. Yeah right, a plan. Well, what better way to find out if someone was after "Ronald" than to follow him myself for a while?

Ronald had given me a bit of information about himself, his address, where he was working, what he did . . . a construction worker, and a hunky one at that. But that about covered it. There wasn't a long explanation of why he thought he was being followed and I appreciated not having to listen to a bunch of crap that would just confuse things. I really can't deal with people who bullshit. I guess that's because I'm from New York where people tell you exactly what they think, whether you want to hear it or not. This particular trait is one that happens to appeal to few people, but I don't concern myself with that; I've been there, and caring what other people think is too much work. It only took me twenty-seven years to figure that one out!

First off, I decided I'd better contact a private investigator friend of mine who, more than once, has come to my rescue when I found myself in over my head. Frank is a former policeman. His short haircut makes him look like a military officer, and he is built like a truck and quite intimidating at first glance. Actually, the real Frank is more fun loving than anything really, unless of course, you upset him, in which case he has a tendency to turn ugly. He has a great hearty laugh, prefers to wear blue jeans, and complains endlessly if he has to dress up for anything. He is also well into a third marriage that does not seem to be going well.

Frank and I are friends, and since we are both nosy, and can lie a blue streak to get the information we want, we understand each other pretty well. His work is much more interesting than mine, needless to say, but we often find ourselves trying to figure out why the people we come in contact with seem to be so universally stupid. We also both spend a good deal of time hoping someone finds themselves in trouble and calls us to get them out of it.

As I waited for Frank to call me back, I realized I had to get to the bank before my rent check bounced and I got another lecture from Mrs. Bennett, a well tanned old lady of about seventy-two, who has a permanent chip on her shoulder. Mrs. Bennett happens to own the house I live in, and ever since the passing of Mr. Bennett two years ago, she lives to tell me how inconsiderate and irresponsible I am which means that I avoid her at any cost, even when I'm in her good graces, which admittedly is not very often.

I was so focused on the impending lecture to come that the ringing of the telephone about knocked me off my chair. Obviously I've had too much coffee as usual.

"Hey, Sam, what's going on?"

"Hi, Frank, I'm glad you called. Listen, I've got a guy who dropped twenty-five thousand dollars in my lap in return for finding out who's following him."

"No one gives anyone that kind of money for a simple job like that, Sam," he told me. "Take my word for it, he's lying."

"Of course he's lying, that's why I called you, I figure with your demented mind and experience in police investigations you could tell me what this guy is about. Why give me twenty-five thousand dollars if he's lying? Is he setting me up?"

"Sammy, how do these people find you?"

"I'm just lucky I guess. So, where should I start?"

"You tell me. What's your first move?"

"Background check to see if anything he's told me so far is true. Then tail him for a while, and see where he hangs out."

"Call me if you need some assistance with this. You know my fee."

"Yeah, expensive. Bye, Frank."

As I hung up the phone, I thought maybe I should have asked Frank to help me out with this one, fee or not. But that would be too easy and I'm not known to take the easy route. Never have or I'd have some cushy, high-paying job in one of those high-rise stuffy law offices in San Diego, a thought that literally made me sick. No, I'd figure this one out on my own. I rarely know what the hell I'm doing when I start working on something new, but I have pretty good instincts, and I can always call on Frank if I need to. He loves this shit. After all, I do have twenty-five thousand dollars sitting in my safe.

I spent the next two hours searching the databases that I have come to know so well, and love or hate depending on whether or not I find what I am looking for. As I checked to see if Ronald Gregory has an insubordinate past, I saw that although it appeared that "Ronald" had used more than one nomenclature, the name he was currently appearing under was one he also used more than twenty years ago, while living in Arizona. Apparently he was attending the State University there when he had his first brush with the law while posing as a campus security guard in order to inspect the girl's dormitory during the evening hours. This seemed to me like a fairly harmless prank. What guys will do to meet girls is beyond the realm of even my imagination. But with my limited access I was unable to find anything else.

I started listing the names that my new friend had used over the years, hoping Frank still had friends at the department who owed him a favor. If I could get a full picture of this guy's activity, I might be able to start putting this puzzle together. Still, at the back of my mind I wondered where I fit into all this. If he really thought he was in danger, he could have gone to the police or contacted a licensed PI but he didn't, he had come to me and I wanted to know why.

Gathering together the file I had so far on Ronald, I headed out with the idea of stopping by the bank and then locating Ronald Gregory at his construction site although I knew I'd rather put sharp sticks in my eyes than sit in my car all day in pursuit of this guy. But before I tried to find Mr. Gregory, I decided to get his file to Frank to see if his guys could uncover anything else.

The bank was empty so I ran in and deposited the two hundred and fifty bucks I'd earned on the living trust I completed for a nice old couple who just moved into the area. The Casey's, Carol and Harold, are in their mid-sixties and great storytellers. I must have spent about five or six hours gathering the information to complete their trust, although to be honest, they don't own a whole lot. They seemed to want to chat about old times and although I had a lot on my plate, as usual, I was happy to listen.

They moved to California from Chicago, where, according to Carol, it was cold as hell in the winter, but to quote Harold, "We're not going to go to Florida and wait to die. We figured we'd come here and maybe be too busy golfing to worry about dying." They reminded me of a couple of kids the way they were always joking with each other. They even pulled out the photograph albums, to introduce me to the family. Okay, so maybe I do become too friendly with my clients but I have found, through experience, that people like to share information, and that information, after all, is how I get my snooping jobs. And besides, it's not like my social life is booming with excitement.

Once I was assured my rent check wouldn't bounce, I was off to the small office Frank shares with an investigator friend of his located on Front Street in Old Town Temecula, the cultural and historical part of the city that was brimming with history. As I pulled into the parking lot, I saw Chuck, Frank's friend, driving off. Chuck is a quiet guy who acts like a real private investigator is supposed to, very serious. I always pictured him saying, "Just the facts, ma'am, just the facts." He also makes me a little nervous. Probably because I've never seen him smile or heard him laugh. He's just too damn serious for my taste.

As I walked up the stairs to Frank's office, I realized it was almost noon. I'm not a big eater, and when I do eat, I'm pretty particular about what I eat. Most of my friends say that I am much too fussy. I say selective, which goes to show that it's all in how you look at it. I admit, when I think too much about how particular I am, I wonder how I survived this long without some wait person punching me out. Oh well, life is short and if I'm going to eat, I want it the way I want it!

I had just reached the top of the stairs and was about to open the door when it flew open and Susan, Frank's present wife, just about knocked me down on her way out. She was obviously upset and to be honest, I don't think she even saw me, but then who knows what was going on. I try to stay out of other people's love lives since my experience in that area is pretty limited. I have a boyfriend but it's as casual as it could be and still be considered a relationship. I'm not the dependent type and most guys, after a while, can't understand why I'm not bugging them about the "M" word. I like being able to do what I want when I want without asking permission. Selfish? Definitely. But who cares?

I waited while Susan jumped into her red bug and flew out of the lot, almost causing an accident as she took off going north on Front Street thinking that giving Frank a minute to calm down would be a smart move on my part.

"Hey," I said finally, giving him a heads up, "do you live in a barn? Your door is open."

He stood by the window, gazing out over the lot. His face reflected irritation and I knew I'd have to watch my step.

"I know you saw her, Sam," he said, flatly. "I was looking out the window, watching you come up the stairs when she decided I was more interested in what was outside than listening to her problems."

"And were you?" I asked him, as I gently played with my hair. Yeah, I know, but the timing just seemed right.

"As a matter of fact, I was," he admitted. "It's getting real old listening to her complain about what I'm doing wrong on a daily basis."

"So, what are you doing wrong?"

"Are you hungry?" he said, avoiding the question. "I need to get some lunch and have a cold beer."

"Where do you want to go?"

"Let's try The Bank, just in case we need to have a margarita chaser."

We walked down the street to The Bank, a popular Mexican restaurant. As we got closer, I could smell the tortillas and hear the Salsa music coming from inside. Even on a Monday, the atmosphere was festive. Just what Frank needed, I thought.

"So what's going on with you two?" I asked, as we took a table near the window.

"I don't know. We just can't communicate anymore."

"Frank, don't take offense to this, but do you even care?"

"I don't know," he admitted. "You'd think I'd have learned something after two divorces."

Not wanting to spend my afternoon as a marriage counselor, I decided to lighten things up a bit.

"I know what the real problem is."

"Well . . . let's hear it. I'm on the edge of my seat."

"You're secretly in love with me," I said, only half joking.

"So now that you know, what are we going to do about it?" he said, going along with the gag.

"Not a thing, Frank, not a thing."

He just stared at me with that big smile on his face, like he knew something that I didn't. I quickly took a sip of my beer. After sucking down a cold one, we decided to order.

Peter, our waiter, was a tall, very blonde, pale complexioned kid of about twenty-two who was wearing thick dark-rimmed glasses too big for his face which made him look to be the kind of nerd who would be more comfortable in a science lab or behind a computer than in a restaurant, taking orders. He gave us the spiel on the specials, none of which sounded special to me, and we ordered. As usual, Frank looked at me like I was crazy as I explained to Peter what I didn't want on my salad, after which we ordered a couple more Beck's.

I watched Peter as he left. He seemed oddly self-assured in a way that was almost defiant. Whatever the difference, it made me uncomfortable. As I looked back at Frank, he was staring at me the way he does when he wants information, personal information.

"What?" I said.

"You tell me," he said, raising an eyebrow. "What's going on with you?"

"What do you mean? My love life?"

"Do you have one these days?"

"Yeah, I'm still seeing Jack, you know, when we're not too busy."

"You mean, when you feel like it, right? Is he happy with that arrangement?"

"He's fine with it, and besides, if I spent more time with him, we wouldn't be able to keep up this steamy relationship we've got going."

"Stop teasing me, Sam."

I knew he really meant it but I just couldn't resist. I think deep down he enjoyed it too.

After lunch, Frank paid the check, despite my protests. Sure, I may go a bit too far asserting my independence, but you'd think he'd at least agree to split the check, after all, doesn't he recall a little thing called women's lib?

We walked leisurely back to Frank's office, discussing my next move as far as investigating Ronald. I gave him the little information I had and he said he would check it out and let me know if anything showed up, no charge. In the meantime, he made it clear that he didn't think I should follow my new client, money or no money, which of course, made me even more determined to get on Ron's tracks as soon as possible. Once back at my car, Frank made me promise I'd stay out of trouble. I reluctantly agreed. I knew in order to move forward I'd need some basic information, and took off to find out what Ronald was driving. I thought that if I got his license plate number, I might be able to gain access to Frank's computer and see what else comes up.

As I headed out to the construction site, I thought about what information I had so far, and realized it really wasn't much. I'd have to get something solid soon and I knew it might take a bit of game playing to get it. Lucky for me, I love games.

CHAPTER 2

Ronald had given me the name of a new housing development located about ten minutes from my home office as his current place of employment. I probably shouldn't have believed this, due to the fact that he had lied about his name or should I say names and the fact that my gut still told me he was lying about why he had hired me. However, for some reason I knew I'd find him there among the twenty or so other sweaty guys working on the framing, roofing and plumbing of those new dwellings. If nothing else, I'd enjoy searching for him among those muscular men in their tight T-shirts.

One thing that really irritated me about all the development is that all the houses look the same. As you drive down the street, it's like your watching a cartoon in which you see the same background over and over again. This can make looking for someone a bit difficult because when you get a description of the house they were last seen at, it doesn't mean much except that you could be watching the wrong house. I guess I should stop whining; at least we have nice weather most of the time.

I didn't want Ronald to see me snooping around so I drove my black Toyota Corolla up the hill to another home site, where, standing at the edge of an empty lot, I had a clear view of the workers below me. Since the area is full of beautiful mountain views, it was not unlikely that someone would be up here checking them out. As a matter of fact, there was a young couple walking around one of the lots, probably making plans for their new backyard. I tried to make it look as though I was doing some planning of my own, all the while sneaking glances at the workers below, searching desperately for Ronald.

It took me about five minutes to locate him, but there he was, hiking around the site, talking to all the other workers and pointing a lot. It occurred to me that he might be a supervisor of some sort which would help to explain where the money had come from. He was wearing a black T-shirt, blue jeans that fit perfectly, and black work boots. In fact, he looked so great from that angle that I found myself wondering about his personal life. He hadn't mentioned that he was afraid for anyone's safety, such as a wife or child, but he was too good looking not to have someone. Those beautiful crystal blue eyes had captivated me, and that was not an easy task, as any one of my former suitors would happily expound upon.

Clouds were gathering overhead, making it look much darker out than usual. This time of year is when we usually have our rain and although we haven't seen too much yet, our weatherman promised we would be having various rainstorms moving in over the next several weeks. Promises, promises.

I hadn't waited long enough to even find a decent radio station when a rusted out, light blue Dodge pickup truck pulled up to the sidewalk. The driver shouted out the window and Ronald hopped in. It took off down the street quicker than I had expected, so in order to keep up without getting too close, I decided to take a chance and cut through the neighborhood to catch up with them on the other side.

Bingo! When I had arrived at the light, there they were, waiting for the light to change on their side. I tried to get a good look at the driver, who appeared to be tall and thin, with dark-brown shoulder-length hair. As the light turned green and they pulled ahead and I made a note of the license plate number. I was glad that I could turn right on red because I was able to stay within one-car length of them without the worry of them making a quick turn and losing me. For someone who was willing to part with twenty-five thousand big ones because he was afraid someone was following him, Ron seemed strangely oblivious to the fact that I was on his tail.

As I followed them down Margarita Road going north, I realized the clouds were moving in steadily. Maybe the weatherman was right for a change, since it did look like a storm was approaching. I was hoping the rain wouldn't start for a while, it will definitely make it more difficult for me to follow Ronald and company, and I wasn't up to dealing with too many complications. I continued to follow the truck when it suddenly took a right into an apartment complex. They slowly followed the driveway around to the back, and stopped at Building D for a moment, before pulling into a parking place by the steps in front of the building. I moved cautiously into the complex and around the corner. Turning my car around, I backed into a parking place where I could easily see the truck just as Ronald and his buddy got out and headed toward the walkway.

As soon as they had disappeared into the apartment, I hurried over to hide behind a dirty green minivan parked across the parking lot. This was a vehicle that was involved in a lot of car pooling from what I could see. There were soda cans and McDonald's bags on the floor, French fries were everywhere and several of those cheap little toys that come with the kids' meals were on the seats. I often wonder how one can stand to get in a vehicle that is so disgusting, and not be bothered by it. Do you just stop noticing the mess? Are parents immune to it? Or do you just give up on trying to keep things in order? It's like when a kid has a nauseating runny nose and the only ones who don't notice it are the parents. This is why the whole marriage-and-kids thing is so unattractive to me. I just don't think I could handle being so unaware.

I had a perfect view of the stairs through the dirty windows, one of which had, "Wash Me" written on it, an understatement if ever there were one, but there were a couple of spots clean enough for me to see them go into the second door on the right. I walked around to the back of the building to observe if any windows were ajar. I didn't expect to see any open due to the cold weather, but you never know. As I moved around slowly I discovered I was right. No open windows.

Standing there in the cold, I decided to go back to my car, listen to the news for a while and make up my mind whether to wait for the group to come out. I didn't have much else planned for the night beyond putting on my most comfortable pajamas and cuddling up on my couch with my candles and fireplace lit, reading a good book, which, by the way is my favorite pastime. It was just about five-thirty now and with the impending storm, I couldn't think of anything I'd like better.

On my way back to the car, I heard someone behind me. Ignoring a flicker of fear, I whirled around and saw a couple of guys so close they were almost stepping on my heals.

"Hey, guys, what's up?" I said.

Just then, lights came on throughout the complex and suddenly, I could actually breathe again. This was when I noticed that one of them was my waiter, Peter, from lunch that afternoon at The Bank. The other kid was short, stocky and had dark hair and eyes. Unlike Peter, who looked so innocent, this one looked pretty tough. I don't think Peter recognized me, and I didn't say anything that would make him think he'd ever seen me before. I found it's best not to be remembered especially when you're snooping around.

"Not much." Peter's companion said, as they started up the same stairs Ronald and his buddy had gone up earlier. I sent them a nod as I watched them go into the same apartment. I couldn't believe it. Now I'd have to stay. This was getting interesting.

By the time I got back to my car, the rain was coming down so heavy that I could barely see through my windshield. I asked myself why it was that I was putting myself through this shit. Then I remembered. Twenty-five thousand dollars, that's why! I should just stop complaining and think about this case. I was very intrigued and although I was more confused than ever, I was loving it.

CHAPTER 3

I woke up to the early morning sun beaming through my car window. I was desperate for a cup of coffee and a shower, in that order. I hoped I hadn't missed anything, but if I had, C'est la vie. I looked through my purse for some breath mints, which I make a habit of carrying regularly, when I remember them, that is, and ended up chewing on almost the whole pack.

I felt restless and needed to stretch out and get some fresh air so I stepped out of my car and walked around a bit. As I looked out at the beautiful mountains, the colors seemed to jump out at me. The varying shades of purple, pink and orange were so soothing. The only sight more beautiful is the beach at sunset, and since I live an hour from the coast, I have learned to appreciate the views I do have.

I got back to my car in a hurry when I heard someone laugh and saw five guys walking down the steps of building D. I could see right away that it was Ronald, Peter, and the other two guys I had seen but at this point could not identify, and another guy whose hair looked like he'd put his finger in an electric socket and decided to go with the look. He also wore black clothes and the kind of dark glasses that gave you the feeling he was not to be messed with. Ron and his friend got into a truck while Peter and the other two commandeered a shiny black Lexus with gold trim. I settled for taking down the license number, figuring that it was better to stick with Ron, who was, after all, the target of my investigation, such as it was.

As it turned out, they didn't go far, just across the freeway to Denny's, which occupied them long enough for me to go back and get the apartment number. It was, as it turned out, twenty-five, and although I knew I was taking a big risk, I turned the knob. Finding the door unlocked, I let myself in. Might as well take a quick look around while they soaked up the fat at Denny's. The apartment was unembellished. The curtains were made of a heavy material, like the ones in cheap motels, and opened wide to allow in the sunlight. The sliding glass door was open a tad and through it I could see a tiny balcony with one rusty lawn chair occupying most of the space. The living area, to the left featured a green-striped couch that looked almost new. Over it hung two pictures of horses, dogs and what appeared to be hunters. A long wood coffee table stood out in front of the couch and a beige armchair sat to the right with a tall black lamp between them.

An entertainment center stood on the wall directly across from the couch and contained a large TV and a stereo system. The room was also equipped with a small brick fireplace with a slender mantle, on which sat three purple votive candles and a yellow cigarette lighter.

The undersized kitchen was to the right and next to it stood a small, round, glass top table with a plant in the center of it, taking up the place that was supposed to be the dining area. Down the hall there was a bedroom on the left and a bathroom to the right. Straight ahead there was another door, this one closed. The apartment was clean. No dirty dishes in the sink or on the counter tops, nothing except car racing magazines and wooden coasters on the coffee table.

Voices from outside made my heart skip a beat and I moved to the slider to check it out. Just a couple of girls walking across the lot. I knew I didn't have much time but I wanted to see what was behind that door. That was when I noticed something sticking out from under the chair.

At first glance, it looked like the remote control but as I got closer I noticed it was a gun. Not wanting to touch anything, I used my sneaker to swipe it out. It was a small semiautomatic, which I carefully pushed back into place. With my heart pounding, I headed down the hall and opened the door.

The room looked like drug lab containing all types of drug paraphernalia including a couple different-sized scales, pipes and some other stuff I couldn't identify. My heart stopped when I heard a car door slam so I quickly closed the door and ran to the entryway. Stepping out of the apartment I closed the door behind me.

As I drove home, all I could think about was what I had found. I wasn't sure if these guys were drug dealers, thieves, or what, but it disturbed me. I almost wish I hadn't even gone in.

Later, as I gratefully sipped my first cup of coffee, all I could think about was this new twist. I was exhausted but my mind wouldn't stop working. Had Ronald known I was following him? If so, had the door been left unlocked on purpose? And if that was the case, how could he know I'd try the door and have the nerve to go in? I concluded that I was overtired and apparently it was affecting my ability to think rationally. Big surprise.

I knew I should call the police and report what I had found but I must admit, I was concerned that it might screw up my search for whatever it was I was looking for. Not that I knew exactly what that was.

What if I called the cops about a handgun and it was legally registered or disappeared before they got there? The drug paraphernalia could also disappear, so I had to be sure it would be worth it to call them. I hate the thought of looking like an idiot, especially as I knew it would probably mean charges would be brought against me for breaking and entering, definitely not something I was willing to risk, not without good cause anyway.

With all my questions, I knew I had to go back, so after a nap, I packed a small cooler and a thermos of hot coffee. As I opened the car door, I saw Mrs. Bennett snooping around by my side gate. I wanted to just ignore her and drive off but I could tell by her stiff jaw that she was disturbed with me, as usual.

"Samantha Parker," she snapped, "you must remember to bring in those garbage cans in a timely manner. I have been getting too many complaints about them sitting out for too long after pickup."

"You got it," I said, as cheerfully as possible, figuring if I mix it up with her I would never get out of here.

"Oh, and your gate should be closed at all times, as we agreed when you moved in."

"All right," I said, sliding into my car. "Whatever."

Probably, she missed Mr. Bennett because it was after his death that she became so harsh and cold. Not that she was the jovial loving type before, but, you could see by the way she looked at him that she had adored him. Kim believes that Mrs. Bennett is lonely and wants me to be her friend. Yeah, in my next life, maybe.

Once I got there I saw the heavyset man I had seen earlier, walking about on the balcony outside apartment twenty-five, talking with some urgency into a cell phone.

"Damn it, you had better be sure," I heard him say. "The last thing we need is to have them find out, so make sure

29

you do handle it." Folding the cell, he swore softly before retreating back inside.

I was relieved to get out of there unnoticed, having told myself it wouldn't be smart to try to get back in, at least not now. I bought it, hook, line and sinker.

I woke up early feeling quite refreshed. My coffee was brewing, due to the gift of a coffee machine with a timer on it that I gave myself for a valentine's gift, and the day was sunny. I decided I should start my day by getting out for a long bike ride. I have an eighteen-speed mountain bike that I have come to rely on as part of my almost daily workout routine. I also lift weights, run, and do my share of step aerobics, all with hopes that it is good for me as promised by the experts.

When I returned, I started thinking about what I have on my list of things to do today. I really wanted to goof off, but I knew I needed to get a hold of Ronald and see if I can get a rundown of his friends. I also have to remember to do some laundry or I'll be out of undies, a fate worse than death.

After my shower, I turned on the news as I do every morning, wondering why there is never any good news. Since Temecula didn't have local TV coverage, I got my news from a Los Angeles station that also reports on Riverside County. As I put on my makeup, I heard Laura Dietz talking about a robbery at the promenade mall in Temecula. Just hearing the word Temecula brought me out of my bathroom, brush in hand.

"Yesterday afternoon a man entered the Unique Jewelry Shop at the Promenade mall in the Temecula Valley," Kristy White, a perky, blonde field reporter, announced cheerfully. "He held up the owner, Margaret Wilson as she was working alone in the store. Mrs. Wilson was not injured but said that the robber had a gun and told her in no uncertain terms that if she even flinched he would shoot her. She explained that

30

she is not usually there alone but that her employee, Peter Manning, had left early due to illness. The robber got away with an assortment of diamonds and gold worth about one hundred fifty-thousand dollars."

As the reporter mentioned Mrs. Wilson, her picture appeared in the upper right corner of the television and I saw an Asian woman of about forty-two. Then the picture of Peter Manning followed.

I couldn't believe it was Peter. The waiter from The Bank and the guy that was hanging out with Ronald! What the hell was going on?

Pulling myself together I drove over to the construction site to see if Ronald had any information about this guy, Peter, who seemed to be popping up too often to ignore. As I arrived at the construction site, I heard all the usual sounds like sawing and hammering, along with the oh-so-familiar melody of Bruce Springsteen's "Born to Run" coming from a boom box.

A tall white man wearing blue jeans, a white T-shirt, work boots, and a baseball cap that was bright yellow and carried the logo of the Los Angeles Lakers on it was busy using a table saw by the side of the house.

"Can I help you ma'am?" he asked, putting down the saw.

"Yes, I'm looking for Ronald Gregory, is he here?"

"Who's asking, ma'am?" he said, in a thick, Southern accent.

"I'm Sam Parker and I'd really like to speak to him." I said, looking around.

"Well ma'am, he's not here today but I'm not sure why, let me go ask some of the guys if they know where he is."

"Hey guys! Hold on! Stop the hammering for a minute, will ya? Any one of you hear anything from Ron today or know where he is?"

I liked the way he walked as if his feet weighed a ton and it took every bit of strength to get them off the ground. He moved back to me shaking his head.

"None of the guys know anything."

I looked at him, thinking, no shit, Sherlock. I don't know any construction guys but I always had the impression that they are not the smartest bunch, although I know it's not completely true.

"Well, thanks for your time," I said, "if you hear from him, will you ask him to call me?"

I wondered if hearing from him and seeing him is considered the same thing to this guy, worried that they were not.

"Sure will," he said with enthusiasm. "I'll be sure to let him know you stopped by."

"What is your name?" I asked.

"I'm Jon James, nice to meet you." His hands were large and rough and he had a tight grip that just about crushed my fingers. I wasn't sure if he disliked me or didn't know his own strength.

I waved as I left and they all waved back. It was a bit freaky and I was eager to get out of there. It felt like I was in the twilight zone or something, they were so polite. Construction workers with manners? I don't think so.

When I passed by Frank's office, on my way home, I thought about stopping in to say hi but decided against it. He would have me singing like a canary about the information I have retrieved so far, which admittedly was not much and I wasn't ready to share what I had, not even with Frank.

The red light was flashing on my answering machine so I pressed the play button and sat down at my desk with a pen in hand. In order to keep track of my clients, I kept a log of my calls with some notes on the reason for the call as a quick reference, having discovered that by remembering them and their issue, they tend to feel more confident in my work and me. It is a practice that I have found to be very beneficial since I get many of my clients after they had first hired and fired someone else who couldn't remember them once their check cleared.

"You have seven messages," said my machine in that unpleasant monotone voice that I keep forgetting to have changed. There was nothing exciting until the fifth message.

"Sam, it's me, Ronald. I need to talk to you. I can't give you a number so sit tight and I'll call you back as soon as I can."

I rewound his message and listened to it again. He sounded so anxious and I knew something was wrong.

I tried to concentrate on my paperwork but just couldn't keep my mind off the sound of Ronald's voice. Up to now he hadn't called me at all, and now he sounded distressed. I had to speak with him. I needed some answers and waiting was definitely not one of my strong points. When the phone rang, I jumped to pick it up.

"Hi, it's me," Ron said in a low voice. "I need to see you. When can we meet? It should be someplace quiet"

"Go over to the Temeku Hills golf course and meet me in the club restaurant." I told him. "I'll be sitting in the back corner,"

"I'm leaving now," he said, and abruptly hung up.

Grabbing my jacket, purse, and a note pad, I headed for my car. It only took me about ten minutes to get to the club and I was relieved to see Ronald had not arrived yet. The club is a small, one-room restaurant with several round tables scattered throughout that overlook the golf course, which is usually quite busy, as it was today. As usual, the club itself was nearly empty. The golfers come in to grab a quick bite but don't hang out. I liked it here, the views are beautiful and watching the golfers do their stuff can be quite amusing. I don't get the attraction to the sport, although I admit, I've found it a bit more interesting since Tiger Woods has taken over the game. But still, it's a bunch of grown men and women hitting a small white ball into a small hole. Duh!

Sally, dressed in her usual uniform of khaki shorts and navy blue polo, brought me my tea with a nice-size lemon wedge hanging on the side of the tall chilled glass. She put it on a cocktail napkin and said she'd be back soon, and then she disappeared into the kitchen. Sipping my tea, I wondered when Ronald would decide to show up. My stomach was doing somersaults as I watched the door. I guessed it was because I didn't know what to expect.

About fifteen minutes later, Ronald walked through the door looking stressed out to say the least, with disheveled hair and bloodshot eyes. He looked as though he hadn't slept in a week. As he sat down, he looked into my eyes and it felt as though time had stopped for a moment. I took a deep breath and pulled myself together.

"What's going on?" I said. "You look terrible."

"I'm not sure, but a couple of the guys I do a little business with have been acting really strange, I'm getting weird vibes from them, like they're hiding something, you know what I mean? It's gotten pretty intense."

Intense! Had he actually said "intense?" What was it with this guy? I knew it could get ugly but I had to know what I was dealing with here.

"Are you into drugs or anything like that?" I asked him. "I have to know what you're doing and who you hang out with if I'm going to help you."

"I've done a little dealing on the side," he admitted, "but only to people I already know. I'm not into it for big bucks or anything like that. I just did it so I could get my stuff for free."

So that's what all this is about. Drugs. This pansy ass has some drug dealer after him and he's looking for a way out. Boy, if Frank were here I know what he'd tell him. He'd tell him to "get lost, pal." and so should I. The only thing is, I have all this money.

"What kind of stuff?" I demanded.

"Just a little weed, I don't like coke or any of that other stuff, I've seen what that shit can do."

I don't know why, but I believed him, I guessed he seemed so vulnerable to me now. Really afraid.

Sally, as promised, came back to check on us. "Hi, can I get you something, an iced tea and some lunch?"

"I'm okay," Ron told her, as he took a pocket watch out of his left breast pocket and opened it to check the time. "I don't have time to eat."

"Who are these guys you're talking about?" I asked him when we were alone again. "I need you to be honest with me on this."

"I know, Sam," he told me, wiping the sweat from his forehead. I've just got to be careful."

He moved in closer and lowered his voice. "These guys are into gambling, loan sharking and serious drug dealing. They don't put up with any crap from anyone. Not friends. Not family. Hell, they'd shoot their mothers if she interfered with business."

"How did you get hooked up with this bunch in the first place?" I said, trying the sympathetic act. "You just don't seem the type."

"We've all been friends since grade school," he explained, looking over his shoulder. "We grew up in the same neighborhood, and have always been hooked up. I just never broke away, even when I realized they were heading down the wrong road. I guess I still wanted their approval. I spent so many years earning it that I couldn't walk away. But you have to believe me, I'm not involved in their heavy drug business. I think they resent the fact that I'm no longer willing to just follow along. That's why I started my construction company. I was finally ready to move on. But they wanted to use it for a cover."

"A cover for what? Are they laundering money?"

"That's just part of it. They all use my company as their place of employment for tax purposes and whatever else they need a cover for. They hustle deals and have even recruited some of my guys into the business. These guys who work for me all have families and if they got caught it would be real bad."

"Why do they get involved then?"

"They do it because they see it as easy money and think they'll stop when they pay off their bills. But that never happens. Because they really can't get out, even if they want to."

"What do you mean, they can't get out?"

"Look at me, Sam. I tried to walk away. Now one of them is on my tail, just waiting for the right time to take me out. My friends have gotten out of hand. They have money and power and a place to hide. They think they are invincible. They do things that would shock you, they still shock me, for God's sake."

"What I don't understand is why you didn't tell me all this in the first place," I told him. "We need to go to the police. This sounds like more than I can handle."

"I know," he said. That's what we *should* do, but we can't. Not yet anyway."

"Why not?" I asked him.

"Because the police would never believe that I wasn't part of all this and you know it. I have to get some hard evidence to prove I'm innocent and until I do, I won't go to them. I know you can go anytime, I can't stop you, but I think, deep down, you want to believe me on this."

He was right. He could be setting me up, God knows I've been snowed before. But not often because I do have pretty good gut instincts. And this was one of those times when I could feel it that I was right.

"Okay, I'll wait," I told him, "but if anything gets out of hand, I am going to them. Got that, Ron?"

"Sure, Sam." But in the meantime, I'm going to continue to gather as much information as I can. But I want you to keep this for me." He said, handing me an envelope. "This is everything I have so far. If anything happens to me, or you think you're in danger, read this."

"Who's going to come after me?" I demanded. This was not part of our deal.

"Sam, I hope nothing will come of this, but if they find out what I have been doing over the last few years...well, it could get ugly. I want you to know that."

I put the envelope in my purse, making a mental note to put in my safe deposit box immediately if not sooner. I had no intention getting myself into any kind of a scuffle over this guy. Doesn't he know, I don't do pain?

Ron was looking at me in a way that unnerved me. I had the feeling that I was way out of my league. I found myself wishing that it was someone else sitting across from Ron right now, hearing about the possible danger that might or might not occur. This was why I never became a cop; the shit they do is way too dangerous.

"Ronald," I said patiently. "Why did you call me in the first place? I'm not a cop. I'm a nosy paralegal for God's sake, it doesn't make sense."

"Well, I have to tell you that I did think about going to the cops," he admitted. "But to be honest, the police would want to jump in and start arresting everyone right and left.

Including me, and I don't want that. I hired you because I've heard you're stubborn and intense and have connections in law enforcement."

"You hired me because of my connections?"

"Sam, look, this is serious. I hired you because I knew you wouldn't quit when you found out that it could be potentially dangerous. I thought I'd be able to trust you to stay with me and keep the information I have spent the last three years of my life collecting, safe. There is no information linking you and me. I've only called you once and that was from a pay phone and I kept the call short. I just need to know that, if something happens to me, you will get the information to the cops. I have to know that they will go down, even if they take me first."

"Look, Ron, or whatever your name is," I said, "this is my life you're screwing with, and you don't even have the balls to be straight with me."

"You want to know everything?" he asked me, frowning. "It could be more dangerous for you."

This was unbelievable. I was listening to Ron tell me I might be in danger and all I could do was look into his dreamy blue eyes with thoughts of doing things to him that were down right nasty. Shame on me!

"Don't you think I deserve at least that much?"

"Okay, Sam, but I don't have the time to tell you. Can we meet again tomorrow morning?"

"Where and when?"

"What time does this place open?"

"Five-thirty for the lunatics that play this game."

"I'll meet you here at five thirty then," he said, as he got up. "Don't be late. We have a lot to talk about."

I sat there dumbfounded as he walked out the door. I hate to get up early and don't even consider it morning until at least seven. What have I gotten myself into? I was eager to find out the whole story but knowing that I could get hurt was causing me some distress. Okay, I was scared shitless. All I could think about was calling Frank to get his input on this, but since he can be too protective of me and would probably do something to interfere, I decided I would wait until after my meeting with Ronald to clue him in. I had to have more information than what I'd been told so far, which was close to nothing.

Although I didn't feel especially hungry, I ate a Cobb salad and tried to forget about Ronald by focusing on some of the more mundane tasks I needed to get done such as the divorce paperwork for a girl who had a husband overseas. They haven't seen each other in two years and she was pregnant. Because she didn't want him to find out about it, for obvious reasons, she was in a great hurry to have this finished and she wasn't the only one. A simple case had turned into a nightmare mainly because of the fact that we had to have him sign all the forms and him being in another country equals time. A small detail that my client seemed unable to grasp. After that, I had to finish up some research on a real estate transaction gone bad, a project I had been working on for several months now. Just thinking about all the excitement I was going to endure gave me chills all over.

Leaving the club, I remembered the envelope and thought I'd better get it in my safe deposit box. As I headed to the bank, I tried to stay calm, but felt the tension rising by the minute because of my present situation, although I was really not sure exactly what that situation was. I found myself looking at everyone like they were about to take me down. Paranoia was setting in fast. This couldn't be good.

My machine told me I had three messages. The first was from an old friend, who now resides in Arizona. Linda and I have been friends for over twenty years and are like sisters, fights and all. The second was from Lori, my divorce client, and the last was from Frank who was just checking up on me to see how much trouble I have found myself in since we last saw each other. I decided to wait until tomorrow to call him back.

I had set my alarm to go off at four-forty five A.M. but since I wasn't able to sleep all night anyway, I figured I'd just get up, It was four thirty. I savored my delicious cinnamon coffee and browsed the paper, feeling like I had a big head start on my day. After two cups, I found I was not only wide awake, but up to date on all the happenings in town too. I loved this coffee machine with the timer on it. I don't know why it took me so long to part with the fifty bucks to invest in one. It was so worth it.

I slipped into a pair of crisp new jeans, a white T-shirt and sandals and headed to the club. The roads seemed deserted at this time of the morning. Anyone in their right mind was still cozy in their beds.

As I pulled into the parking lot, I saw Ron getting out of a green pickup truck. I watched him as he walked toward the club, reflecting on the fact that he really was a good-looking guy. Even this early in the morning, I had to remind myself that this had to be strictly business. Besides, I didn't even know if he thought I was even remotely attractive. I watched as he went inside and got out of my car. I felt a sense of calm and hoped there would not be an impending storm to follow. Instinctively, I checked out my surroundings and noticed a couple of cars in the lot. They must be the die hard golfers, you know the ones who are overly competitive and feel compelled to be there even before the doors open. I just don't get it.

Ron was sitting at "our" table. "Good morning, I wasn't sure you'd make it." he said.

"Good morning," I said, ignoring the comment.

This early they don't serve any food but put out a tray of assorted doughnuts and rolls and have coffee available on a self-serve basis. Ron brought back a tray with two mugs of coffee and a couple of doughnuts. As he took a bite out of a cream filled doughnut he gestured for me to help myself.

"No thanks." I said.

"Not hungry?"

"No, I can't eat this early." I told him, ready to get started. "You want to tell me what's going on? Isn't that why I got up at this ungodly hour?"

"Yes, it is," he said. "Look, I know I should have filled you in, but I wanted to be sure you wouldn't bail on me, so, I figured I'd give you a little information and tell you about the possible danger and if you didn't call me last night to tell me you were out, I'd give you the whole story."

"You were testing me?" I asked.

"Sam, I wanted to be sure you were with me."

"You son of a bitch." I said, my anger rising.

"Look, do you want out or can I continue?" he asked, sharply.

I was tempted to tell him to take his money and fuck off, but I have to admit, I was intrigued. Why he felt the need to put me through his little test after giving me twenty-five thousand dollars, was beyond me. On the other hand, I was pretty sure that I had sealed the fact that I wasn't the one that was paranoid.

"I'm still here, so let's hear it." I told him.

"Sam, as I was telling you yesterday, I've known these guys as long as I can remember. We've grown up together and have all been involved in each others' lives. I guess it all began when we were in elementary school. We started pulling things like breaking into neighborhood houses and stealing a beer from the refrigerator or just leaving a light on, to make them wonder, you know? Juvenile pranks. We were little kids. As we got older, our crimes got more serious. We'd break into houses and steal stuff for our fort. We even used to break into the schools and steal the clocks and phones and whatever else we felt like we needed at the time. Every once in a while one of us would get caught but because we were too young to go to jail, the authorities really couldn't do anything except tell our parents. Now don't get me wrong, this was a big deal then, most of us had our asses kicked by our fathers, and some of us got beaten up pretty bad."

"Including you?" I asked

He shrugged. "Let's just say I definitely got the message that my behavior would not be tolerated. But I also had a father who started to teach me about business, and how I could get what I needed if I worked hard and smart. The other guys had fathers doing the same shit we were doing on a larger scale, and they thought beating the crap out of their kid would teach them a lesson or at least make it look like they were. These are uneducated street guys. They didn't know any better. Unfortunately, as a kid, when you see the power that your dad has, where people fear him, you think it's cool. You just get pulled into it by the power trip."

I couldn't believe how he was describing his childhood. It sounded like a scene out of *The Godfather*. "Was your dad like that?"

"No, my dad was no tough guy. He was a businessman. I have to admit I was a little embarrassed by the fact that he never intimidated anyone."

Wow, this guy was a messed up little dude. It's good to know his dad had some sense. "It sounds like your father was really smart in raising you."

"Yeah, but my pals didn't know anything about it. They never would have understood. These guys just don't get it. Never did, and probably never will. Anyway, the point is that I stopped all the stealing because I didn't want to let my dad down. He taught me more than just business. He taught me the value of money, the importance of self-respect and respect for others, as well as how much more fun and challenging it is to win legitimately in business."

"Well, then why did you continue to hang out with them?" I said, annoyed he didn't stand up to them.

"I told you. These guys are like my brothers. We've always been there for each other."

"Until now," I said.

"Yeah, until now," he said, as he dropped his head, shaking it slowly from side to side.

"Are you okay, Ron?"

He closed his eyes and slouched into his chair. A moment later, he looked up. "Ya know . . . You think you know someone, you spend your entire childhood and most of your adulthood as friends, close friends, and then out of nowhere, they blow you away with this new attitude. Suddenly, you are no longer a brother. They shut you out, just like that. And now, well, one of them wants to take me out. How the hell does something like this happen?"

I felt sorry for him. He was losing part of his family and it was killing him. I decided that no matter how dangerous his friends were, I was going to have to help him. I would have to be careful. I knew that if they associated him with me in any way, shape or form, I was history. The thought of it scared me to death, but I didn't feel like I had a choice, not now, not after hearing his story.

"Look, they used you. They wanted you to get into the drugs and theft so they would have control of you. And when you wouldn't go along with their plan, they talked you into letting them use your business as their cover, jeopardizing it, and you." I told him, angrily.

I hoped I hadn't overstep my boundaries but I was pissed off about what had happened to him.

"Ron, I . . ."

He stopped me. "Sam, you're right. I can't let them take everything I've worked for. I'm going to need your help. Can I count on you?"

I was pumped up and ready for a fight. "Damn right you can count on me. Let's go kick some ass."

CHAPTER 4

I hadn't heard from Ron in days and it was affecting my behavior as well as my mental state. I was uptight, nervous and pissed off all at the same time, liable to snap at everyone who got near me. This, as anyone who is acquainted with me knows, is one of the ways in which I deal with stress. The other way, which I hope no one knows about, is that I tend to stop eating. I am a recovering anorexic, which explains why I tend to be a bit of a control freak about myself and my environment.

As I thought about my last meeting with Ron, I couldn't help feeling that maybe I had missed something. He seemed so eager to take back his life and not let his "friends" take him down. But now it's been four days since I've heard anything from him and I wasn't sure what I should do about it. He had asked me to help, so why hasn't he called me? Since waiting for a telephone call was definitely not working for me I decided to head out.

Ron lived in an expensive neighborhood in town called Los Ranchitos where the homes are all custom built and sit on at least one acre of property. It was an area that has always reminded me of the East Coast or mid-West, with quiet country roads lined with big, sprawling elm trees. Some of the roads were not even paved, creating the sense of being deep in the country, when in reality, you're just a hop, skip and a jump from town. It was, in short, a place I could get used to living in. Well, I can dream, can't I?

Ron's house was big, but simple and comfortable looking, painted white with black trim and shutters and enclosed in a wrap around porch. There were flower boxes in the windows filled with geraniums and flowerpots containing clusters of daylilies that were set on the porch along with white wicker furniture. It looked so delightful that I thought the Cleavers just might come out the front door any minute.

I'm not much of a gardener, but I appreciate the beauty of a well-landscaped yard, and this place was impeccable. The garage was set back a bit so as not to take away from the beauty of the home itself, and out back was a white barn, also with black trim and black shutters. I didn't see any horses but if he had a couple, that would complete my dream.

I took a deep breath and turned off the ignition. As I opened my car door and got out, I stood thinking how nice it would be to come home to this place. As I walked up the stone path and through the gated entryway I realized I was getting too caught up in my own little fantasy and had better get back to the reality of why I was here in the first place. On the porch, a newspaper and a coffee mug sat on the table. I took in the scent of cinnamon and almost began to drool on myself. It was after all, my favorite.

I knocked on the door and waited anxiously.

No answer, so I tried again, knocking harder this time.

Still no answer.

That was when I heard what sounded like a chain saw at full throttle. As I rounded the corner behind the garage, I saw a man in jeans and a red flannel shirt cutting wood. Sometimes I amaze even myself, with my keen ability to be so damn observant.

He was busy working and didn't notice me standing there at the corner of the garage, but I watched him, trying to remember if I'd ever seen him before. He was a stocky man, approximately 5'10" with sandy blonde hair and handsome features. I wondered if he might be one of the crew on Ron's construction site. Whoever he was, he was not a part of my memory bank and I would have to get his attention in order to be sure I was in the right place.

The day was cool and clear and there was a fresh smell of cut wood in the clean air. Fall is my favorite time of year and although it was winter by the calendar, Temecula's seasons were not like those of the rest of the world. Our fall happens in the winter and we don't really have a winter at all.

I decided to follow my intuition and not ask this guy about Ron. After all, this could easily be one of the so called "friends" he was telling me about, and since I wasn't suppose to have any connection to him, for fear of having my face rearranged, I thought I'd skip it and move on to plan B. But just as I turned the corner of the garage to leave, I found myself face to face with Peter! Startled, I almost screamed. We were standing so close that I had to take a step back to look at him. He was wearing dark-rimmed sunglasses and jeans with a long-sleeved blue shirt and brand new sneakers and the expression on his face was one of mild amusement. But he gave no indication that he recognized me.

"I'm sorry I scared you," he said, "Can I help you with something,"

"Well, yes," I told him, saying the first thing that came to my mind. "I'm looking for the Andrews, we have an appointment."

"Come with me then," he said, "Matt Andrews is just out back cutting firewood."

I couldn't believe this was happening! I had used the first name that came to me and here I was going back to meet Mr. Andrews. Damn, now what was I going to do? Well, for one thing, I was going to have to be on my toes and come up with something fast.

"We don't need to bother him," I assured him, turning on my heels." I'll come back later."

"No, really, it's okay," Peter assured me. "What's your name?"

"I'm Sam Parker," I told him, deciding that it would be just as well not to remind him he had once been my waiter. "I'm a paralegal."

"Well, it's very nice to meet you, Sam, I'm Peter. Hold on a minute. Matt! Hey Matt!"

Just then the chain saw ground to a halt.

"No need to yell at me, Pete," he said with a laugh.

He had a big wonderful smile and I thought he probably had a great sense of humor as well. He just looked like he loved to laugh. I knew right away he was someone I would like.

"Well, it is very nice to meet you, Sam," Matt said, after Pete had given a remarkably formal introduction. "Who do I thank for having you come looking for me?"

"Well, to tell you the truth," I said, prepared to do anything but, "I had a message on my machine asking me to come over to discuss putting a living trust together for a Mr. and Mrs. Andrews. I tried to return the call but got no answer, so I thought I'd just stop by. I hope that was all right. I must tell you that I just love your home. It's so beautiful." I was babbling but it didn't matter because if the look of his eyes were any indication, he was buying my story.

"Well, Miss . . ."

"Please call me Sam."

"Well, Sam, I have news for you. First of all, I never called you, and second . . ."

"What?" I said anxiously.

"There is no Mrs. Andrews."

Yessss . . . was the first thought that crossed my mind. I only hoped he couldn't see that I was lying through my teeth.

"Do you like coffee, Sam?"

"Yes. Yes, Matt, I do like coffee very much."

"Then why don't you come inside and have a cup with me and we can straighten this mix up out."

"Uh, I'd better get going," Peter said, clearly uncomfortable. I could feel for him because I have been in the middle of these situations myself, more times than I'd ever like to admit. But for the moment, all he represented was some unanswered questions. Who is this guy that seemed to know everyone and have a job everywhere? It would take some looking into but I had to know.

"Shall we?" Matt said as he gestured toward the back door. "I'll take you on the grand tour if you like."

Right inside the back door was a small coatroom that looked as though it ought to be used for snow gear. It reminded me instantly of an East Coast home, where they actually have snow, although it was decorated as a garden room with white wood paneling and garden tools hanging from hooks. Above were white shelves on which flowerpots, watering cans, and many other colorful garden paraphernalia were arranged, giving the room a quaint feel to it. I liked it right away because it felt comfortable and homey.

Next came a big, bright room with pretty pale yellow walls and white cabinets stacked with expensive looking floral dishes. In the middle of the kitchen stood an island with a flower arrangement in the center, and above it was a wheel type of thing with pots and pans hanging from it. I liked the look and couldn't help thinking that one of the pans could come in handy if I found myself in any trouble while I was here. Isn't it great that my twisted mind is always working?

"It's just beautiful," I said. I must have been beaming because I felt so damn good. You see, I don't let little things like the fact that I don't have two nickels to rub together get in the way of my fantasy life.

"So, you're a paralegal?" Matt asked. "And you are supposed to put together a living trust for me and my non-existent Mrs.?"

"Well, that's what I thought," I said, feeling crappy for having to lie to him. "I could have sworn that this was the correct address. Do you have an ex-wife who might have called about it; I've had that happen before. The ex thinks that they should have access to their former spouse's assets after they die."

"You're kidding right?" he said.

"No, I'm not kidding," I said, hoping to convince him that I wasn't lying, which of course, I was. "There are some pretty screwed up people out there.

"That's unbelievable."

"Yeah, I know, but it happens. So, do you have an ex-wife?" I asked, deciding that blunt was best.

"No, I don't have an ex-wife. What about you?"

"I don't have an ex-wife either," I told him.

"You're funny," he said smiling. "How about an ex-husband?"

"No, I don't have one of those either," I said, struggling to keep a straight face.

As he took me from room to room, giving me a few details about the architecture and history, I suppressed the urge to ask him what his relationship to Ron was. Instead, I spent this tour looking for any indication that Ron lived here. Because I was doubting his story now and I really did have every reason to do so. He had lied to me, given me almost no information about himself, and it was pissing me off now that he was "missing" and I was trying to find out what the hell happened to him.

The master bedroom was much larger than the other rooms. It had a vaulted ceiling with a ceiling fan and to the left, separated from the rest of the room by French doors was a large nook containing a fireplace, a stereo, a large screen TV and a computer. Around the walls were bookcases that held a good many books. Yet it was not cluttered at all, something that bugs me more than I'd like to admit. Just another one of my many quirks. In the bedroom there was a big bed with a white quilted coverlet, a good-sized oak dresser and matching night tables, on one of which was a clock and Stephen King's *The Dark Half*, an excellent book in my opinion. I do tend to like that scary stuff. Apparently, only one person slept in this bed, if the fact that one of the two night tables was bare of any of the items that covered the other was any indication. I wondered who slept here alone, the man beside me or perhaps my missing client.

Across the room, there was a beautiful bay window. It was quite large and had a cozy window seat with a few oversized throw pillows on each end. It looked like a great place to sit with a book and a cup of coffee or a glass of chilled wine. I walked over to look out.

"Not bad, huh?" Matt asked me.

He was now standing right behind me, very close. I didn't let on the effect it was having on me, but I'll admit, I was feeling a bit flushed.

"This is really beautiful," I said. How long have you lived here?"

He hesitated for a moment.

"This house has been in the family for quite some time, but I have only been living here for a few months. I moved in after one of my brothers decided to move out."

"Oh, is Peter your brother?"

"No, no, Pete is an old family friend, I've known him since I was a kid . . . Actually, now that I think about it, he is like a brother to me. He's always been around."

This conversation was sounding strangely like the one I had with Ron and I wondered if Matt was one of those lifelong friends that had turned their back on him. If so, where could Ron be? This was supposed to be his house yet there is no sign of him and Matt was telling me a different story. Would he have left town without a word to me, knowing I was on the case? Or has something happened to him?

"How many brothers do you have?"

"I have seven brothers and two sisters."

"Wow, that's quite a big family," I said.

"Yes, the parents were very good Catholics," he said with a laugh.

I had to smile. Growing up in New York, I understood exactly what he meant.

"So where are you in the lineup?" I asked, slightly regretting my choice of words.

"I am number six, lucky number six."

"Why lucky number six?"

"I am just far enough down the line that my parents had loosened up their rules, so I had a lot of freedom, much more than the older kids had had."

"And this was a good thing?" I asked, wondering exactly what kind of freedom he had growing up.

"Well, yes. I was able to make my own choices and do a lot of things that some of my friends couldn't do."

"Such as . . ."

"I could stay out late, go to bars, and not have someone question my every move."

"That must have been nice, but if your friends couldn't hang out, who did you do all this cool stuff with?"

"My other friends, some of whom were out living on their own or had mellow parents as well."

"Oh, so you lived a double life?" I said with a smile in my voice.

"What can I say, I'm very mysterious. Do you like men of mystery?" he asked with a bit of a bad French accent.

"What red-blooded American girl wouldn't? You men of mystery are very exciting."

I was so enjoying this flirtation I almost wish I wasn't there on such false pretenses. I was not lying though; I did in fact find him very mysterious and exciting.

"Sam?"

"Yes, Matt."

"Would you consider having dinner with me tonight?"

"Tonight? Oh, I'd love to but I can't. I have an eight o'clock appointment with a client." It wasn't true, of course. But I had learned a few things over the years and one of them was to never jump at the first offer. It makes you look desperate.

"Okay. How about tomorrow night then?"

"All right, tomorrow night."

What was I thinking? This was probably the guy that Ron told me about. The one that might hurt me if he found out I was snooping around. Why did I say yes? I didn't even know this guy and here I was, accepting a dinner invitation. Not the first one though, so at least he wouldn't get the wrong idea about me.

CHAPTER 5

I got in my car and drove off, wondering why I had just agreed to dinner. Granted that I did want to spend more time with Matt. He was fun, friendly and possibly would give me some of the answers I was looking for, and I have to confess, I was very, very attracted to him. But, at the same time, a definite red light was flashing in my head, signaling this was a mistake and I was not listening. Sure he seemed nice and all, but in the back of my mind was a picture of a criminal who would take his mother out if she interfered with business. Matt could be that guy and I had to stay alert, if only to save my own ass.

I decided to go back to the construction site to look for Ron or anyone else who might be able to tell me something about his whereabouts. Maybe someone had heard from him by now. I really felt like he would be there. Probably so I could go out tomorrow night and enjoy my dinner with Matt without worrying about if he was dangerous. Hey, I'm being honest here.

Asking around, I discovered no one had heard from him. I have to tell you, I found it rather unsettling. First of all, I had the feeling they were playing with me. They acted like dumb ass construction workers, answering my questions with questions of there own. So, I decided to ask Jon James about Ron's address and all he could offer was, "it sounds right." What the hell does that mean?

I wanted him to be there so bad. This was the first time I had really believed wishful thinking would make it real. All I could think about was the fact that on one hand, I thought I might just be "in love" again and on the other, I was breaking all my own rules getting involved with someone that could be a piece of the puzzle in my investigation. Not to mention my relationship with Jack, no matter how casual. How the hell had I let this happen? Shit.

I tried to convince myself that this was all part of what I had to do to get the job done. After all, the truth was what I was really searching for, and sometimes you do things you know you shouldn't do in order to get to the truth, right? I knew I was fooling myself and would ultimately lead to trouble but what could I do now? I couldn't just let this all go. It was against my better judgment. Okay, so Matt Andrews was the only lead I had to go on. That was good enough for me.

Since I didn't really have an appointment tonight, I thought I'd use this time to attempt to come up with a plan to get back into the house. I needed some time to find something that I could connect to Ron, but what?

I arrived home to find Mrs. Bennett outside, watering the plants. She was one strange lady. I knew she was waiting for me, why else would she be watering in the dark. As usual, she had a sour look on her face.

"Miss Parker, do you know anything about the exterminator coming out here?"

"Yes, I do." My reply was as friendly as I could muster.

"Why did you call?"

"Because I have ants, Mrs. Bennett."

"You know you are supposed to call me and I'll make any arrangements that I feel necessary."

"Well, last time I asked you to take care of it, it took you so long to call that ants were coming out of my faucet as I brushed my teeth. Do you have any idea how disgusting that is?"

"There is no excuse for going against my wishes."

"Mrs. Bennett, the rental agreement I signed states that you will take care of these things in a timely manner which is identified as a fifteen-day period. Three months is not timely." I was getting agitated and knew it would not be a good idea to take this much further.

"You know my friend was ill at that time, Miss Parker, and that is why it took me so long to respond to your request."

"Requests."

"What?"

"Requests, meaning more than one," I said, correcting her. "Goodnight, Mrs. Bennett."

I walked into my house and closed the door as she stood there with the hose running, trying to think of something else to say. Even though I loved my little house, I knew deep down I longed for a place of my own, without a Mrs. Bennett to stick a thorn in my side at every turn. "Someday," I told myself.

I lit a fire and some of my scented candles, put on my sweats and poured a glass of white wine, which I like sufficiently chilled. I sat on my floor and took out all the notes I had so far on Ronald and company. I had to acknowledge the fact that I did not have a whole lot of information and felt more like I was on a wild goose chase than working on a case. I attempted to put together the notes that related to one another like a flow chart. I do this because it helps me to clarify my information and organize my course of action, as well as pinpoint missing pieces and identify things that don't make much sense. I also thought it might be time to call Frank to see if he'd stop by and bring me anything he had recovered for me.

When I finished my glass of wine I felt my mind loosen up enough to let my thoughts flow freely. I dialed Frank's cell phone and left a message. It was too late to get him at his office and I wouldn't dare call his home. Not with what was apparently a tempestuous state of affairs evolving there.

I awoke to the test pattern on the television and the sound of my big eucalyptus tree brushing against the house outside my front door. The wind was blowing fiercely and I could hear the faint sound of rain on my windows. It was still dark so I decided I'd go up to bed and see about getting a few more hours of sleep. Turning off the TV, I took a look outside my back door to see if anything had blown away. Not too much damage, although one of my plants had been blown over and was rolling around the patio. Just as I stepped out to bring it in to safety I thought I heard something that resembled the cry of an injured animal. I stood motionless, listening, but the blustery weather made it difficult to hear anything except for the sound of the trees and bushes. The gusts continued as it started to pour rain harder than I can remember.

Suddenly aware of a strange, unsettled feeling, I locked the back door and checked to make sure the front was secure as well. Once satisfied that I was safe from the outside world, I went up to my bedroom where, taking one last look out the window into the backyard, I thought I saw something moving. Finally, deciding that my imagination was getting the better of me, I got in bed and fell asleep listening to the pounding of the rain.

It was almost eight by the time I woke up, much later than I usually sleep, even on a weekend, but I felt good, really rested. The day looked so crisp and clear that it was hard to believe we had had such a terrible storm. Or had we? For a moment I wondered if I had been dreaming. But when I went downstairs for a cup of coffee, I found my plant safe and sound, sitting in my kitchen sink where I had placed it last night, confirmation that I was not hallucinating, and that's always a good sign. My coffee machine sat empty however. Damn, I had forgotten to set it up.

I looked out the back door and observed the strewn branches and leaves in the backyard as I waited for the coffee to brew. There is no other sound or smell that is quite so captivating as a pot of delicious hot coffee brewing in the morning. I cradled my cup in both hands as I went to my office, a cozy room decorated like a small beach cottage. It's painted blue and hanging on the walls are various pictures of beach scenes. The furniture, a desk and matching chair are white and in the corner is a most comfortable easy chair. Sitting in it feels like a big hug and it's where I do my best thinking. As I waited for my computer to connect to the internet, I sipped my coffee, enjoying the blissful feeling that comes with a good night sleep and thoughts of a new man.

When the phone rang, I was tempted not to pick it up for fear that whoever was on the other end of the phone might jolt me into reality before I was ready. And I was definitely not ready. However, duty called. After all, the business day had begun-more or less.

It was Frank, sounding way too happy. Apparently he wasn't going to announce another divorce. Not today anyway.

"It's me, your secret admirer, calling to ask if you're free for a breakfast meeting," he said.

"Why are you so happy?"

"What kind of question is that?"

"A good one, given that you never sound like this."

"Meet me and I'll tell you."

"All right, where?"

"How about Rocky's Diner?"

"Sounds good. Will you bring me anything you have on the license plate numbers I've given you and the rest of the file on Ronald? I'll bring what I have. I might need some assistance; I've run into a little snag."

"Sure," he said, still sounding unreasonably agreeable. "I'll stop by the station and pick up what Chuck has retrieved for us and we'll figure this out, I'll see you in about an hour."

I dressed in blue jeans, a black cashmere sweater and my black boots. A touch of make up and a dab of perfume and I was about ready to go. As I put my file together I thought about all gaps that needed to be filled in and I was hoping some of the information Frank had uncovered would assist me in doing just that. I was also contemplating telling Frank about my dinner plans with Matt. I didn't think he'd approve, and probably for good reason. I just wasn't sure if I wanted to hear it. Besides, I needed to get back into that house and find out why Ron had lied about it being his home, if indeed he was the one lying. This might be my last chance to wrangle an invitation. The only other alternative was called breaking and entering, I'll do that if I have to, of course, but I really would hate to go to jail.

My car was cold and since I wasn't in too much of a hurry for a change, I decided to let it warm up before I went barreling down the street. I have been told by every man I know, including my dad, that you are supposed to warm up the car before you drive it. I don't happen to do this on a regular basis and have found myself in trouble because of it, often breaking down on the side of the road and all too frequently showing up embarrassingly late for events.

As I ventured toward Rocky's, a cute little old-fashioned diner that aims to take anyone who steps across the threshold back to the 'fifties, with red leather booths and a jukebox, as well as all the old-time movie memorabilia, and of course, the waitresses in their foo-foo skirts and saddle shoes, I couldn't help but feel anxious about Frank's news. Frank doesn't get excited easily and when he does I never know how to react. You see, without my instincts I'm nothing. I base every move I make, both personal and professional on them, and so far I'm doing fine. Well, I could be doing a lot worse.

The first thing I saw when I spilled into the parking lot was Frank's truck. Taking my files off the passenger seat, I went into the diner.

"Good morning," a tall, red headed waitress in full fifties garb said, cheerfully. All I could think of was where were these people getting the happy pills and why was I the only one not on them.

"Hi, I'm meeting someone," I said, as I spotted Frank. He was wearing that goofy smirk on his face as I approached.

"It's killing you, isn't it?" he asked me.

"What?"

"You know, my news."

"I haven't thought much about it to tell you the truth, I just want to see what you have for me," I told him.

"You lie, you haven't been able to think about anything else and you know it."

"All right. So what is it?"

"I have to give you a little background so you will be able to appreciate the magnitude of it."

The redhead on happy pills took our order and disappeared with an abruptness that made me wonder if I'd ever see her again.

"So, what is going on?" I asked eagerly.

"Do you remember when I told you about that case I've been working on for the last six plus years, and had run into a dead end?"

"Yeah, you called them the big guys, or . . ."

"Tough guys, Sam."

"Yeah, whatever."

"Do you remember?"

"Yeah, you said you had been tracking down some punks who were into some pretty bad stuff and that you kept uncovering layer upon layer of information that tied them to insurance fraud, and money laundering among other things. Then, all of a sudden, you came to a dead end. You couldn't find out who the leader was but there were so many guys involved that it was like a crime ring. Haven't you been assisting in putting some of those guys away?"

"Yes, Chuck and I and a couple of cops on the force are working together to shut down their operation. We think we might have stumbled on some new information that will also put murder on their résumé."

"What do you mean? I thought they were teenagers running into each other's cars on the freeway, and screwing the insurance company."

"Sam, there are over twenty-five guys involved in this ring, all different ages, and as we are finding out, all different crimes. Insurance fraud is one of their gigs but they are also into auto theft, robbery, bank fraud, loan sharking, illegal possession and sales of firearms and racketeering."

"You're kidding, right?"

"No, I'm not kidding! These thugs do a lot of bad things. For God's sake, Sam, they will do anything for money. Along with everything else, they have a scam going to swindle the elderly out of their dough with different types of home improvement scams as well as selling fake insurance policies. Most of these poor old folks don't even find out until something drastic happens to them, then they realize they have been ripped off and in most cases, have lost their entire savings."

"Why are you telling me all this?"

"Because I found him, Sam. The big guy, the head man, the boss of the whole fucking operation."

He opened the folder in front of him, and took out an eight-by-ten glossy and turned it upside down on the table.

"This is the biggest score of my career," he told me, looking like he was going to explode from the excitement. It's taken a lot of work and some very dangerous undercover operations. I shouldn't even be telling you about this but I know I can trust you. Are you ready?"

He turned the picture over and slid it in front of me.

"Oh my God, I know him!"

"What the hell are you talking about?"

"I met him yesterday, I was following a lead on locating Ron and I ended up meeting him. Are you sure it's him? He just doesn't seem to be the type."

"Where did you meet him?" Frank demanded, "I need to know where, when and how." all business now.

"I hadn't heard from Ron in a few days and in fact, I've been trying to find him."

"What are you talking about? He's lost?"

Since it was clearly time to fill him in, I did just that, adding as many details as seemed necessary to get him up to speed on the events of the past few days, including why Ron had claimed he wanted help and the fact that he had apparently disappeared. And then, of course there was the business of going to Ron's house and finding this guy working out back.

"I didn't know who it was," I said, "but Ron had told me his "friends" were dangerous. I was scared so I hid the fact that I was looking for Ron and made up a story, that's how I met him. We started talking and he seemed really nice."

"Sam, he's not nice. In fact, he's very dangerous," he said, rubbing his forehead. "So, what are you not telling me?"

"Don't freak out, okay?"

"Oh shit, Sam. What?"

I knew he was going to blow a gasket when I told him. Bracing myself, I took a deep breath.

"I'm having dinner with him tonight," I said.

"You're what?"

"I'm having dinner with him tonight."

"You can't, Sam. You have no idea what your getting into here!" he told me, pounding his fist on the table.

I knew he was going to do everything he could to stop me, but I was determined to stick to my guns. I knew it could be dangerous if what he was telling me was true, but I didn't really feel like I had a choice. Ron needed help.

"Look, I promised Ron I'd help him. In fact, as you recall, I took a sizable amount of money from him and now he's disappeared. I have to get back into that house. I know there is something there that will help me find him. So please don't try to talk me out of it. If you're so afraid for my safety, then help me."

"Sam . . ."

"Look, I'm going whether you help me or not." I got up and grabbed my files. I turned and started for the door, hoping I did know what I was doing.

"Okay, Sam, okay."

Frank shook his head back and forth slowly, his head down ever so slightly.

"You are one stubborn little lady, Sam," he muttered.

"I know, Frank. Thanks."

"Don't thank me yet, this could get pretty ugly."

"I'll be careful." I assured him. "I know what I'm doing. Well, at least I have some idea."

"Sam," he said, "you're going to have to trust me here, and listen to what I tell you. If you don't you could find yourself dead, so no bullheaded moves, you follow my directions. Do you understand?" he scowled. Clearly my effort to reassure him had fallen short

"I understand. I'll do whatever you think is right." I must admit, I said this not completely convinced I was actually going to follow his directions, but I had to at least be open to his ideas, after all he was the professional. Not that it mattered to me in the least because it was my ass on the line.

CHAPTER 6

I spent most of the day with Frank, who dressed casually in jeans, and Chuck, who was in his usual gear. Chuck was an uptight sort, who took himself much too seriously. He wore his perfect brown hair parted on the side and his lean body was always dressed in a suit and tie reminding me of the officers in the old *Dragnet* series, always appearing as the picture of perfection. We spent the afternoon going over the many rules for my "date" tonight. They wanted me to wear a wire but I declined, arguing that Matt and I had met completely by chance and he would never think I knew anything about his criminal behavior.

"Do you really think it would be smart for me to take a chance on having him find out I know anything about his job?" I argued. "You and I both know he will not hesitate to do some major damage to me if he even suspects I'm setting him up."

Chuck was getting irritated with me but I didn't much care. That's what really bugged him. He puts on this act like he's so macho, instead of just a control freak.

"Jesus, Frank, what the hell is wrong with her?" he professed.

"Me? Chuck, you really expect me to do something that will probably get me killed?"

"Why do you think it will get you killed?"

"Look, this guy and I have made a connection, all right?" I said this as calmly as possible.

"You don't really believe that do you? Chuck demanded. "This guy is all about business, so get real Sam. He hasn't been sitting around all day thinking about you in anticipation of your 'date,' and even if he keeps it, which I seriously doubt he will, don't expect him to get all sappy with you. This guy is about making money and hurting people to get what he wants. He doesn't care about anything else, so stop acting like a schoolgirl and get with the program so you don't get yourself hurt."

"I don't need your crap, Chuck. I'm not wearing a wire and if you don't like it you can go screw yourself."

Chuck gave me a dirty look and walked out of the office, cussing as he descended the stairs.

"Oh, that was good, Sam. You really know how to make friends. Do you have any idea how good Chuck is at his job? He was a great cop and now he heads up some of the most important investigations that come into this office and works as a special investigator for the cops and the FBI."

"I'm sorry, Frank, he just rubs me the wrong way. I'll apologize to him okay? But I can't wear a wire, you have to trust me on this."

"You said you would listen to me. That was the deal. If you're not going to do what I tell you, I can't help you on this and you will be compromising an investigation."

"Can't we do something else? I'd feel safer if I didn't have anything on my body, that way if he discovered it, I could try to bullshit my way out of the situation."

"Fine, but I've got to talk to Chuck and see what he thinks. Will that be okay with you?" He was just slightly condescending.

"That's fine. You know, I am really sorry." I hate having enemies and making Chuck one was especially bad news.

Frank told me to sit tight while he went to get Chuck who we both knew, was probably across the street, having a beer to cool down. I hate to apologize, so I sat there thinking of a way to do it that would cause the least amount of pain.

When I heard the grumble of their voices outside I knew Chuck was not going to be very forgiving.

"Chuck," I said, trying to get him to look me in the eye. "I'd like to say I'm sorry. I really didn't mean to disregard your expertise. I'm a little freaked out by all this, that's all, and I'd feel really self-conscious if I wore a wire. I hope you'll forgive me." So, I laid it on a little thick, but what could I do. The last thing I want is to have my ass hanging in a sling and have my rescue crew too pissed off at me to come to my rescue.

Frank and Chuck finally agreed on a small listening device that fit into my cell phone which would allow them to sit in Chuck's Corvette listening to every word while keeping out of sight. As for me, I was just hoping to get through the evening intact. I was a bit uncomfortable with the thought that Frank and Chuck would hear everything that went on while I was on my so called "date" since I really was quite captivated with Mr. Andrews. I hoped I wouldn't make a fool of myself because if I did, I'd never hear the end of it. Chuck would tell the story of the lovesick chick who fell for a crime boss to all his cop buddies. They'd be whooping it up for years about that one. God, I hate being humiliated.

When Matt called me at two to confirm our dinner plans, I convinced him to let me come pick him up that evening. I told him my place was a mess, adding that I was embarrassed about him seeing it in that condition. A shameful lie, I feel horrible about it, really.

He said he had a late-afternoon appointment so we decided I should come over at seven. Pete would be around, so if he was running late I should make myself at home, a thought that instantly brought a smile to my face. Maybe I'd be able to get a look around. I'd have to be careful though.

Now that I had an idea what I was dealing with, I must admit that I was scared shitless. I was just glad that I was confident that Matt did not suspect that I had any idea what he was doing.

I decided to dress up for my big date so I put on my tan jeans, a black low-cut shirt and my black boots. I also put on my sexiest bra and undies, just in case. Yeah, I know, it could never happen, but I do my best flirting in them and felt the need to remain confident this evening. Also, if something went wrong I needed a backup plan and that was all I could think of. I added a bit of perfume, because I've heard that if a guy likes how you smell you captivate him. Hey, I am not above trying anything to save my ass. And of course, the thought that Frank could be wrong about Matt did enter my mind, in a sort of hopeful way.

Frank had instructed me earlier that he and Chuck wanted to come by at about six to check out the equipment, give me some instructions, and answer any questions I might have. I agreed. As I waited for them to arrive, I did a little channel surfing and found an old episode of *Magnum PI,* God, I love that shit. I'm going to be as cool as Magnum tonight even if I didn't have a great car, not to mention the fact that I was a woman.

The bell rang and I got up to answer it, ready to eat humble pie again in order to placate Chuck. I knew I was nervous because I didn't really feel sorry for what I had said, I just didn't need him for an enemy.

"Hey !" Matt was standing there with a dozen red roses, a big smile and a big shiny black limo parked out in front.

"Hello, I thought I'd surprise you," he said. "I'm sorry about being early. Are you ready?"

"I thought you had a meeting." I replied, hoping that I didn't sound too disappointed.

"I told them I had an important engagement this evening and would have to postpone," he told me, smiling. "Get your things. We have a big night ahead of us."

"We do? I thought we were just having dinner?"

Matt laughed as though he didn't have a care in the world. His eyes were bright and his smile was magnetic. I couldn't help but relax, thinking Frank must be making a mistake; this guy was just too nice. I got my purse and checked to be sure my cell phone was in it. As a precaution, in case I was the one that was wrong.

Matt was dressed nicely in black jeans, a gray T-shirt, a black jacket and black boots. The only thing missing was a big black cowboy hat. If he had had one on, he could have passed for a country-singing star. He looked very handsome and I realized that the little tidbit about being captivated by someone who smelled good was true. I was sure of it now.

He glanced into my small house, which was immaculate since I have a compulsive thing about clutter and dirt. I felt myself getting warm, realizing I had told him my place was a mess, and that's why he couldn't pick me up. I hate being caught in a lie. I took a deep breath.

"I was a little embarrassed for you to see my little house," I told him. "Yours is so big and beautiful. I apologize."

He smiled, "You shouldn't be embarrassed, this place is really great, very comfortable looking. You've done a fantastic job decorating it."

"Thanks, I really do love the house. Unfortunately I'm renting it right now from someone who makes it tough to really enjoy it, but I hope to be able to buy it when my landlord is ready to sell." I told him, realizing that Mrs. Bennett would finally be out of my life forever.

"Maybe by then you'll have other plans." He handed me the roses. I smelled them and gave him a big smile.

"I guess you never know," I said, all of the sudden realizing I desperately wanted to leave, before I had more company.

As he escorted me to the limo he made a comment about how nice I looked. I was happy to hear it because I didn't have any intention of going back and changing.

The limousine driver opened the door and I slid in just in time to spot Frank and Chuck driving up the street. They strained to look in the limo windows as they passed, but the tint made it impossible to see inside. I hoped they would keep going. I should have known they would. After all, they were both private investigators.

As we drove down the street, Matt closed the window between us and the driver, put on some soft music and asked if I'd like some champagne which was fine with me although I'd rather have a beer any day. I had no idea where we were headed but hoped we would be going back to his house at some point. It was killing me not knowing if I'd be able to get a look around. I thought I'd better just chill out though if I wanted to have the opportunity. If he felt I was too eager, it could cause a red flag to go up. Not a good thing.

We turned onto 15 Freeway heading south. We were leaving Temecula!

"So, when are you going to tell me where we are going?"

"I would really like to surprise you," he said. "Don't you like surprises?"

"I just haven't had very many good ones I guess. Maybe that's why I'm a little hesitant to receive them."

"Anything you'd like to talk about?"

"No, not tonight."

He nodded and smiled as to say he understood.

"If you really need to know, I'll tell you what I have planned for us."

"No, I can wait," I said, being super cool about it when what I wanted to say was, "yes, yes, yes!"

I knew Frank and Chuck were probably cussing me out about now, particularly if they couldn't hear me. I just wasn't really sure they could since we hadn't had an opportunity to check the listening device they had planted in my phone, but unless they were pretty close behind us, I might be out of range. There was one way to make sure. They were driving Chuck's 1967 silver Chevy Corvette. You don't see many of these on the road anymore so it should be easy enough to spot.

"God, it's beautiful out tonight. How about opening the sunroof?" I asked.

"That's a great idea."

"Wheee, this is fantastic!" I said, jumping up and sticking my head out. Chuck's Corvette was about four car lengths back and over one lane to our left. I ducked my head back in.

"Matt, you have to check this out, it feels great to have the cold air blowing on your face."

He was hesitant.

"Come on. You said you loved surprises. Just for a minute."

And so there we stood, smiling at each other until he collapsed onto the seat laughing.

"Doesn't that feel great?" I said enthusiastically.

"You know, as many times as I've been in this limo, I have never done that."

"You're kidding!"

"No, really. I never have. It was great, thanks."

"You're welcome. I guess you like to get surprises as well as give them."

"You know, I never thought about it."

I made an attempt to smooth out my wild hair, probably I looked as though I had been in a wind tunnel. I had the boys to thank for this, I thought.

As we drove down the freeway, we talked about our families and our friends and growing up. I tried to ask him a lot of questions. I thought if I kept him talking maybe he'd say something that would help me to determine if he had anything to do with Ron. No, I hadn't forgotten that the whole reason I was here was to find Ron. I was looking for something, anything that would bring me a little closer to locating him.

As we talked, Matt had mentioned something that struck a chord. There were, it appeared, a group of guys he has known "forever" and would do anything for. He said they were like brothers, always there for each other. Ron had talked about his group of friends the same way. Coincidence? I don't know. It could be I guess. I just don't happen to believe it myself.

We drove over the long bridge that led us onto Coronado Island. I was curious to know if Frank and Chuck were still on our tail but I had no way to check it out that wouldn't attract some attention. I wondered why we had to come all the way down here for dinner. It didn't make much sense.

The closer we got to wherever we were going, Matt became more spirited. By the time we pulled into the parking lot of a marina he was literally beaming. To tell you the truth, it freaked me out a little. But that's just me.

"This is it," he told me, "this is where I like to spend my time. Come on, I'll introduce you to the love of my life." I must have looked a bit startled because he quickly told me not to worry. I wasn't worried, much.

At the end of dock B there was a fifty-foot white and red sailboat with the name *Lucky Man* written across its stern. I had done a little sailing as a kid, but this was way out of my league.

"Sam, this is my passion, isn't she beautiful?"

What could I say, she was truly breathtaking.

Yeah, she's beautiful alright, I thought, realizing that if we were going to go out for a sail, Chuck and Frank wouldn't be able to keep track of me. Oh, shit. Here I was with this guy, possibly a dangerous one, and what happens? He wants to take me out where no one would be able to contact me. I have Ron to thank for this!

CHAPTER 7

Once we were on the boat, Matt introduced to me the "off season" crew, which consisted of the captain, who, surprisingly enough was a long-legged blonde with wide blue eyes and soft skin, dressed in a navy suit with a short skirt and a white silk blouse. Christina apparently didn't think I was worth her time, barely muttering a decent greeting and poor me, I had no idea what I had done to piss her off.

The chef, a short, heavyset Frenchman by the name of André, was friendliest. I was just hoping I would like whatever it was he would be serving because I didn't want to offend him, too.

"I have one more person to introduce you to," Matt said smiling. He was humoring me, but I wasn't up for it. I hoped we could get the show on the road so we could get back.

The low ceiling dining room was furnished in mahogany and featured a beautifully set table, complete with red roses and white candles. Peter was just putting a bottle of champagne in an ice bucket.

"Hello, Miss Parker," he said, "it's nice to see you again."

"Hi, Peter. Thank you. It's nice to see you, too. Please call me Sam."

When he reached out to shake my hand, I noticed a cut across the top of his right hand, just above the knuckle. As we shook hands I also noticed a slight bruise under his left eye, by his cheekbone. It looked as though he might have been in a fight, but I didn't think it would be a good idea to ask about it now. He excused himself and Matt pulled out my chair, indicating I should sit down.

"I haven't had the full tour," I said.

"We'll get to that," he assured me. "I'd like to eat so I can let André get back to the restaurant. He gets a little nuts if things are not done properly. Then he starts firing everyone. I can't risk that now."

"So what you're telling me is that he's a little temperamental?"

"That's an understatement, but he's a master in the kitchen. And he is also a great guy."

"What did you mean when you said you couldn't risk him firing everyone? Isn't it his business if he fires everyone at his restaurant?"

"Actually it's my restaurant, although he'd object, saying I don't have my heart in it."

"Is that what you do, own a restaurant?"

"Yes, I actually have a couple of them, I'm a silent partner though, I don't have my hands in the day-to-day operation. Anyway, let's not talk about that tonight. I'd really just like to enjoy being away from that life, even if it's just for a while."

"God, I'm sorry," I said, uncomfortably aware of what appeared to be a growing uneasiness on his part. "I don't know what I was thinking. I hate talking about work during off hours. So, tell me about your sailing adventures instead."

"Now that is what I'd call interesting conversation," he told me grinning. You're a girl after my own heart. Do you sail?"

"I used to go sailing with my parents a lot as a kid. We loved it. We went out just about every weekend." As I thought about those times I must have been smiling.

"You should see your face right now. You look so happy."

"Those were great times, I really do love being on the water, it makes me feel so free."

"You're not the only one."

"How long have you been sailing?" I asked, wanting to get inside his head.

"I've been sailing since I was a kid," he told me, "but I've really gotten passionate about it in the last seven years or so. It's really the only place I feel totally relaxed, being on the water away from the stresses of real life."

"It is unquestionably the best way to escape from the day-to-day routine. On the water, there is no schedule, no hustle and bustle of doorbells and telephones. It's really the one place you can really escape."

"That's why I love it so much. It's a place to think, to enjoy, to just be."

"It must be nice to be able to afford the luxury." Did I just say that out loud? Shit.

"Actually, yes, it is nice. I am very lucky. I have had a few things go right for me and I am able to enjoy this, as well as a few other luxuries."

A few things go right? Is that what all this is? I think things are going right if I can pay my rent and still eat.

A moment later, Peter was approaching our table with two plates in hand. He set them in front of us and opened the champagne. The meal consisted of swordfish, with a side of lemon, fresh asparagus with some type of yellow sauce, wild rice and fresh baked rolls with butter. Yes . . . I scored. This could have been a total disaster but fortunately for me, tonight I wouldn't have to offend the chef.

"André had to get back to the restaurant," Pete announced, "but he said to enjoy your meal and your evening and he'll call you later. Can I get you anything else?"

Peter was very professional. As I watched him I thought about the many roles he seemed to play. A jack of all trades, master of none. Maybe not. It sure was odd that ever since Ron contacted me, he had become so ubiquitous. I wasn't sure what his part was in all this, but whatever it was, it was more than what it appeared to be. I was sure of it.

After we had finished our dinner, Peter dutifully cleared our table of everything but the candles and our champagne glasses. I asked about the full tour, hoping that once we were on our feet and I was shown the boat, the natural progression would be to head back to Temecula and the house that, as far as I knew, really belonged to Ron.

Forfeiting more champagne, we decided on a cold beer and with a Beck's in hand, we began the tour.

"Where would you like to start?"

"How about at the top?"

"Good idea," he said.

As we walked toward the corridor, Pete informed Matt that Christina was in her cabin, going over the charts for their trip. He seemed pleased, so I had to ask where they were going.

"Catalina Island," he said, "fishing."

"Sounds fun." I responded, even though the thought of catching a fish on a sharp hook seemed to be cruel, to say the least.

The upper deck was quite large with the bridge at the forward, housing what looked like an extensive array of navigation and communication equipment. Matt told me about what most of it did but I must admit, I was not paying as close attention as I should have been. Not that it wasn't interesting, I just couldn't get past the extravagance of the vessel. The interior was a beautiful wood, mahogany I think, as were the ceilings and cabinetry throughout the yacht.

On each side of the bridge were glass doors that led out onto the deck which was wide enough so that you could walk around without feeling that one wave would knock you into the water. I was comforted by this state of affairs, since the last thing I wanted to do was trip and end up freezing my ass off waiting to be rescued at sea, so to speak.

When Christina opened the door of her cabin, she looked annoyed to see me. Not that that came as a surprise. While she and Matt talked, I looked around and saw a desk with a half dozen framed photographs including one of Matt and Christina looking very cozy by a pool. Several eight-by-ten photos hung on the wall as well.

As Matt gave the tour guide speech, I felt awkwardness in the room. I glanced at Christina and saw her staring intently at Matt with a look that was forceful to say the least. I quickly turned away, not wanting her to notice me watching her. As Matt talked about the architecture of the yacht, I walked over to the pictures and looked at each one closely.

Besides the pictures of Matt and Christina, there was one of a group of guys on a boat holding up a big fish. I recognized Matt, Peter, Simon, and the chef, André, right away. As I glanced from face to face I thought one of the men looked familiar but I wasn't sure where I had seen him before. Then it hit me. It was Ron. He had a beard and mustache then so it was difficult to recognize him at first. But it was him, I'd swear it. I was still staring at all the picture, when Matt came over.

"Looks like fun, doesn't it?" he said.

"You sure have a lot of fishing buddies," I replied. "Do you get together often?"

"We do about two long trips a year but fish pretty regularly all year long. Some of the guys are married and are not able to go out as often so they really let loose during these trips."

The next picture was of four guys: Matt, Ron, Peter and another man I didn't know. All posing in a clear attempt to show off their tanned, muscular physiques, on what looked like Matt's boat.

"And who are these guys?" I asked, almost afraid of what I'd hear.

"These are my best friends in the world." He told me, picking the picture up as Christina stood behind him. "This is Peter, as you know. He hasn't changed a bit, has he? He still looks like a teenager. This guy here is Nick, he's the jokester of the group. Loves to play practical jokes and goes to great lengths to make them work. I'll tell you about them sometime. This is Ronnie. He's the smart one. He has been the rock of the group. Ron is a great thinker and the one we all go to for advice and can count on to always be there for us. He is a true friend and like a brother to me."

There was a knock on the door and Christina went to open it.

"Hey, Matt. Can I talk to you for a minute?"

"Sure, Pete." Matt turned toward me. "I'll be right back."

"All right," I said, although I wasn't particularly keen about spending quality time with a woman who looked as though she'd like to see me walk the plank.

"Where did you meet him?" Christina said coldly as soon as the door closed behind him.

"It was a mistake really, I had thought I was going to a client's home but got the address wrong and ended up meeting Matt."

"At the house? I mean . . . his house?"

Why, I wondered, had she hesitated and corrected herself.

"Yes. In Temecula."

"Oh, when?"

"Just a few days ago."

"I see."

"Is there a problem?" I asked a bit perturbed. Just then the door opened and Matt came flying in.

"We have to get going, Sam," he said. "We'll finish the guided tour another time."

"Um, all right."

I looked at Christina, "It was nice to meet you."

"Likewise," she said.

We were both lying but what the hell.

CHAPTER 8

As Matt escorted me to the limo, he explained to me that one of his employees had been in an accident and that he was going to have to go with Peter, but that his driver would take me home. He wanted me to enjoy the ride back and told me to make myself comfortable, adding that there were movies and CDs as well as a full bar, and not to be shy. Like that would ever happen.

He explained to his driver, whose name, it appeared was Simon, to make sure I had an enjoyable ride and apologized again, asking if he could call me. Now that I knew he had a connection to Ron, I was very eager to have another "date" with him as soon as possible. He leaned in to kiss me but then reached down and took my hand and kissed it instead. Before I knew what was going on, he was gone. I stood there dumbfounded, wondering what I had done to deserve that because I wanted to kiss him. Yes, even if he is a bad guy. It's no big deal really, a harmless kiss. It's research!

As Simon opened the door to the back seat, I hopped in front, announcing that I would be more comfortable up there, and after all, those were Matt's instructions, were they not?

Simon looked surprised. "Ma'am?"

"Please call me Sam," I told him.

"All right, Sam," he said, "are you sure you wouldn't rather sit in back?"

"I'm sure."

It was very dark as we drove out of the parking lot, and what few lights there were created an eerie orange haze. What was the point of having lights that didn't brighten the area? I didn't know. All I knew was that I was not able to see Chuck's car and I had to wonder if they had lost me along the way. Whatever. The important thing was that I still had a job to do and that consisted of pumping Simon for all he was worth, and keeping my fingers crossed that he wouldn't realize what I was up to. If these characters were as dangerous as I thought they might be - and this, unfortunately included Matt - I didn't want to end up wearing cement shoes at the bottom of the San Diego bay.

"So, how long have you been a driver?" I asked him as we drove toward the bridge.

"I have been driving for Matt . . . Mr. Andrews, for almost four years."

"You must enjoy it then."

"I do. I get to meet some very interesting people. He's a very successful businessman, you know."

"I gathered that whatever he does he's very successful at it." I laughed with what I hoped might sound like careless abandon. "But speaking of his friends, you know, Matt was showing me some pictures of his buddies on a fishing trip. I noticed you were in one of them."

"Only one?" he said.

"Well, I only got to see the few that were framed in the captain's quarters. You know Christina, don't you?"

"I know her, yes."

It was clear that, know her or not, he didn't seem to want to pursue the subject, but figuring I'd better give it my best shot I continued.

"She didn't like me much," I said. "I think that as far as she was concerned, I was some kind of interlude."

"Sam," he said, "let me tell you something about Christina. She's a different type of gal. She is tough and possessive and just plain rude most of the time. Please don't let her attitude scare you off. After a while she does warm up a bit. But keep in mind, it will be 'just a bit' if at all."

"Why is that? What have I done to her?"

"You exist and Matt is taken with you. That's all she needs."

"Matt is taken with me?" I asked, as a shiver moved through me.

"You do feel the same, don't you?"

Oh, great, now I have some dangerous man that is "taken" with me. What could I have possibly been thinking to go out with this guy? I knew it was too good to be true. I thought I'd slip in and get what I needed to find Ron and slip out just as easily, but no, now he's taken with me, so where does that leave me?

"Well, yes, I just wasn't sure about him. He did get rid of me pretty suddenly tonight."

I knew this conversation would be giving Frank and Chuck a heart attack, if they were, in fact still listening.

"Don't let that bother you," Simon told me. "He has a lot of responsibilities and he has to spread himself thin sometimes. You just need to trust him."

"Can I ask you something?"

"Shoot."

I hesitated, wondering about his choice of words.

"How long have you known Matt?"

"I've been driving for him . . ."

"No, how long have you known him? Are you one of the lifelong friends he was telling me about?"

My heart pounded hard in my chest as I though about my current situation and I felt like I was starting to loose it. All

I wanted was to be home safe. Maybe if I kept him talking, he wouldn't see that I was scared to death.

"I met Matt and the other guys when I had moved to the neighborhood in the fourth grade," he told me. "I was ten. He and his buddies were planning to beat me up."

"No. Really?"

I guess this confirms why my gut is doing somersaults. It's true, Matt is dangerous and probably has been since he was a kid. I had to figure out a way to get out of this.

"Yeah. I had just moved in about two days before and on my first day of school they decided I should be initiated into the neighborhood. You see, they didn't want any wimps living on their turf."

"So what happened?"

"Well, as I came around the corner Nick and Matt jumped me. I had done some boxing and held my own against the two of them beating on me, and from then on we just started hanging out."

"So it was just Nick and Matt who ganged up on you?"

"No, the other guys were there, too, but they stayed back, it was already unfair with two against one." He said, shaking his head as if it had happened yesterday.

"Can I ask you a question? Matt was telling me about your friend, Ronnie. Is he still around?"

"Oh yeah. We see him all the time," he said. I hoped the shock I felt didn't register on my face.

"When did you see him last?"

"Do you know him?" he demanded.

"No, I'm just curious. Probably it comes with being taken with Matt." I said, attempting a giggle. "Have any of your buddies left town?"

"Why would they do that? We're like family and enjoy hanging out together."

He was being more cautious. I could sense it. I'd have to back off a bit. I was asking too many questions.

"Matt speaks so highly of all of you, I hope we get an opportunity to hang out sometime."

Simon seemed to relax a little as I noticed his hands loosen on the steering wheel.

"From what Matt has told me, I'm sure that will happen."

"What did he tell you exactly?"

"All I can say is that he enjoys your company."

This was a definite junior high conversation and I felt foolish engaging in it, but I was fishing. It had to be done.

"That's good enough for me," I said.

"Now that we've covered my life," Simon said, with just a touch of irony, "why don't you tell me a little about yourself?"

I hate talking about myself but I knew that in order to gain his trust I was going to have to divulge something.

"Tell me everything about your life."

My life? He obviously is mistaken me for someone who actually has a life.

"Well, I'm a paralegal and I live in Temecula." I said.

"What kind of work do you do as a paralegal?"

"Mostly divorces, living trusts and wills."

"Do you like the work?"

"It's okay. I really don't enjoy doing the divorces, as you can imagine, it gets pretty depressing."

"What firm do you work for?"

"Oh, I don't work for a firm now. I've done that several times and have discovered something."

"What?"

"I hate lawyers."

He let out a big hearty laugh.

"You and me both!"

The rest of the ride we engaged in conversation about music. The best concerts we've been to and our favorite bands, etc. We also discovered that we share the same birthday, making us both twenty-seven.

When we pulled into my driveway it was clear that Simon was protective of Matt and certainly wouldn't betray him. Smart guy.

He got out of the car and opened my door.

"Can I walk you up?" he asked.

"No thanks. I'm okay." I told him, as I took out my keys.

I hit the light switch inside the door. Shit, the bulb was out. Starting into the living room I stumbled and struck my shin on one of the end tables.

"It's about time you got home," Frank said as I snapped on the lamp.

"Oh, shit! What the hell are you doing here sitting in the dark? Are you trying to give me a heart attack?"

"Your landlord was snooping around again so I thought it would be better to keep the lights off. So, how did it go tonight?"

"Have you ever heard of knocking on the door? It is customary you know. How did you get in here anyway?"

"Bathroom window, you need to get that fixed, someone could break in."

"Thanks, Frank."

"So tell me all about your evening."

"Weren't you listening?"

"Yeah, we were listening, but I want to know what you saw."

"Where's Chuck?"

"I dropped him off, he had plans for the evening."

"I need a drink," I said. "Do you want something?"

"Sure, do you have a beer?"

"You got it," I said as I limped to the kitchen.

For the next hour, I filled Frank in on everything about the evening, while he, methodical as usual, took notes.

It was after midnight when we decided to call it a day, making plans to meet at his office the next afternoon at one, to go over the events again. He said Chuck would be there, and that I should be on my best behavior. Probably, Chuck was going to rip me a new one for all the things I did that were not "by the book," and I was already dreading it. Once in bed, I fell asleep almost before my head hit the pillow. I slept restlessly all night though, going over the events of the evening in my head.

When I woke up, I felt as if I'd been hit by a truck. My mind hadn't stopped working all night and I could feel it. I was just plain bushed. I sucked down my usual three cups of coffee hoping to regain some of my energy. I knew I'd have to be at my spunkiest for the meeting if I was to survive the wrath of Chuck, but honestly I was not feeling the part.

I decided I'd better get to the gym for a workout and went up stairs and donned my cutest workout shorts and top. I felt like if I looked good I'd start to feel good, too. I got my gym bag, a water bottle and headed out.

I returned from the gym about an hour later after having a great workout despite the fact that I could barely get out of my car when I arrived. I felt much better and was starting to think there actually was a possibility that I would be in good shape for my meeting this afternoon. All I needed now was a hot shower.

I dressed casually in blue jeans, a black shirt and white tennis shoes, knowing anything more would be too much. I was comfortable and feeling pretty good now. I did have something on my mind though and knew I'd have to tell the boys about it. The envelope that Ron had given me was still in my safe deposit box and I had not yet opened it. I know I should have done that immediately after not hearing from him for the first twenty-four hours but I kept thinking he would get in touch with me. I also naively thought if I opened it, it would solidify that he was in fact, really missing.

I decided I'd better stop by the bank and pick it up on my way to the meeting. It definitely wouldn't be a good idea to tell them about it if they couldn't see it. I knew that would cause more trouble for me and I wasn't up for it.

While at the bank, I ran into Henry Sullivan, an old friend who had left Temecula last year after an ugly divorce. He was an outgoing friendly guy and I couldn't help but to wonder what had gone wrong. I told him I'd give him a call so we could catch up, and I took off.

Although I thought it would be best to go home and take a look inside the envelope in order to be sure I should share the information with Frank and Chuck, I decided just to head over to their office. I took the scenic route and drove slowly, enjoying the quiet moment before the impending storm. The fact that the envelope was still sealed would be beneficial if the information turned out to be bogus. At least I had something in my favor.

Upon my arrival I was reminded, once again, to keep my cool when Chuck arrived. Frank didn't enjoy the friction and would have to ask me to leave if I didn't hold it together. I promised I would, although it was clear that he didn't believe me and, of course, he did have a point. If I got heated I lost control, and that was a fact. Sometimes I think that he knows me better than I know myself.

"Frank," I said. "I have to show you something. I should have brought this up before, when I first discovered that Ron was nowhere to be found. You see, he gave this to me."

His jaw tightened and he rubbed his temples. I could see the frustration building up but before he had a chance to bark at me I held out the envelope and he clutched it away from me. I lowered my eyes, not wanting to see his reaction, knowing it would not be a positive one.

"Did he say what was in it?"

"He told me that this would lead me to the information that he has spent the last few years gathering on his buddies' illegal business practices. He didn't want his friends to get away with all of this, even if they got to him first, he wanted me to stay with it. He wanted them to pay."

. Frank stared at the envelope for a minute and then opened it. He pulled out a video tape that was unmarked. We both stared at it, probably wondering the same thing; what was on it? Just then Chucked hiked into the room with the mail. Frank moved to the safe and deposited it inside, muttering something about this case getting stranger and stranger. As far as I was concerned, it felt so good to have someone else making the decisions. So good in fact, that I didn't even argue about not watching it right then.

Hey Chuck, Sammy's ready to go over the events of the evening." Frank said, eyeing me.

"Sam, can you think of anything you didn't tell me last night that we should know?"

"I don't know, Frank, I was exhausted. Can we go over it again?"

"Why did you take off before we got to your place?" Chuck said this, obviously annoyed. I moved my gaze toward Frank with a look that clearly asked, is he kidding?

"I didn't take off, Chuck. Matt just showed up. He wasn't supposed to come over at all. He said he wanted to surprise me, and believe me, he did."

"So he didn't call you first?"

"No."

"Why would he just show up?"

"I don't know. He said he wanted to surprise me," I said with a flat voice, concentrating on keeping calm no matter how much this man irritated me with his implied criticism. "Chuck," Frank intervened. "I took these notes last night. We went over the evening from beginning to end and all the information is consistent with the tape. Sam filled in the blanks, what she saw etc., so I think we're in good shape. I just want her to go over the notes and make sure she didn't forget anything. Then we need to decide what to do next."

"I'd like to take a look, too, and I have a few questions. Is that all right Sam?" Chuck asked, still tense.

Here we go, I thought. Let the interrogation begin.

"Sure, Chuck," I said. "Anything you say."

I looked over Frank's notes as I thought about the details of the night. Although I was exhausted, I thought I did a very thorough job of filling in the blanks for him.

"Looks good," I said, as I handed them to Chuck. As Chuck looked things over, Frank and I sat quietly, staring at each other, expressionless.

"Good notes, Frank. It looks as though you're getting better at paying attention to the details. Sam, what's the story with the captain? It's a dame named Christina isn't it?"

"Not to me she isn't," I told him. "The lady made it clear I was to call her Captain and I don't know what her story is. I tried to get some more information from Simon, the driver, but he wasn't offering much. Why?"

"Because it's unheard of for gangs or crime families to bring in a female, especially in a leading role. I was wondering if she could be the daughter of one of the honchos. Did you happen to get a last name on her?"

"No, I didn't even think to ask. I must admit I was a little surprised to see a female captain as well. And as I told Frank, when Matt took me with him to her cabin, she didn't look very happy. I wondered if they were involved or had been. If they were, she's not over him anyway. That's for sure."

"What about him, did he seem to have a connection to her?"

"That's what was odd. He wasn't uncomfortable or uneasy at all. It was as if she was the only one who knew what was going on. It was strange because I could feel the tension and wondered why he didn't even seem to notice it."

"Let's make a note to see what we can find on her," Chuck said. "We need to know where she fits in to all this."

"How are we going to do that?" I said rather sarcastically.

"Well, Sam, it looks like we're going to need you to see Matt again. Do you think he'll be calling you?"

"I don't know. He got rid of me in a hurry. Maybe I'm not his type."

"Don't worry, Chuck, he'll call her," Frank assured him. "Sam has an irresistible quality that you just haven't had time to notice yet."

I looked at Frank and smiled. It felt good to have him on my side. He trusted me and it truly warmed my heart. He was a true friend.

"Okay, so will you see him again and see if you can dig up something on our captain?"

"Sure. I can do that." Didn't he hear Frank? I'm irresistible for God's sake. Some guys are so blind to real sex appeal!

CHAPTER 9

Driving home, I felt as if I had been put into the big game. I knew that if I could get something on Christina I would gain a little respect from Chuck. Actually, of course, I don't give a shit. Or maybe, deep down, I did. Perhaps it was because he was a friend of Frank's or because he was well respected as an investigator. I don't really know. But I do know that I love the excitement of this kind of work and I do have a knack for it. It beats typing up divorce papers for a living.

When I arrived home, I found a package on my doorstep. There wasn't any return address on it but it had been sent through the U.S. mail, and was postmarked Temecula, California. Probably an order from my book club. I left it on the coffee table and went in to take a pee.

When I emerged from the bathroom my telephone was ringing. I was surprised to hear Jack's voice on the other end since he had gone to Vegas for a big sales conference. He never called from Vegas anymore. A pact we had made after last year's conference. A bit too much drinking and gambling. He knows how I hate those 3 A.M. calls from him when he's shit faced, slobbering about how much he loves me and how we should just get married. I have to talk him down and half of the time he falls asleep with the phone still in his hand. It just pisses me off and he feels embarrassed about making a fool of himself. Then we go through an "awkward" stage for a couple of weeks. Bottom line, it just sucks.

"Are you all right?"

"Yes, I'm fine and I'm not drunk I just wanted you to know I miss you. How about us going out for dinner tomorrow night? I'll be back about five and could come by to pick you up after I get cleaned up, about seven?"

My first thought was whether or not I'd be hearing from Matt. It's not that I didn't want to see Jack, because I did. You see, although our relationship seemed too casual for most, it worked for us. We liked the slower pace and the natural way it evolved, seeming all on its own. I just had to keep my options open, you understand, don't you?

"Sure, that sounds good. Will you call me first? I have an appointment I'll need to postpone. I wasn't expecting you in for a few more days. Why are you cutting the trip short?"

"I just want to get home; I'm tired of being on the road."

"You must be exhausted."

"I'm fine, I'll call you when I get in. Try to change that appointment. It would be really nice to see you."

As you know, I didn't have an appointment, but if Matt called I'd need to be free to see him. This wasn't personal, it was business and Jack couldn't understand why I was so attracted to it. He was the safe type. He didn't have an adventurous spirit and didn't understand my need for it.

I poured myself a glass of iced tea and went in to open my package, which was the size and shape of a shoe box but much lighter than you'd expect. It was wrapped in brown paper with my name and address written clearly in capitals directly across the center. Looking at the box, I thought it seemed strange, the way it was written. Probably, it was those block letters that did it. Sometimes I think I watch too many detective shows on TV. Anyway, suddenly I felt as though someone was walking all over my grave.

It gave me the creeps and I started to think, why would someone send me an unidentifiable package? I put the box up to my ear to see if I'd hear anything. I listened intently. Nothing. I think my imagination is getting the best of me.

"Just open it, what could happen?" I wasn't talking to anyone in particular, just speaking out loud to prove just how ridiculous I was being. I sat down, box in hand and started to open it slowly. First the edges, then the rest of the paper and was now left with a box that said Nike across the top. At least the sender had good taste in running shoes. I lifted the lid cautiously and stared at the contents. Newspaper! What the hell is someone doing sending me pieces of newspaper?

Here I had been, scared shitless, thinking a bomb was going to explode in my face and I'm staring at pieces of newspaper. I felt around to see if maybe I was missing something, an item that was under this pile and saw a headline that really sent my antenna up. "Five Bodies Found in Lake." I read the article, put it aside, and grabbed another one. More references to violent crime; this time strangulation.

I must have sat on the floor for an hour, reading article after article about the violent acts of the "businessman mobsters" as they were referred to, over and over again. Despite the fact that I hadn't gotten through the whole box, I had to get up and move around, my butt was sore from spending too much time on the hard wood floor. As I paced, I thought about who could have sent this. If it were Matt or any of his "friends" I was dead and I knew it. Was it a warning? Could Ron have sent it? If so, where the hell was he hiding and why scare the shit out of me this way? None of this made any sense to me. All I knew was that I was more confused than ever and scared stiff as well.

I poured a glass of wine and dialed Frank's cell phone number. He picked up on the first ring.

"You have to come over right away, I have something here that you need to see."

"Sam?"

"Yeah, can you come?"

"I'm in the mid——"

"Please, it is urgent."

Silence.

"Frank?"

"I'll be right over."

I hung up, now wondering if I am truly paranoid. What if I've dragged him away from something important and . . . no, this is important, I was certain of it. Even Chuck would agree on this one.

I continued to read as I enjoyed every sip of my wine. It somehow tasted better than I ever remember wine tasting to me. Fear for my life? That was it. This might be my last glass ever so I'd better enjoy it.

The knock on the door gave me a start.

"Sammy, it's me," Frank called. "Open the door."

It wasn't until I got up to let him in that I realized I had stopped breathing.

"My God," he said. "You look like you've seen a ghost. "Are you all right?"

"I don't know," I said, feeling very vulnerable. "Let me show you what was waiting for me this afternoon when I returned home."

We sat down together on the couch. I gave Frank one of the articles to read. He skimmed the contents. I handed him another one, and then a stack. As he read, I watched his expression change from bewilderment to comprehension.

"Where did you get these?" he demanded.

"They were waiting for me on my doorstep when I got home," I told him. "There isn't any return address but the postmark is from Temecula."

"So, who sent them?"

"I wish I knew. I have to tell you, Frank, this is starting to scare me now. Why would someone send articles about alleged mob hits to me?"

"Sam, think. Who would want you to have this information?"

"The only one I can think of is Ronald but . . ."

"Who else?"

"I hate to think about it, but what if Matt or one of his guys found out I have a connection to Ronald and sent them as a warning to me?"

"Do you really think that is a possibility?"

"I don't know. I'm not sure what to think anymore."

"Well, let me take them to my office," he said. "We'll get with Chuck and see what his take is on all of this. In the meantime, I want you to think about everyone who knows about Ronald contacting you. Everyone, Sam, no matter how insignificant you think the connection may be. Oh, and get some sleep. I'll call you in the morning."

"You expect me to sleep?"

"Try."

"Yeah, sure."

I closed the door behind Frank and locked up. I checked the house and made sure it was secured for the night. Having repaired the bathroom window with a new lock, I felt satisfied I was safe. Even so, I knew I wasn't going to get a wink of sleep so I decided another glass of wine and a good cheerful movie was in order. I pulled out my most recent addition to what had become a fairly extensive movie collection, *Meet the Parents*, with Robert De Niro and of course, the hysterical Ben Stiller. Yes, this was just what I needed.

It was about eleven thirty when the movie ended and I was feeling much better. Laughter is the best medicine. But because I was still a bit jumpy and needed to blow off the anxiety before I could even think about closing my eyes, I did a bit of cleaning and finally went to bed at three, so tired I could barely see.

The ringing of the phone disturbed me just enough for me to decide that I didn't want to pick it up. My machine picked up on the third ring and as I dozed, I thought I heard the faint sound of a familiar voice. Too tired to complete the thought process I fell back into a deep, comfortable slumber.

The sound of my stomach growling finally woke me at ten and despite the fact that I run best on eight to nine hours of sleep, I felt well rested. After a bowl of cereal, a few cups of coffee and a shower, I was ready for the day. I checked my messages as I drank my third cup of Joe. Frank had called as promised and wanted me to call him right away.

I dialed his office as I paced the floor, eager to hear what he and Chuck thought about the clippings. I had started a list of everyone I could think of that would know about Ron hiring me. A list that consisted, so far of Jon James, one of the guys I spoke with at the construction site, Sally, the waitress from the club house restaurant, Ronald, Frank, Chuck and myself. I was sure I hadn't mentioned the case to anyone else. To be honest, I'm not too much into being around people. I prefer a book and except for my work, I don't spend a whole lot of time socializing. No answer. I left a short message asking him to call me on my cell phone, I was going out.

I grabbed my purse, keys, sunglasses and a water bottle and headed for the door. Because I needed to get a clear perspective on all this a visit to Carol and Harold was in order. A fresh outlook was sometimes all I needed to bring things into light. Having the information is one thing but being able to recognize its value is imperative. Yes, a fresh point of view was exactly what I needed.

But first I stopped at Milano's deli, a great little place run by a couple of New York guys, to pick up some lunch, just in case I was still hanging around their house waiting for Frank to call when mealtime rolled around again. Milano's is as close to a "real" deli as I have found since I've been in California, and believe me I have searched. In fact, I do consider myself to be a somewhat of a sandwich expert. I have after all, been enjoying them all my life and consider any time a good time to take pleasure in one. And seeing as I don't cook, the need to have a great-tasting sandwich is vital, given that I sometimes find myself eating them for all my meals. Equipped with three roast beef heroes and a big bag of chips, as well as a six-pack of Amstel light, I was on my way.

When I arrived at their house, I was happy to see Harold out feeding the horses. As he tossed in the hay, they moved to him and nuzzled him gently.

"Hi, Harold," I called out. "I brought lunch. Do you and Carol have some time to talk? I've run into a snag on something and could use your advice."

"A snag, huh? What kind of snag?"

The property was made up of several large paddocks that sat side by side, separated by tall white fencing and off to the back was an old red barn where the feed and tack were kept. There was a long winding path that took you up to the main house, which, by any standard, was beautiful but modest.

As we approached the house, Carol, who was doing something complicated with the geraniums that filled one of the wicker boxes that lined the porch, seemed glad enough to take a break and before you knew it, we were parked in three of the four rocking chairs that Harold had found at a flee market over in Murrieta, with our feet on the railing shooting the breeze. It was the kind of setting I liked best with a great meal, a cold beer and good conversation.

At twelve noon sharp, I produced the heroes and beer and Carol came back with a tray in hand, holding some plates, napkins, salt and pepper, butter and homemade potato salad on it. Harold followed with some chilled beer glasses. We all gathered around the main table settling down to eat and talk.

"So Sam, what is going on?"

"Oh Harold, give her a chance to take a bite of lunch first," Carol protested.

"No, it's fine." I told her. "I'm here to get some input from you both. I need a fresh perspective in order to move forward with this."

Harold had spent forty years as an insurance executive, specializing in fraud and Carol was a crime reporter for *The Post*. Because of their combined experience and ability to identify a scam from a mile away, I felt it was important to share what I knew so far and hope they would be able to fill in some of the gaps. I wasn't disappointed. Harold's take on it was that Ron, for reasons not yet known, wanted to disappear. He had seen it a million times, it was about money. "Find the money and you'll find the answer." He said. Carol, on the other hand had suggested that he was running from his "friends" and that I needed to stay away from Matt. "He's bad news," she told me. Either way, I was now convinced that I could be in more danger than I originally thought, because if Ron had decided to disappear, then he had purposefully led me right to Matt's door, knowing he was dangerous and if that was what happened, I had to know why. Why me?

CHAPTER 10

That evening, as I stood in front of the fridge, checking out its contents, the phone rang and instinctively I knew there would be a change of plans. Sure enough, it was Frank, wanting me to meet him at the cantina.

"Chuck will be there, too," he added, "so no attitude. It's important."

Attitude? I was in no condition to give anyone any attitude. All I wanted to do was get closer to knowing what the hell this was about and why.

Running upstairs, I pulled a comb through my hair, brushed my teeth, checked my clothes; black jeans, white top, leather jacket and sneakers, and ran back down searching for my purse and keys.

My hand was on the door when the phone rang again. I picked it up, hoping to God it would be Ron.

"Hello?"

"Sam?"

"Jack?"

"Yes, I told you I'd call, remember?"

"Sure." Oh, shit. I forgot he was going to call. Now what was I going to tell him?

"Are we on for dinner tonight?"

"Um, Yeah, but I'm just on my way out to a meeting. Can I call you when I know how long I will be?"

"Damn it Sam, we have to talk. I told you I needed to see you."

"This shouldn't take long, Jack. I'll call you in an hour."

"Fine, Sam. Fine"

He hung up abruptly, pissed off at me for not clearing my schedule for him, I'm sure. Like he'd do it for me. Maybe I wouldn't call him. I don't need this shit.

The phone rang. Probably Jack to lay a guilt trip on me.

"This is my job," I said, "so fuck off!"

"Sam? It's Matt. Did I interrupt something?"

Matt? Oh my God.

"Oh, hi Matt. Sorry. I . . . never mind. What's up? It's nice to hear from you."

"Are you sure you are all right?"

"Yes, I'm fine. I have a client that is a bit of a nightmare sometimes but it's really no problem."

"Are you sure? Maybe I could talk to him."

I suddenly remembered who I was talking to. "No, no really. I can handle it myself." I didn't even want to entertain the idea of what having this man talk to anyone might mean.

"Well then, would you do me the honor of having dinner with me tomorrow night?"

"I'd love to, Matt, I really would love to."

"Shall I pick you up at seven?"

"I'm not sure that is going to work," I told him, fabricating furiously. "You see I have a late-afternoon meeting in San Diego and I'll be driving back up from there. You know how unpredictable the traffic can be. Would you mind if I just meet you at your place when I get back into town?" I hoped he would agree, I really wanted to get inside the house again.

"Sure," he said. "In fact, why don't we plan to order in?"

"That would be wonderful!"

"Great, see you tomorrow night then."

"Bye, Matt."

I hung up wondering if I had pulled myself together as well as I thought I had. I looked at the clock. Shit. Frank was probably wondering where the hell I am.

Arriving at the cantina, I saw Frank and Chuck looking at their watches in unison. Here we go.

"Hi, I'm so sorry I'm late. Just as I was . . ."

"We don't care about your excuses."

"Nice to see you, too, Chuck. As I was saying, just as I was walking out the door Matt phoned. I didn't want to rush him, you know?"

"Good thinking, Sam," Frank said as he gave Chuck a warning look.

"So what is going on? You said you had some information."

"Have a seat. Do you want a beer or something?" Frank waved the waitress over.

Taking out a large folder, Chuck chose a few pictures to lay on the table in front of me.

"Do any of these people look familiar to you?" He asked.

"No. Are they supposed to?" Why was it that I found it so impossible not to be flip with this man?

"Now look at these." He placed three more black and white photos down. "Would you believe that any of these men are the same person?"

Examining them closely, one by one. "No," I said. "It doesn't look like any of them could be the same person. Their features are very different. It doesn't even look like they could be related."

"Are you sure, Sam?"

Both Frank and Chuck were solemn, expressionless. I looked at the photos again.

"I'm sure," I said firmly.

"Tell her, Frank," Chuck declared in a flat voice. "Tell her what we found out."

"Sam, these photos represent the work of one of the best plastic surgeons in the United States."

"Meaning?"

"See these two?" he said, pointing to the top two photos. "Take a really good look, compare them,"

"I see them," I said, as Frank pushed one of them closer. "They don't look alike."

"This is Clarence Fuser, better known as 'the Fuse,'" He explained. "When he discovered that there was a hit put out on him several years back after he was caught fooling around with one of the Casio crime family's wives, he went to the FBI, turned himself in and cut a deal to bring down the family in turn for protection. They had been into everything, including prostitution, which is not a business the mob usually likes to have anything to do with. After he testified, the FBI set him up with a doctor for a face job, and put him into the witness protection program. He put another picture right next to the first one. "This is what he looks like now."

"You're kidding, right?" I said. "This can't be the same guy. Just look at them."

"We know. It's unbelievable," Chuck said, sounding as though he had done the make-over himself.

"So you're not pulling my leg," I said. "This is for real? Holy shit." I sat back and took a deep breath. What have I gotten into? If there are doctors and witness protection programs in this...Shit. "Obviously you think this has something to do with Ron's disappearance." I went on.

"That's correct," Frank told me. "Chuck has uncovered some interesting information. Here is the file. We need to investigate all the possibilities here. And in the process, we're going to need you to get up close and personal with our friend, Matt. Are you up for it?"

Me? I don't even know how I got involved in all this. The job was supposed to be simple, and now...I think I'm going to puke. "You know I am."

Frank gathered the photos and the rest of the thick, heavy, file and handed it to me.

"When are you supposed to see Mr. Andrews again?"

"Tomorrow night, I'm going to his place and we're planning to order dinner and eat in."

"Are you opposed to a wire?" Chuck's sarcasm had vanished.

"Sorry, Chuck, I can't risk it. You said yourself that Matt is a dangerous man, and if that is true, I can't even imagine you'd want to put me in that situation. Can we do the cell phone bug again?"

"Sure, Sam," Frank replied. "If that would make you more comfortable, a bug it is. I'll get it all together and we'll set you up."

"When should I meet you?" I asked. "I'm due to arrive at Matt's at seven."

"Let's be safe this time," Chuck replied. "Better meet us at our office at four. We need to discuss your thoughts on the file and make sure the equipment is working. Do you think that will be enough time to cover everything, Frank?"

"It should be. And Sam, here's the file. Study it."

"I will, I'll do it tonight," I told him. "Oh, shit, I'll be right back. I have to make a call." Jack picked up on the first ring.

"Hi, Jack," I said. "Look, I'm sorry but I have some work that I need to get done tonight."

"Sam, this is just too much," he protested. "We need to talk, I won't take up too much of your precious time but I'm stopping by your place tonight. I'll bring over a pizza and we'll talk. What time should I be there?"

Although I knew I needed to meet with Jack, my heart just wasn't in it. He wasn't the kind of guy that would understand my current situation or be all that supportive. He wanted Susie Homemaker and was getting Miss Congeniality instead.

"Meet me in a half hour," I told him and headed back to the table where Frank and Chuck were sharing a laugh over their rookie days.

"Are you all right, Sam?" Frank inquired.

"Oh, yeah. I'm fine."

I wasn't fine; I had a strange feeling about tonight. Jack has wanted more from our relationship for some time and I haven't been able to give it to him. I know he wanted to start a family soon but emotionally I was stuck. I could feel the pit in my stomach.

"I've got to go," I told them. "See you both at four. I'll be home studying so if you need me to come over earlier just give me a ring."

They stood up to see me off. Frank gave me a hug and whispered in my ear to hang in there, and that he'd call me later. I smiled at him and left.

On the drive home, I was feeling anxious. Exactly how did I feel about Jack? I hadn't asked myself that question enough. In fact, I've always taken him for granted. The casualness of the relationship had been safe. And I like safe. No, I'm comfortable with safe. We had fun when we were together, no hassles, no dependency. But was that enough? I didn't know. I guessed that I would have to see what he had to say and then, if he wants more from me than I was prepared to give, I could deal with it. Somehow.

Pulling into my driveway, I turned off the car's engine and just sat. I hate feeling emotionally vulnerable, but here I was, my ass hanging out in the wind, exposed. As I got out of the car, Jack's white Toyota pickup truck pulled in front of the house and he got out holding a pizza.

"Perfect timing," he said. "Are you hungry?" Clearly he was in a good mood. I hadn't expected that.

"What kind of pizza did you get?" I said, trying to act as if nothing had happened. My usual cop out.

"Your favorite, sausage and pepperoni. I got some spicy wings, too!"

"Sounds great."

He unlocked the door for me and while I got some plates and a couple of beers from the kitchen, he lit some candles and made a fire in the fireplace. Talk about making himself at home. But I found that I really didn't mind.

We took off our shoes and ate in silence, sitting on the living room floor.

"Sam," he said, finally. "Exactly what do you want from this relationship?"

"I don't know."

"You don't know, or you don't want me to know?"

"Look, Jack, I'm not really sure what you are looking for here. Why don't you tell me what you want and I'll tell you if I can give it to you."

"I want more of a committed relationship," he said. "I'm tired of it being so damn casual. I'd like to get married someday and have a family but you keep me at such a distance, like your afraid or something. For God's sake, if you want to stay together you're going to have to let me in."

"What do you mean let you in? You're in."

"No, Sam. Do you know that you've never even told me about your past, I don't know what your childhood was like, what dreams you've had that have or haven't come true. I don't even know if you've ever had your heart broken. I don't really know who you are."

I knew what he said was true. I did have trouble opening up and trusting others. It was no big secret. The weird thing was that as he continued I didn't think he was upset for himself, but that he felt sorry for me.

"What difference does it make that you don't know about my childhood." I told him, defensively. "I'm not blaming anyone for anything. I'm not carrying around any baggage. You do know me. What you see is what you get. You act as though I have this secret life or something!"

"No, you act like you have a secret life! I don't even know where the hell you are most of the time, and you certainly never offer any information to me."

"Why would you care?"

"You just don't get it! People who love each other do care."

"I know some women who would bore you with every detail of their lives. I don't want to hear that shit so why would I expect you to be interested in it?"

"That's what you think? That I'm not interested in what you do? We've been seeing each other for some time now and have had some great times together. Why would you think I don't care about what you do?"

"So that's it? You want me to bore you with the minute details of my life, that will mean we're committed?"

"Sam, you just don't understand."

"I guess I don't."

Jack got up and walked to the door. He was walking out on me, right when I was spilling my guts!

"You're leaving?"

"I'm sorry, Sam. I can't do this."

"Before you go, tell me what made you suddenly get so serious."

"When I was in Arizona last month I met someone.. . ."

Oh my God. I couldn't believe this was happening. He wasn't concerned about me or our relationship. It was always about him!

"Fuck you!" I told him. "Get out!"

Slamming the door and locking it, I went upstairs and sat on the edge of my bed, shaking from the rush of adrenaline that surged through my body. I felt sick to my stomach, my head was pounding and my emotions moved from anger to self-pity and back again. Here I had been, forced to open up emotionally and he had already met someone else. What an idiot! He didn't have to come over here and go through his act, as if there was a decision to make. There were no options here. Not for me. A decision had been made, and he had made it. I went to bed, unable to think about anything else. The file would have to wait until morning.

CHAPTER 11

My sleep had been restless, thoughts of Jack crowding my brain. After tossing and turning for a few hours, I finally got up at 3 A.M., deciding that a diversion was in order. I got myself a cup of coffee and brought it and the file back to bed and got under the covers. As I read, I was amazed at what the information suggested. There were articles about the plastic surgeon, Dr. Everett Weatherbee, and the miracles he had performed over the last twenty or so years. Disfigured children, burn victims, people wounded in war and car accidents, all have benefited from his expertise.

The FBI recruited him to assist in changing the identity of their witnesses, a practice that was regarded as extreme but often necessary in the success of the witness protection program. Some very interesting stuff.

Also in the file, were the records of Ronald and all his cronies. The information depicted the good, the bad, and the ugly of their lives since they had been in little league. As well as containing all the information that Ronald had passed on to me, it also included a bevy of Ron's talents that he had neglected to mention. Ron, it seems, wasn't the angel he painted himself out to be.

I spent the next four hours reading and studying all I could about "the boys," paying special attention to any information pertaining to Matt Andrews. He was a born leader, very smart. He also had the reputation of a smooth talker with a first-class sense of humor, as well as having a way with people and a confidence that most adults don't have, much less a kid. Trust . . . yes, they trusted him, and coming from a large wealthy family, he found himself in situations that gave him occasions to mingle with the rich and to gain their confidence. In a word, he was everyone's friend. He hung out with his father's associates, and was included in their golf outings and fishing trips. He was always charming, it seems. Some things never change.

Too tired to read another word, I clung to the thought of sleep but after thirty minutes I gave up and decided that what I really needed was a good workout so I set off for the gym.

I don't usually pay too much attention to the sweaty bodies at the gym, but for some reason, my new status made me wonder about what type of guys worked out there. It really had been a while since I was "on the market" and although my relationship with Jack was pretty laissez faire, I felt no need to look for something better. I was content. Of course, now, with the imminent reevaluation of self I must put myself through because that is what you do when you get dumped, I figured I'd better get a handle on what I might be facing. I haven't had to flirt or be interesting in a while and to be honest, I wasn't sure if I was up for the challenge. I'm not saying that I have to get another boyfriend right away; I have no intention of doing so. But when I am ready, I'm not sure I'll know what to do.

As I ran on the treadmill, I paid close attention to the free weight area where all the guys were busy counting reps and grunting from lifting weights that were obviously too heavy for them. Dressed in muscle shirts, shorts and expensive sneakers, they worked out vigorously. Some of these guys were so built up that they had no necks.

There were a few women there too, some really working out hard, sweat dripping from their foreheads, arms glistening. Then there were a select few who wore a full face of makeup, hair done perfectly and donned tiny workout outfits that made me blush just looking at them. I felt as if I were peeking into their dressing rooms, yet they were strolling around as if they hadn't a care in the world. Sure, they picked up a weight or two, acting as though they were working out, but as I observed them, I noticed they were spending more time assessing who was examining them than getting a workout. I wondered what their purpose was here, having a good sweat didn't seem to be the goal, that's for sure. All in all it was quite a show and made my thirty-minute run fly by faster that I can remember. Maybe depression makes me more aware of irrelevant details. Now that would be something.

Home and showered I decided to get some breakfast and get back to my file. I had to be sure I had a real grasp of the facts in order to probe for the right information tonight.

In an odd way, this position I was in didn't frighten me now. I felt almost numb to the danger. I had to forget about the threat that was apparent in dealing with the mob and follow my gut. It helped that Matt Andrews was pleasant and good looking, like a regular guy. Only, he wasn't a regular guy. The influence he had was so overwhelming it was difficult to grasp. How could someone live like that? I spent the next few hours categorizing the information I had collected and entering it on index cards and a story board, outlining the players and indicating what tied them together. When I finished, the one thing that was absolutely clear to me was that there was still a lot of work to be done. Actually, all I knew to date was that Ron was missing, he had some sort of connection to Matt and that Matt was a mobster. Not much. What I really needed was a new source of information.

That's when the good news fairy looked my way. The phone rang and voila! It was Henry. As I had mentioned, Henry bolted from Temecula last year after an ugly divorce having come to the conclusion that marriage was a waste of time and that it might be fun to live life on the road for a while and see everything he wanted to see and even some of the stuff he had no desire to see at all, just to do it. Henry always seemed to know everything about everyone and had no qualms at all about sharing this information with friends, which make me glad to be one of them. This was the reason he had acquired the nickname, "the Mayor." And believe me, he enjoyed the reputation for being the one to call if you needed dirt on anyone. His strong features and boyish good looks gave the overall impression that he was a laid back sort that didn't take life too seriously. Yet he was a competitor at heart and he knew that his smooth talking ways were worth their weight in gold. Fortunately, I knew it too. I could almost see the grin on his face when I asked him if he could assist me in gathering some information.

"If it involves gossip, you know I would love to help," he said. "Are you going to fill me in or is this confidential."

"To tell you the truth, it is. But in order to help, I'm going to have to give you some information pertinent to the client."

"Information is the name of my game," he said cheerfully. "When do you need me to start sleuthing?"

"Yesterday," I told him. "It's pretty important."

"I'm at you service. Is this a paying gig?"

"Of course. Your talents haven't gone unnoticed. Believe me!"

Henry arrived about thirty minutes later with a smile and a six-pack. I had decided that he would be most helpful in providing me with details on Christina, since I was positive she hated me and would be only too happy to tell me to go screw myself if I even attempted to approach her with my fake, *oh, we just got off on the wrong foot, buddy, buddy attitude.* Henry was smart and had style. He cleaned up real nice, too, which he just might have to do in order to get her to notice him. That would be his call.

Obviously, it would be dangerous to fill Henry in on the details of the case, so I didn't. What I did tell him was that I needed to get the particulars on Christina because she might be involved in blackmailing wealthy men. I explained that I had attempted to become "friends" with her in order to gain access to her "secrets" but that she was not the type to open up, especially to another woman. His mission, I told him, was to sweep her off her feet, or at least thaw her out a bit.

I gave him some specific information to fish for, such as her full name, family background, where she's from, where she lives now (if she resides anywhere other than the boat), and social security number or license number, if possible. The sort of thing that might be taken care of by snooping in her purse. Anything else he cared to add to the repertoire of information would be much appreciated. Then we discussed what character he'd be playing and the ground rules. He had to be a wealthy guy from out of town and he couldn't mention my name. The rest was up to him. I gave him a description of her and told him he would find her at the Coronado Island Marina on the *Lucky Man.* He was supposed to spot her there and set up a "chance" meeting.

"Piece of cake, Sam."

"She's a cold fish, so just do what you can."

"I'll call you in a day or two and let you know what I have."

"Thanks, Henry, be careful, It's possible she could be dangerous."

Henry took the information I had put together for him and left, clearly eager to get started. When I indicated that he might have trouble with Christina his eyes widened, he loves a challenge and he would certainly find one in her, I was sure of it.

I was due at Frank's office soon so I ran upstairs to shower and doll myself up for the evening. I wasn't sure what to wear since we had planned on staying in, but I felt like dressing a bit sexy anyway. Part of the reason was to irritate Chuck after the lecture he had given me about being in my fantasy world as far as Matt was concerned. Yes, I do so enjoy rubbing it in when I'm right.

Because of the cool February evening I thought it best to wear a pair of my new, relaxed fit Lee jeans, a low-cut white top and my navy blue suit jacket with a pair of navy blue heels. The look comes off sexy without being so blatant about it. I brushed my teeth, put on light makeup as usual, and wore my hair down. Adding a spray of my favorite perfume, Escape, so fitting for the occasion, and I was ready to go.

My adrenaline was in high gear by the time I reached Frank and Chuck's office even though I knew that I had to appear to be at ease with Matt. *Appear* is the operative word here because I knew my fears would return as soon as I saw him again. I just hoped the numbness I had been feeling since my new found freedom would continue until the evening was over. Not too much to hope for, but with my luck, reality will set in way too soon.

I hoped the looming rain would hold off a bit longer, at least until I returned to my digs. If we're going to have a storm, I'd like to thoroughly enjoy it in the comfort of my own home where I can cuddle up in my favorite cozy pajamas with a good book.

Pulling into the lot I parked my car next to Chuck's mint corvette, I was careful not to ding the door when I got out. Chuck was there alone in the office, talking on the phone.

He signaled he'd be a minute so I put down my briefcase and stepped outside onto the balcony to give him some privacy. As I watched the clouds move in, I wondered where Frank was. I felt uncomfortable being alone with Chuck and I was pretty sure that he felt the same way.

Chuck came out and stood next to me as I gazed out at the darkened sky. The low gray fog that was setting over us made the air feel dank and chilly.

"Hi, Sam. Thanks for giving me a minute to finish my call."

"No problem. Where's Frank?"

"He's home. Something is going on with Susan."

"So, he's not coming?"

"He said he'd try but he wants us to get started without him. He wanted me to be sure you are still up for this."

"I'm fine with it," I assured him. "Let's get to work."

"Did you have an opportunity to read through the files?" He asked me as we moved inside and sat across from each other at the small circular table.

I was amazed at how vulnerable I felt having to spend time alone with Chuck. I guessed Frank's presence gave me the courage to be flippant with him because, without him around to protect me, I didn't feel brave enough to send out even the slightest bit of sarcasm.

"Yes, I spent quite a bit of time reading and rereading the material."

"What do you think?"

I was relieved that Chuck had apparently decided not to knock me about verbally and wondered if we were in fact, coming to a truce.

"What part are you referring to?"

"Let's start with the files on Matt Andrews and Ronald Gregory. Had Ronald shared any of that information with you prior to his disappearance?"

"Some of it, but he did leave out the fact that he had been arrested on numerous occasions. He had me believing that he had stopped all criminal activities a long time ago."

"Well, we think he had tried to get out but was strongly encouraged to stay. We have some conversation tapes indicating this, if, in fact, it is Ronald on the tape. Did he mention that any of the others felt the same way?"

"No, he just said he felt ousted. He told me he was afraid for his life."

"He could have been telling you the truth. We've been following these guys for a very long time and have many hours of conversations regarding their activities. If one of the guys shows any signs of having second thoughts they don't have any trouble eliminating them."

"So you think Ron is dead?"

"Look, Sam, the reality is that it is very likely. Don't you find it strange that he comes to you and offers you a ridiculous amount of money for your services because he thinks he's in danger and then just disappears, just like that? Think about it."

"So then, what I am doing? I was paid to find out who was following him, or so I thought. If he's dead then no one would be following him and I'm done."

"What if he's not dead? Don't you have a responsibility to continue to finish the job or at least work on it until you've earned your pay?"

"You're right, I do have that obligation. Ron came to me because he said I was stubborn and wouldn't give up. I owe it to him to get to the truth."

"Sam, I don't think he is dead."

"But . . . you just said . . ."

"I said that it is likely."

"So, if he's not dead, where is he?"

"Let me ask you something. What did you think about the file on Dr. Weatherbee?"

I sat for a minute, allowing my thoughts to flow.

"No! You think Ron went to him?"

"I'm not sure. Again, I don't want to rule anything out here. There is too much at stake to dismiss some very real possibilities."

"Well, let's say he has had his identity changed. Do you think he'd still be hanging around here?"

"I agree that it's doubtful. But he could be."

"But why? It would seem pretty risky to me to be hanging around where the people he's been afraid of still reside."

"He may have fled, but since we don't know for sure, we have to keep in mind that he could still be around somewhere."

"Or he might be dead."

"That's right, you have to be open to all the possibilities or you'll focus in the wrong area. That's what makes a good investigator, following all leads and being aware of all the what-ifs. You gather the facts and the evidence and put all the pieces together like a puzzle. If you can do this, you will be successful, most of the time."

"I was wondering about this doctor," I told him. It was amazing to me how easily we seemed to be working together without either of us rubbing the other the wrong way. "Is it just the faces that he changes? Because what if the person has other identifying marks on the body, like a birth mark?"

"Well, I think the main objective is to alter the face but I have some other data on the good doctor that backs up your theory. If there is an identifying mark, changing just the face would seem ludicrous."

"So we're dealing with the possibility that the only way we will be able to identify Ronald is by his . . ."

"Yes, his fingerprints and dental records."

We looked at each other and smiled. I had the feeling that Chuck was satisfied that I seemed to be "getting it" or at least thinking on my feet. I felt pretty good about it as well.

Chuck got up to stretch his legs and get a soda.

"Here, let me take a look at your cell phone," he told me. "I'd better be sure our listening device is working properly before I send you out there."

Opening up the back portion of it he looked up at me. "You're sure this is what you want to do?"

"Yes, I told you that wearing a wire would make me too nervous." Our eyes locked and we both looked away anxiously. Silence filled the room for a long moment, and then Chuck's attention moved back to the cell phone.

"No, I don't mean the wire. The whole operation, are you sure you still want to participate? I'd understand if you wanted to bail out. Things are getting pretty heavy."

"I don't want to bail out. I'm ready to do whatever I need to do. Is it working?"

"We're all set."

"Where are you going to be?" I asked.

"You're planning to stay put at his house, right?"

"As far as I know. That's what we talked about, but don't hold me to it, just in case Matt has alternate plans."

"I'll be close by just in case something happens so don't worry."

For some reason, hearing Chuck assure me he would be close by felt comforting. Were we starting to like each other?

"I'm not worried, Chuck."

"All right then, let's do it."

I looked up at Chuck. "Thanks," I said, meaning it.

"You are going to be fine, I'll be there if anything happens."

Outside, he opened my car door for me. I slid in, tossing my briefcase into the backseat.

"Talk to me on your way over," he said. "I want to check volume and clarity while you are on the move. This wind could affect it. If I flash my lights at you then pull over so I can take care of the problem before you get there."

I backed out of my slot, and drove out to the street, once again heading towards Matt's place.

"Hello, Chuck," I said, when I was about a mile away. I have to say that I was feeling pretty foolish talking without even knowing if he could hear me. "I just want to tell you I'll do my best to get some valuable information tonight." A glance in my rearview mirror showed no flashing lights so apparently everything must be in order with Chuck. As I drove, I thought about what the evening would bring. My nerves had settled and I was feeling good.

Even with the gloom of the big black clouds that were hovering close to the roof, Matt's colonial house or was it Ron's house, had a special charm. I checked the mirror, hoping I still looked fresh. Satisfied, I emerged from my car just as the rain began to fall heavily. Slipping on the step leading to the porch, I twisted my ankle.

Matt, who apparently had come out to greet me, was sitting on the wicker chair, half hidden by a wisteria vine.

"Sam, are you all right?" he said, rising, his face in the shadows.

"I think so, my ankle is a little sore, I think I landed on it wrong."

"Sit down, let me take a look at it."

Wiping the moisture from my face with the back of my hand, he knelt in front of me, putting my foot up on his leg. Taking off my shoe, he held my ankle gently as he moved my foot in a slow, circular motion.

"Does that hurt?"

"A little."

"Let's get you inside and put some ice on it before it really swells up."

He lifted me up, carrying me across the threshold and into the study, setting me gently on the couch.

"Stay put," he said. "I'll get some ice. Can I get you a drink? A glass of wine?"

There was just time for me to relish the charm of the book lined room before he returned, carrying a large zip-lock bag filled half way with crushed ice, and a chilled glass of white wine. Moving in close, he bent over me and handed me the wine.

"I am so sorry, Matt," I said as he sat down beside me and pressed the ice pack against my ankle. "I feel like a real klutz."

"You're not a klutz," he said grinning. "You're quite a runner. Do you work out regularly?"

"Yes, it's supposed to be good for me."

He laughed. "Well you're doing something right because you look really good." He leaned in close to me and I felt my heart flutter as he pressed his lips to mine. Our first kiss ended with a feeling of rapture that illuminated my body and possibly my soul as well. As I sat mesmerized, the realization that was most paramount in my mind was that his kiss, as wonderful as it was, had created a complication that I just didn't see coming.

CHAPTER 12

The evening was going well despite the fact that it had started out with me making a complete fool of myself, injuring my ankle in the process.

We ordered Chinese and listened to old music, a secret passion of Matt's. He had quite a collection of forty-fives and old albums such as Rama-Lama-Ding-Dong by the Edsels and Run Around Sue, by Dion that still played well on the old phonograph that had been handed down to him from his grandfather. He liked to use it so he could connect somehow with the past, and remember how lucky he was. A *lucky man*, yes, but for how much longer?

The rain was coming down in sheets now, lashing the windows. We went outside with a bottle of wine and a big blanket and sat on the wicker couch to watch it. The rumble of thunder blended with the music and the beating of my heart as lightening streaked the sky, surprising us, like kids experiencing it for the first time.

I should have felt nervous and uptight but I didn't. Not even a little. I felt comfortable and protected. Whenever I remembered that this man sitting so close to me, keeping me warm, could be part of the mob, I quickly dismissed the thought, or tried to. But the reason I was here kept intruding on my consciousness and I found myself trying to think of questions to ask that wouldn't seem as though they were coming out of left field. Unfortunately, everything I wanted to ask sounded that way. What the hell.

"So what's the story with Christina?" I said.

"Christina? What do you mean?"

"She doesn't seem to like me."

"Where did you get that idea?" He asked, as his arm tightened around my shoulder.

"She appeared to be upset about me having dinner with you that night on the boat. Why is that. Is she an old flame or something?"

"Sam, Christina is my sister."

How wrong could anyone be? I suppose it was because she was so beautiful, I had simply assumed that there was something between them. But his sister!

"She's a bit protective," He went on thoughtfully, "so she often comes across like a real bitch. She's not too bad once you get to know her. It just takes a while."

"It's just that she seemed so angry at me," I told him. "I didn't know what I had done to deserve it."

"Don't worry about it," he said. "I'd really like to forget about her tonight. I am really enjoying spending time with you. You're very special, Sam. I don't usually say this sort of thing but I have to tell you that I haven't been able to think of anything else but you since we met."

"I feel the same way." It was unfortunately, too close to being true. I looked into his eyes and took a deep breath. "I have had such a great time tonight but it's getting late, I should go."

My ankle wasn't so painful now but it was swollen and Matt was determined that I shouldn't drive, especially in this rain. I was staying and that was that. I was sure Chuck was going ballistic about now, cussing me out about everything under the sun, but I had an idea.

We went inside where the fireplace was burning bright with a warm glow that radiated throughout the room as the wood crackled and sparked. I sat down in front of it and took in the warmth. The heat felt good on my back, and I could feel myself relax as I listened to the soothing sounds of "My Girl" playing quietly in the background.

Matt brought in the wine and filled our glasses. He sat next to me, so close our knees touched. He leaned in and kissed me again, this time more urgently than before.

"So, are you ready to go up?"

There was no doubt in my mind as to what he meant.

"Matt," I said. "I would love to but it's just too soon. I really should go home."

"We've already decided you shouldn't drive, the rain hasn't let up and it could be dangerous, especially with your foot not exactly in prime working condition. I'll set you up in the guest room, that way if you change your mind I'll be right down the hall."

"I won't."

"I don't want to rush this. I can wait as long as it takes for you to be comfortable. I'm not in a hurry."

"Thanks, Matt, It's just . . ."

"No need to explain anything. Let me show you to your room."

When he switched on the light, I remembered the room from my tour, and found myself glad I would be staying in it. The furniture was a white wash with a slightly weathered look to it. There were some photos on the dresser and the bookcases on each side of the bay window, displaying an old collection of Dickens and some art books, as well as some decorative items such as a tiny tea set and some antique dolls. The rest of the room was also white with accents in lavender. It was a soothing and feminine room and I was curious about who resided here. Ron hadn't said he was married or involved, or that he had children. Or maybe it was where Christina stayed. I'd have to look around and see if there was something that could give me some answers.

"You'll find clean nightgowns in the bureau and fresh towels in the bathroom," he told me. "Is there anything else you need?"

Nightgowns? So this was a woman's room. I wanted to ask him if it was Christina's room but given the way he had more or less refused to talk about her earlier, I decided not to.

"No, thank you, I'm all set." I said.

"Well, if you need anything, don't hesitate to let me know."

The look in his eyes was tempting, to say the least. But I had my work cut out for me tonight. It would truly be a lost opportunity if I didn't take advantage of it and search the house.

"I will," I murmured. "Good night, Matt."

He kissed me gently and said good night. I closed the door and sat on the bed, smiling. What was happening here? I was actually falling for this guy!

I took my phone out of my purse. "Don't worry Chuck," I said in a low voice. "I know what I'm doing. I'm fine so go get some sleep, I'll call you tomorrow." I put the phone back, glad that I couldn't hear him yelling at me. I know he was probably pretty pissed off. This was not part of the plan and Chuck doesn't approve of deviating from a plan. Too dangerous he says. But this was different.

I put on the nightgown, a white cotton number by Victoria Secret, with lace around the neckline and wrist, not exactly the sort of thing I would have pictured Christina wearing and certainly nothing I would have picked out for myself. But surprisingly enough, it made me feel very much like the kind of woman who puts her life on the line by searching strange houses with a flashlight in the middle of the night. Which, by the way, was exactly what I was about to do, all with hopes of finding anything that would give me something on Ron.

I moved about the room taking a close look at all the photos, I didn't recognize anyone. I went to the dresser and searched each drawer. Sheets in the bottom, blankets in the middle, and some handkerchiefs and knickknacks in the top. Decorative pill boxes, small antique picture frames, a dulled money clip, some small change, numerous pieces of jewelry, buttons, and a buffet of old coins that looked as though they were from various countries were all scattered about. Nothing significant. But when I picked up the pile of handkerchiefs, a gold pocket watch fell out, hitting the side of the drawer and falling to the floor with a thud.

I sat down on the floor, shining my flashlight on the watch, inspecting it carefully as I held it, using the pajama top so I wouldn't leave fingerprints. It reminded me of something. What was it? My grandfather had one. Maybe that was it. No. Where had I seen this before? Think, think. Oh my God! That day at the club, Ron had been carrying a pocket watch! And I remembered there was something distinctive about it, I quickly opened it up. His initials, RG, were inscribed in script on the inside cover. This was it. This was Ron's watch!

I thought I heard a noise so I stood in place, listening. But it was only the wind, thrashing the trees against the side of the house. The rain tapered off but the wind seemed to be picking up speed, creating a harsh blustering sound that was unsettling to say the least.

Opening my door deliberately didn't keep it from creaking, and the sound seemed to echo down the hallway.

Passing the master suite on tip toes, I headed for the stairs, gliding down them in my bare feet. The house was dark except for the suggestion of light that radiated in from the street, and the spotlights on the outer sides of the barn out back, that created a shadowy glow throughout the first floor. The wind added movement to the silhouette.

What I hoped to find was photos or letters, some tangible evidence that Ron had been here. This was supposed to be his home. There must be something with his name on it. Bills, letters, advertisements. There had to be something. There was a small, built in desk in the kitchen, the top littered with mail. Flipping quickly through the stack, I was surprised to see so many different names on the various pieces, yet they contained only one address, and this was the place. I couldn't imagine why there were so many people receiving mail here. As I sifted through again I noticed they were all men. Matt Andrews, Peter Manning and Jon James, not to mention the other fifteen or so names that I didn't recognize.

I opened the side drawer and saw a bundle of letters bound by a thick rubber band. I steered my flashlight to the name written on the front of the top envelope and scribbled on it was the name Ronald Gregory. No return address. Releasing the envelope from the bundle, I folded it and tucked it inside the elastic on my sleeve just as the light came on.

"Can you find everything all right?"

I jumped, letting out a scream. I was only too well aware of how I looked.

"Water," I said. "I came down for a glass of water."

"It's okay."

"You don't mind that I'm helping myself?"

"No, of course not, but I do have a question."

My heart stopped, this was it. He knew what I was up to. I'd been found out and despite the kisses and the wine and the cuddle under the blanket, this man could be dangerous. This man might, in fact be the reason my client had apparently disappeared.

"Really? What is it?" I asked, trying to keep my voice even.

"Do you always carry a flashlight with you?"

I looked at the counter where my little flashlight stood upright.

"Actually I do," I told him. Determined to brazen it out. "I was a girl scout." Yeah right, me a girl scout. That's a laugh.

He smiled at me.

"Can I walk you back up?"

"Sure."

"How's the ankle feeling?"

"Much better."

He walked me up stairs and back to my quarters. I had put myself through enough for one night. I needed to get some sleep. I tucked the letter in my purse and got into bed. Exhausted, the sound of the wind lulled me to sleep.

When I woke up, sunshine was piercing its way through the windows. Remembering where I was, I bolted upright, and jumped out of bed, searching my purse for the watch and the letter, relieved to find they were still there.

When I went downstairs, Matt was sipping coffee.

"Good morning!" he said. "How did you sleep?"

He looked fantastic in a pair of faded blue jeans, a white shirt and white sneakers. His hazel eyes were bright and his sandy blonde locks were parted to the side and slightly disheveled. And he was in a festive mood. Any concern I might have had last night about his being suspicious faded away.

"Come with me," he said. "I have a surprise." Out back, a table for two had been set up under a sprawling oak tree and beside the table was a champagne bucket, in it champagne chilling. In the center of the table was a vase with three perfect red roses in it. The air was cool but not too cold for this time of year. It looked so inviting.

"What is this?" I inquired casually.

"Breakfast."

It was a terrible irony that I should find myself so attracted to a man who almost certainly was a criminal. I remembered what Ron had told me about Matt and his other friends. And now Ron was missing, perhaps dead. Matt had taken over his house and God knows what else. And in the process of trying to bring some justice to the situation, I had allowed myself to become attracted to this man. No, more than attracted, if I were honest with myself.

I followed him into the kitchen and helped him get the coffee mugs and some plates. We also took out a basket of assorted muffins and butter. We sat across from each other and sipped our coffee. The sky was clear and the air was warming up. It felt good to be outside.

"What are your plans today?" he asked, nonchalantly.

"I have to check my appointment book," I told him. "But I think I have to get to the law library today. I'm researching the legality of a pre-nuptial agreement."

"Sounds interesting."

"Not really. This guy is a real pain in the ass. He's checking this out after only being married for three months. I think he wants to dump her and take her for half of everything she's got. And she's loaded."

"Who is she?"

"It's confidential," I told him, feeling as though I were treading water. "I could get in a lot of trouble for telling. What are *you* doing today?"

"Well, I was hoping I'd be able to see you."

I smiled. I had hoped to turn the tables on him but he was one step ahead of me.

"That would be nice, but I really have to get this work done, I'm meeting with the client Monday morning."

"Can I call you later?"

Did he really have to ask? "Sure. I'd better get going now. I really enjoyed our evening," I said, meaning every word. "Thanks for taking care of my ankle."

"I had a great time too, I'm glad you stayed over."

As he leaned in to kiss me, I closed my eyes and took it all in. He held me in close to him, his grasp tight around my waist. When I felt myself losing control, I moved away, regaining my balance, emotional and otherwise.

"I need to see you again, Sam," he told me. "I'm going to call you later."

I wanted to go back in the house and roll around in bed with him all day but I knew I couldn't do it. I had never felt passion like this in my whole existence and yet now I was feeling it for someone that I couldn't ever be with. Life is so unfair!

"Okay, I'll talk to you later." As I drove home I was so overwhelmed with emotion that I started crying. I knew I wouldn't be able to see him again. How could he be the danger that Frank and Chuck were so convinced he was? I had to know, to be sure, so I could let this go.

When I arrived home, Chuck's car was parked in front of my house. Furthermore, Mrs. Bennett was up to her usual tricks, making a big deal out of watering her petunias while keeping an eye on anything going on around the neighborhood. I wondered if she knew I was coming home from an overnight stay. I wiped my eyes, hoping neither of them would notice that I had been crying.

"I heard you crying, Sam," Chuck said as soon as we were in the house. There was compassion in his eyes. "You've really fallen for him, haven't you?"

I felt too miserable to be embarrassed even though this was the one person I did not want to see me so beaten up. I wondered how much he had heard and how much he had imagined during the last twenty hours or so

"Look," I said. "I know. I'm really not in the mood for a lecture right now."

"I'm not going to give you one," he assured me. "I just want to tell you that I understand what you're dealing with. You are going to come out of this just fine."

I couldn't believe what I was hearing. This was Mr. Serious. Mr. Don't Fuck This Up. Mr. Perfect, telling me he understands what I'm going through.

"How would you possibly know what I'm feeling?" I demanded. I didn't like him taking advantage of my sorry ass, trying to humiliate me even more than I had already done myself.

"Because I had something like this happen to me," he muttered, avoiding my eyes. "I experienced a very similar situation."

"What happened?" I asked him.

"It was a long time ago. Maybe we can talk about it another time."

"I'm sorry, I didn't mean to pry."

"You just hang in there. You'll be fine."

"He wants to see me again."

"I know. Why don't you get some rest. Come by the office later and we'll figure out how to handle that."

"Okay," I said, thankfully. "I'll call you later."

I should have given him the letter and the watch to take with him but I wanted to hold on to them and get a good look. After all, I nearly gave myself a freaking heart attack retrieving the stuff. I should be able to check it out first.

Securing the door, I immediately went to my kitchen, put on my rubber gloves and took out the watch and the letter and placed them on the table while I put some coffee on. I sat down to inspect my findings, my eyes staring at the watch. I picked it up and studied it. I'd have to get a collector to look at it and let me know if the markings were significant in any way. Probably not but you never know. I flipped it over. It was old but in pretty good condition. I didn't recall if I had commented on it when Ron had looked at it that day. I do remember thinking how unusual it was to see a pocket watch. Not too many people carry them anymore.

I opened it up and stared at the initials RG engraved in an odd-looking script. It was unusual for the initials to be placed on the inside of a watch. I wondered what that was about. It was working, keeping perfect time which had to mean that it was wound regularly. The question was, who was winding it? Why would Ron's watch be in a woman's bedroom. Had he been staying in the room with someone? Or perhaps, his belongings were being hidden so he couldn't be identified easily. I couldn't stop thinking about who occupied that room. I gave it a little shake and heard a slight pinging sound. Hoping I hadn't broken it, I inspected it closely and found a small latch that opened up the face, exposing a small compartment. In it was a tiny key, one that looked as though it belonged to a little girl's jewelry box. It was silver, old fashioned in style. I couldn't imagine why it would be concealed in a watch . . . Ron's watch.

Putting both the key and the watch in a plastic baggy, I set it aside and picked up the envelope, noticing that it had a Coronado postmark, dated February 9. Whatever the reason for the block letters that had been used for the envelope, the letter inside had been written in what looked like a woman's writing, although I couldn't tell for sure. I have seen plenty of men with way better handwriting than mine. The letter read:

Ronnie,
   I need to see you. We have to make this thing work.
                                                        T

Wow! Now we're getting somewhere. Unfortunately it wasn't signed, so I'd have to do some more snooping in order to find out who "T" was, and what "this thing" signified. I took out another bag, reread the letter and placed it inside, wondering what it meant regarding Ron's sudden disappearance, if anything at all.

Pondering this new lead, I couldn't help but to entertain the thought that maybe Ron wasn't dead after all. Was it possible that he was being held by a woman? Maybe he pissed off the wrong gal and she lost it. Or was it possible that Matt was in on this after all? The fact that he and Ron were friends would give him plenty of opportunity. And the fact that he had taken over Ron's home was too big to ignore. But the handwriting was so feminine looking and since I found the watch in the woman's room, was it possible that Matt didn't know anything about it? At this point, I didn't have answers but I sure had a lot of questions. So where did this new lead leave me? Hopefully, one step closer to finding out what happened to Ron.

CHAPTER 13

The next morning my cell phone rang me out of restless sleep.

"Something has happened down here, Sam." Henry's voice was almost an octave higher than I have ever heard it. I knew whatever had happened had to be bad news, I just didn't want to think about what it could be.

"Sam, you're not going to believe what's going on down here."

"What's going on?"

"I hooked up with Christy as planned, I'll tell you about that later. The thing is that this morning I got a frantic call from her. Some guy was found dead, floating in the harbor. I guess she recognized him. Anyway, she called me around seven all freaked out. I took her to the Harbor House. The cops have taped off the area and she wasn't allowed to go back to the boat. She said she had some calls to make. She's wound up pretty tight. Anyway, I told her I'd be back in a few hours. I thought you..."

"So who's the dead guy?" I interrupted him. I suppose it was only natural that the possibility that it was Ron came to mind. For a moment I saw his face. Bloated. Grey. Almost unrecognizable. I had been unable to protect him after all. And if it were Ron, did someone else know about me? "Who's dead?" I repeated.

"I don't know. The cops haven't released any information on him yet. You know, they have to contact the next of kin. Christy says..."

If it is Ron, I wonder who they would call. But maybe it's not him. If Christina knows who it is, I'd bet that Matt knows too. I imagine since Christina reported it, the cops would be all over Matt's boat. I imagine he'd want to get down there right away to check things out. It's natural curiosity.

"What's this with calling her Christy?"

"That's how she introduced herself to me."

"Are you sure you've got the right girl?"

"She looks exactly like the description you gave me. Why?"

"Because Christina is definitely not a 'Christy' type of gal."

"Well, that's how she introduced herself. I don't know what to tell you."

"Okay, okay. Where should we meet?"

"There is a little hole in the wall we stopped by last night. It's around the corner from the Harbor House. The patrons all look like criminals but they have cold beer and some great fries. It's called Keno's."

"I'm leaving now," I told him. "I'll meet you in about an hour, hour and a half."

"See you then."

I hung up, wondering what the hell I would find. My first thought was Ronald. Would it be him? And what's with the Christy shit? She was no Christy, no matter how she introduced herself. Putting those thoughts out of my mind I realized that soon enough I would be learning the identity of the floater. The image sent shivers down my spine.

Frank was waiting for me so I decided to run by there first and get the watch and letter off my hands. I wasn't comfortable hanging on to them and I was eager to see what he and Chuck thought.

"This is what I found it in Matt's house," I told him. "Look at the engraving on the watch. On the inside. What do you think? Does it mean anything?"

"I don't know," Frank said, frowning. "Maybe we should ask a jeweler."

"I'll make some calls."

He put the watch down. "What's the key for?"

"I found it inside the face of the watch. I don't know what it belongs to. I didn't discover it until this morning when I got home," I said, trying to rush things a bit. "Look, I have to go. Can you check this stuff out for fingerprints? Maybe it will give us something to go on."

"What's your rush?"

"A body was found in the harbor, I want to check it out. I'll see you later."

"Call me!"

As I ran down the stairs, I shouted, "I will!"

I drove on 15 Freeway going south, heading to Coronado Island. The drive from Temecula takes about an hour and a half, depending on traffic. I was lucky that I was heading south, the cars going north were at a standstill around Miramar, all wondering, I presumed, what the problem was.

The fact of the matter was that besides the horrible daily traffic that begins at about three, every afternoon, there was also an accident. Two fire engines and four police cars lined the freeway and as I was driving by, an ambulance sped up to the scene. I turned my radio to an A.M. station, looking for some news about whatever it was that happened. But all they had to report was that there was an accident and it was holding up traffic. Well, golly gee whiz!

I arrived on Coronado Island, stopping at the tollbooth to pay my fee for the pleasure of entering this lovely locale. I was due to meet Henry at Keno's so I asked the heavyset lady, wearing an old, yellow, short-sleeved shirt that looked as though it hadn't been washed "ever" what the best way for me to get to the Harbor House was. Looking at me as though I had insulted her, she snapped something about following the main road around and not being able to miss it. I guess I'd be pissed off, too, if that were how I made my living. Anyway, I followed her directions and got lost anyway. I should have known she was messing with me.

Figuring that the Harbor House had to be by the harbor, I followed the boat masts and finally found Keno's, a small wooden structure with an old decrepit porch that looked as though it would collapse out from under you at any minute. Above the door, a large boat's steering wheel sported the name Keno's in large letters at the center. The building looked like a gathering spot for old sailors, and from what I could see, they had been there a long time. No young guys here.

When I walked up the stairs, the porch became silent. These old guys had to be wondering what I was doing here because I certainly didn't fit in. One of the old guys sporting blue jeans, an orange, red, and white Hawaiian shirt and boat shoes, stood up and opened the door for me. I hoped like hell Henry would be inside.

And he was, sitting at the bar in deep conversation with the bartender, a short, stocky, and balding man with an uncanny resemblance to Uncle Fester from the Addams family. Beside him was a little woman who was dressed up like she would be attending some fancy ball later on tonight.

"Hey, Sam, this is Eddie," he said when I joined him. "He owns the place, and this lovely lady is Katie, his gal."

"Nice to meet you," I said as I gave a quick nod.

We moved over to a table away from the bar for privacy. I was now feeling a sense of urgency to know who the dead guy was. I had to know if it was Ron.

"So what happened," I said eagerly. "Start from the beginning, and don't leave out any details."

"Well, I came down yesterday and went directly to the marina," he told me, anxiously. "The boat was docked so I hung around and found myself in a conversation with some guy that has his boat on the next dock over. I had a great view of the *Lucky Man* and positioned myself so I could see it as I talked with him. At first I didn't see any activity at all. Then, all of a sudden, this beautiful creature stood up. She had been sunbathing on the deck. You didn't tell me she was a knockout, Sam."

"I said she was very pretty."

"Very pretty. That's an understatement!"

"Okay, okay, go on." He was irritating me.

"Well, she got up and went down below. A few minutes later, she appeared again, wearing a long white dress, and got off the boat. Christy went into the Yacht club, so I followed her.

"It's Christina," I said firmly.

"Maybe to you."

"No, to me she's captain."

"Captain? Really?"

"She's the captain of the *Lucky Man* from what I understand. She didn't mention that to you?"

"No," he said, apparently unconcerned to have missed a vital point along the way.

"That's odd," I mused. "Well, go on, what happened next."

"You're right about her, Sam, she is a tough gal. I watched several guys go up to her and she shot them all down without batting an eye. They didn't even have a chance. So I decided to play it differently. I went up to the bar to buy a round for the guys and as I stood waiting to give the bartender my order, I dropped a rose at her feet."

"You what?"

"She told me I dropped something so I gave her my most charming smile, picked it up, and handed it to her. Then I just walked away. I didn't say a word."

"Get out of here, and it worked?"

"Like a charm."

"What happened after you walked away?" I asked, still baffled by his methods.

"I went back, sat with Jerry and his pals and sucked down a few more boat drinks."

"And . . ."

"I got up to use the head and when I came out she was standing there, pretending to use the phone."

"What do you mean pretending to use the phone? Maybe she *was* using the phone."

"She hung it up as soon as I walked out, it would have had to be great timing. Besides it was evident she wanted me."

I rolled my eyes. I love Henry but his overconfidence and my lack there of was really bugging me.

"Yeah, yeah, go on," I said.

"She invited me to dinner."

"Are you kidding me?"

"No, not at all."

"Where did you go?"

"I told her I was supposed to be dining with my friends but maybe I could meet her later. She asked me if I could have dinner with her and meet them later. I walked over to the table and thanked Jerry and said good night. The Yacht club has additional seating upstairs so we went up there."

"Unbelievable" was all I could say.

"When we sat down I introduced myself to her and she told me her name was Christy Anderson."

"Christy Anderson? Are you sure it wasn't Andrews?"

"It was Anderson."

"All right, what else did you find out?"

"She said she was staying on the boat for now, but would be moving soon. She is an only child and her parents died in a car accident a few years ago. I wasn't able to get a license or social on her because she wasn't carrying a purse. She must have a tab at the club because she said dinner was taken care of."

"Was that it?"

"Not exactly."

"Meaning? . . ."

"She took me to the boat for a nightcap."

"Was anyone else there?"

"Some young blonde guy. She said he took care of things. I never met him though. He did look at me suspiciously but I just ignored it."

"Did Christina say anything to him?"

"Not much, she just kind of announced that I was an old friend and we would be having a drink. Come to think of it, it all felt a bit strained."

This was so odd. Matt tells me that Christina is his sister and yet she tells Henry that she is an only child and gives a different last name. I'm lost. I thought this might help to clear some of this up but it seems to be getting more confusing. Damn!

"Did you spend the night with her?" I was almost afraid to ask.

"No, we had a drink and went for a walk by the water. She was lovely. Funny and charming but a bit closed off when I asked her anything about her family or what she did for a living."

"Did she say what she did?"

"Interior design. That's why she's staying on the boat. To fix it up. It took a bit of prodding to find that out."

"What did you tell her about yourself?"

"Well, she is supposed to be seeking out rich husbands, right? So I told her that I hadn't had much luck finding my soul mate, and of course, I mentioned how difficult it was to meet unattached women in my circles. I dropped the names of a few places that I vacation regularly and told her that I had a lot of time on my hands because my business practically ran itself and I had good people overlooking the day-to-day activities. I said I owned a couple of oil stations and supplied most of the gas stations around the east and mid west."

"Did she buy it?"

"Why wouldn't she?"

I shrugged. I think Henry is a better liar than me. How scary is that?

"So, how did your evening come to a close?"

"I walked her back to the boat, kissed her good night, and gave her my personal phone line, just in case she'd like to see me again."

"Your personal phone line?" He was smooth. The wording was perfect; it must have made her feel very special. "And you left?"

"I left her, but then I saw this place so I came in for a drink. Then I went over to San Diego and stayed at the Sheraton."

"You said she called you all freaked out, when was that?" I wasn't sure I wanted to hear anymore but I needed to get to the bottom of this.

"She called at about five-thirty this morning. Said she couldn't sleep so she went out on deck. She was sitting out there, and as the sun came up, she saw something floating along next to the boat. She was really afraid and practically begged me to come down."

"Had she called the police?"

"No, she was a mess. She told me she knew him. Sounded scared to death. I told her to call the police but she just told me to meet her at the coffee shop."

"So what did you do?"

"What could I do? I met her. By the time I got there someone had called the cops cause they were all over the area."

"Do you think she called them?"

"I don't know, Sam. I didn't think it mattered; they had been called. You should have seen her. She was shaking like a leaf and she could barely talk, I felt sorry for her. I've never seen anything like it."

"She said she knew him, did she say who it was or give you any indication what her relationship was to him?"

I couldn't stop thinking of the visual I had had of Ron, floating in the water, grey and bloated. Then I realized that Matt had several buddies that he seemed to be very close with. Maybe it was one of them. I tried to convince myself this was the case but I didn't really believe it. The question I kept asking myself was; what if Matt had done this to finally get rid of Ron, once and for all?

The fact that I had been so close to Matt, not allowing myself to even entertain any bad thoughts about him scared me now. And then to top it all off, I actually felt so attracted to him I could barely control myself. But how could I ignore this?

"No, I think she was in shock. She hugged me so tight, and she just wept . . . for a long time."

"Then what?"

"I told her she needed to get some rest and offered to bring her back to the boat. But like I told you, we couldn't get to it because the cops had it taped off. They wouldn't even let her get anything off it, that's when I took her to get a room at a hotel down the street. I'm going to have to get going, I told her I'd be back soon." He sounded genuinely concerned.

"Henry," I said. "I need you to hang out with her for as long as possible and find out whatever you can about her relationship with the deceased. It's really important."

"She said she didn't have anyone else to talk to, so I'll see what I can do."

"This case may be related to something else I'm working on," I explained. "I need as much information as you can get. Do you have a small tape recorder?"

"Not on me."

"Can you grab one before you go back to see her?" I knew I was starting to sound desperate.

"Sure, I'll get one. I suppose you want me to tape everything she says?"

"That is the point. If these cases are related I'm going to need her on tape so the police don't think I'm nuts. Meanwhile, I'm going to roam around down here for a while and see if I can find out anything about the guy. If you need me just call me on my cell."

"Okay. Any idea how long you're going to hang around?"

"I'm not sure. I may have to get back tonight. I'll let you know," I said, wondering if Matt would be calling me.

I didn't know the protocol when there was a hit. I expected he would be as far from the body as possible, being the boss, and have a good alibi as well. One thing was for sure, I'd better check my messages at home. Suddenly I felt like I had to see him again. I had to watch how he acted. Would he be cool? I had to find out if I would be able to tell if it was him. I know, it was only yesterday that I was a blubbering mess, convinced that I could never see him again. But, yesterday, no one had died at his orders.

We got up and Henry walked over to pay for the drinks and bid farewell to his new friends. I waved but I was eager to get out of there and back to the marina to see what was going on. Henry came back over, mumbling something about my lack of charm. I was in no mood for the lecture series on how much further I'd get with people if I paid them a little extra attention. I didn't have the patience to stroke egos, that wasn't my style and I was not about to start now.

"Stop!" I said, fully aggravated, "I'm just not up for this right now."

"Gotcha." Henry said and I expected he did. After we parted ways, I headed back to the marina, wound so tight that my neck was aching. I need to seriously consider dropping some cash for a massage when this was over.

As I suspected, the place was still crawling with cops. The familiar yellow tape that indicated a crime scene secured the area. I took out my cell phone and hit Frank's number at the office. If he or Chuck could hook me up with a friend that was working on this I'd have access to the inside story and possibly learn the identity of the deceased. When the machine answered, I hung up and decided to just hang around and keep my ears open. I'd try Frank again in a while.

Catching sight of the news crew from Channel 7, I sauntered over, hoping to have the opportunity to get close enough to hear what the news reporter was saying. He didn't look familiar to me, probably because I don't have much occasion to see the San Diego stations, considering that Temecula gets stations from Los Angeles.

Accompanying the reporter and the camera man was a pretty young lady hauling cords around. I wondered what she really wanted to be doing; I doubted that this was it. In a business that was so competitive I imagined you must start out doing a lot of grunt work and kissing a lot of ass. I just hoped for her sake she was kissing the right ones.

"What's going on here?" I asked her.

"Someone was found in the water," she responded.

"You're kidding?"

"No, really. Gross huh?"

"Yeah, pretty gross. Who is it, do you know?" I didn't think she'd have much to offer but I had to ask.

"I don't know," she said with a shrug. "I heard that he fell off his boat. Probably drunk. These people can really party, at least that is what I've been told."

"I'm Sam," I said. Are you a reporter?"

"No, not yet. I'm doing an internship through City College. They advised me that the best way to get into this business is to make yourself known, so that's what I'm trying to do."

"But you want to be a reporter, like that guy?"

"Yes, it is all so exciting, don't you think so?" I hoped she wasn't seeking approval from me.

"Will you be able to gain any reporting experience through your internship?"

"I'm not sure. All they told me was to follow directions so that's what I'm doing. I'm hoping if I do a good job they will give me a chance."

I felt like telling her not to hold her breath, that most likely, they were going to use her to get the coffee and haul around dirty, heavy equipment, and then send her on her way. But I decided that stomping on her dream would not be beneficial to anyone, especially me.

"What's your name?" I asked.

"It's Amelia, why?"

"So that when you're a famous reporter, I can tell all my friends I knew you when you were just starting out."

She smiled shyly.

"Amelia, did you see anyone that looked suspicious hanging around?"

Her eyes widened. "As a matter of fact I did. That's what investigative reporters do, they notice the things going on around them."

"So, what did you see?"

"You're not really a reporter trying to scoop me are you?" She asked, suspiciously.

"No." I said. "I'm not a reporter."

She leaned in toward me. "I saw a guy that seemed real nervous."

"You did? What did he look like?" I asked.

He was about 5'10, sandy hair. Really cute." She told me.

"Did you see where he went?"

"Sure. He was with a cop. They went over there, by the cop cars. I lost him after that. I had to follow them around. You know?" She said, eyeing the crew.

"Thanks, Amelia. I have to go but it was real nice chatting with you, good luck with your reporting career." I told her as I surveyed the area.

"Thank you . . . um, I don't remember your name."

"Sam, my name is Sam Parker."

"Bye, Sam."

I saw Frank walking through the crowd of onlookers and hustled to catch up to him.

"Sam, this is an old buddy of mine from the academy, Captain Neil Wessler," he said. "Captain, this is a good friend and associate of mine, Sam Parker."

I nodded. "Nice to meet you, Captain."

"My pleasure," he said with a smirk.

"Am I missing something?" I asked, feeling like you do when someone tells a joke and you don't get the punch line.

"You're not missing a thing," Frank told me. "Neil and I go way back. We were young, macho, stupid and had a rule about pretty women."

"Oh, yeah? What was that?" I was sounding a little defensive but I couldn't help it.

"It was nothing Sam." Frank said, clearly embarrassed. But I decided not to let him off the hook. Although not that young anymore, he was still relatively immature, as evidence of the longevity of his so called marriages.

"Obviously it was something if you're still making references to it now."

"Look, we just said we should never work with a woman you'd like to sleep with. As a cop I can tell you that that gets a little sticky."

"You guys never grow up!" I said, shaking my head. "How juvenile."

"So what's going on," Frank said grinning. "Do we have an ID on the guy yet?"

The captain's manner shifted. "No, not yet," he said grimly. "The coroner is here and we should have something soon. You think he might be a client of yours?"

"Not directly," Frank told him.

"Should I ask?"

"Better not, I don't want to put you in a bind. Will you keep me posted on anything you find out? I'd appreciate it."

"Sure, but then you will fill me in, right?"

"I'll buy you a drink and tell you the whole sordid story," Frank said, without hesitation.

"Okay, I gotta go. I'll let you know what I get."

"Thanks," we replied in unison.

The captain disappeared into the crowd of medical professionals, police officers and detectives, all moving about, doing their various jobs.

I looked at Frank. "So what do we do now?"

"We wait," he said.

He was so intense and serious that I continued to stare at the crowd. I had to remind myself that he might have been at a scene very much like this as a police officer. I myself have never seen a dead body up close, but knowing the stages a human goes through after death—the taut, pale skin, which then turns blue, then a greenish color. The loss of the finger and toenails, the draining of the fluids and the flattening eyes, and the smell . . . then adding the element of extremely cold, salt water, the fish . . . Well, you get the idea.

"Did you ever cover a drowning when you were on the force?" I asked.

He looked at me, stone faced. "More times than I'd like to remember."

"Sorry, Frank."

"Let's get out of here."

CHAPTER 14

I finally had the opportunity to call home and get my messages and wasn't surprised that there were none. I imagined Christina would have called Matt in which case, I would be the last thing on his mind. I decided to check in with Henry and also see if I could locate Captain Neil Wessler to see if he had any information.

Frank had left me in order to return to Temecula where he had another cheating wife to follow. After an odd look from me, he explained to me, in no uncertain terms that not all PI work was exciting and/or gratifying. I guess not.

The marina was pretty well cleared out of the onlookers and only a handful of what I expected to be crime scene investigators were still there doing whatever it was they do to complete their duty at the site of a crime.

I paced about a bit not sure of where I should be going. I had Henry's cell number but was hesitant to call. The last thing I wanted to do was interrupt him if he was in the process of gathering information from Christina. I knew any disruption could halt the flow of the conversation and make her think too much about what she was revealing, never a good thing for the person wanting the information, particularly when that person just happened to be me.

There was no sign of the captain in the area so I decided to head over to the Loews Bay Resort to see if there was any talk about the happenings of the day. I expected it must be of interest to the people who belonged here. It was not an event that would go unnoticed nor one that happened frequently, so someone must be speculating about the details of the event.

As I approached the entrance, I saw a police car in the parking lot. I had, as they say, lucked out. At a table tucked away in the back were four policemen enjoying a bite to eat and some conversation. I hoped it would not be impossible for me to convince the hostess to seat me within earshot of the group. If I hadn't mentioned earlier, eavesdropping is another one of my many talents and I find that if I practice regularly, I do in fact, get better at it.

Since most of the lunch business had gone, the hostess said I could sit wherever I pleased and I opted for a table in the back by the window. Yes, right near where the police officers were seated. Do you think I would really have it any other way? I ordered an iced tea and asked to see the menu. As I sat contemplating my choices, I listened attentively although the conversation wasn't quite what I had hoped for. The officers, all of whom were in uniform, and seemed to be a bit more seasoned (okay, I'll say it . . . old) were discussing shift changes and the upcoming shooting competition, in which none of them would be participating, for a variety of totally uninteresting reasons.

As I waited for my salad, I gazed out the window, thinking about all that had happened. All at once I realized the cops were discussing the floater. I had to strain to hear and I hoped my body language did not give away the fact that I was so desperately trying to listen to them.

Their dialogue was brief but included words that suggested foul play. I thought I heard one of them say the man had been shot, but honestly, it was so difficult to hear them that I couldn't be sure. I finished my salad and checked back at the marina. It looked as though everyone was wrapping up and getting ready to clear out. I knew hell would have to freeze over before these people would disclose anything to me, so I decided to head back home and take a nap. I'd ask Frank to contact the captain for details on the case later.

Once back on my turf I felt much better but still the thoughts of the day's events rattled me. I knew I should call Matt but I wasn't up for putting on a show so I stopped in at Milano's for a quick bite and then opted for the couch and a movie to calm my nerves. When I woke up it was one in the morning, so I headed up to my digs for a proper night's sleep.

I awoke early and had my coffee while watching the news, hoping for a tidbit of information about yesterday's big event. Well, I asked for a tidbit and that's just what I got. They have to be kidding! The reporter basically said that a body was discovered on Coronado Island by the docks and added, "the police are still investigating and we'll bring you more as it comes in." That's it? Unbelievable! Some poor guy is found floating by the docks and that's all they give him? A gruesome death like that and the guy doesn't even get his fifteen minutes of fame. I flipped off the TV, disgusted.

Once showered, I put a call in to Frank to see if he might have heard from the captain. As the phone rang I realized it might be too early to catch him in the office. As I suspected he did not answer. I left my usual charming message and asked that he return my call ASAP. Now to find out what Henry has been up to all night.

It was clear, when he answered, that he had been asleep.

"Hi, Henry. It's Sam. Am I calling too early?"

"Yes."

"Too bad, I've been waiting to hear from you and I can't stand it anymore. What is going on down there?"

"Can I grab a cup of coffee and call you right back?" He asked, as he hung up the phone abruptly.

An understandable request, seeing that it was the ungodly hour of 5:30 A.M.

As I waited, I moseyed into the kitchen and retrieved another delicious hot cup of Joe for myself. I went in and anxiously propped myself on the couch and put my blanket over my legs and held my cup in both hands to keep warm.

"Hi, Sam."

"Feeling better?" I asked.

"A little. Why are you calling so early?"

"I thought I'd hear from you yesterday and when I didn't I just had to call. So far I haven't been able to get any information on our friend in the water and it's killing me . . . sorry, bad choice of words. Christina flipping out over this has me very curious about who it is. Did she tell you anything?"

"Let me ask you something first."

"What?"

"She really isn't looking for rich guys to blackmail, is she?"

"She might be."

"But that's not why you sent me," he said.

"No, not exactly but the reason is because of the confidentially of the case. I couldn't tell and I still can't. I could go to jail."

"So what is it you really want?"

"Christina could be involved in something pretty bad, I need to find out if she is."

"And the body that was found, is that all part of this case?"

"It could be. When you called and said Christina recognized the guy and was freaked out about it, I figured it was someone vital to the case. I still do. Look, I'm sorry I couldn't tell you everything; it could have been and still may be dangerous for you. If you met her by chance, well, that's different. That is why I told you not to mention my name. It was for your own safety."

"Oh, I understand."

"Henry, I am sorry. Really."

"It's all right, Sam."

"Did I screw up?"

"No, I really do understand your position and to tell you the truth, I appreciate you choosing me for the mission."

"So you're in?"

"Of course I'm in, it's all getting so exciting."

"Will you tell me what happened with Christina? Did she tell you who it was floating in the water?"

"She did."

"Did you get it on tape?"

"Yes, I did."

I couldn't help letting out a rejoicing "yes!"

"Are you with me, Sam?"

"I'm here, who is it?"

"Sit down."

"I'm sitting."

"She said it was Simon, an old friend that she has known since she was a kid."

"Simon . . . oh, no."

"You know him?"

"I met him once." I said, feeling a deep pain in my chest. I sat, all of a sudden unable to breath.

"Sam, are you okay?"

"I've got to go. I'll call you later." I hung up still hearing Henry's voice. I tried to calm myself but felt sick and dizzy. I couldn't believe this had happened. I knew I had to finally face the fact that Matt just might know that I was involved in all this. If he did, I might be the next one to end up in the water. The phone rang but I didn't pick it up. What if it was Matt? There was no way I could talk to him knowing what he had done. I felt paralyzed with fear as I lay there on the couch trying to make sense of it all. I just didn't understand it. Why Simon? He was so fond of Matt and I thought Matt was fond of him as well.

As I thought about Simon, I started to get angry and the anger provided me with a reason to get myself together. I had to find a way to make Matt pay. The only thing I could do was to find evidence that would put him away. Life in prison. That might do it.

I called Frank back and he asked me to come over. He had, it seemed, heard from his friend, the captain.

On the way over, I concentrated on one fact. If I wanted to have Matt put away for life, I had to keep it together. Undoubtedly, I would be seeing him again and would have to act in the same manner as I had before as to not give him any indication of what I suspected. It would not be easy for me to do but what were my choices? Give up and back out or stand up and help to take him down. No choice, not for me.

When I arrived at the office, the door was just slightly open and I heard Chuck and Frank in what sounded like a serious discussion.

"You are making a big mistake!" Chuck said in a stern voice.

"She's on the inside. She could be our only hope for nailing this son of a bitch and you know it!" Frank was clearly trying not to yell but wasn't doing a very good job at keeping it down. So they were talking about me. I decided to listen.

"Is that all you can think about?" Chuck demanded. "This is her life. How fucking selfish do you have to be, think about her for God's sake and get your head out of your ass!"

"*I am thinking about her.* You want me to just cut her loose after all she has done? It should be her choice."

"Cut her loose. There is no choice, it's too dangerous!"

I couldn't take it anymore so I walked in.

"Hi, am I interrupting anything?" I said, staring at them as they stood face to face, looking as though they were ready for battle.

They both eased up. Chuck walked over to his desk and sat down.

"We have to talk, Sam," Frank said, as he glanced in Chuck's direction.

"No," I said.

"What?" Frank looked at me and then realized I had heard their conversation.

"I'm not backing out!"

"You don't have a choice," Chuck said as he stood.

"I do have a choice, I'm in."

"God damn it, Sam!" Chuck's voice was strained.

"I'll be seeing Matt Andrews whether you like it or not. So as I see it, I can work alone or we can work together and nail this murderer!"

Chuck shook his head and sat back down. Probably he was frustrated with me. Yeah, whatever. But I knew he was trying to protect me. "I could have you picked up, you know," he said calmly.

"And have me arrested for dating a mobster?"

He mumbled something under his breath. I thought he said dumb broad but I could be mistaken.

"If you have something to say to me, say it so I can hear you,." I said. "Are we finished with this now, Frank?"

"I don't know." He said, looking at Chuck. "Are we?"

"I can't believe you're doing this."

"*We.* You can't believe *we* are doing this," Frank said.

"Yeah, I can't believe *we* are doing this." Chuck had been defeated, this time.

We all moved to the conference table, as we so fondly call the small table sitting to the side of the office.

Frank started, "Sam, the captain called, it seems our floater . . ."

"Can we not refer to him like that?" I said, feeling protective.

"Yeah," he hesitated, "sure, Sam." Looking back at his notes he continued. "Our victim was a fellow by the name of Simon Levey. He worked as a driver for . . ." He moved his gaze to me. "You've met him."

I took a deep breath and held back the tears. "Yes," I said, not wanting to think about him now. Not wanting to remember the long ride, my prying for information. I liked him. I admit, I saw him as a way to retrieve some particulars, but I did, in fact, like him. I really did think I would see him again but I was wrong. I wondered why this was affecting me, I was doing a job and I had not killed him, yet I felt guilty somehow. Why? What was I missing?

"Sam? Sam?" Frank was waving his hand in front of my face.

"I'm listening."

"Was he the one who drove when you went down to the boat?"

"Yes. Matt had some emergency to take care of and had Simon drive me back."

"What kind of emergency?" Chuck inquired, like I would actually know.

"No idea, he said something about an accident with an employee."

"An employee from where?"

"I don't know. Matt said he owned some restaurants. I asked which ones but he told me he didn't feel like talking about work so I didn't push. I thought I'd ask again on another occasion."

"So Mr. Levey couldn't have been that accident." Frank observed.

"No, but I wonder who was." I thought aloud.

"Did you talk on your return to Temecula?" Frank asked.

"Yes, I was asking questions about the pictures on the boat. He was in one with a few other guys, including Ron, so I asked if he had seen him lately. He said they all see each other all the time but when I asked when he saw Ron last, he changed the subject and closed up a bit. I remember feeling like I might have pushed too far."

"So that was it? No more talking?" Chuck said as he got up and retrieved a soda from the small fridge sitting on a stand.

"No, we talked. I spent some time trying to get him to let his guard down and once he did I was careful what I said. I wanted him to trust me and I think by the time we arrived, he did."

"Anyone want a soda?" Chuck said, as he took out two more and handed them to us.

Frank was eager to get back to business. "What was he like?"

"He was nice. He seemed to enjoy driving for Matt. What was weird was that he was so at ease. Thinking back on it now, I wondered why. Being in that position you'd think he would have been more guarded."

"How did he come to be Mr. Andrews' driver anyway?" Frank continued. "Did he tell you that?"

"I asked him that and Simon told me they had known each other since the fourth grade."

"That's long time. He must have been on the inside."

"I guess so," I said. "It's still so unbelievable to me."

"What part?" Frank asked.

"All of it." Moving on I asked, "What else did the captain have to report?"

When the phone rang, Chuck picked it up.

"Sam, some of this is pretty ugly stuff," Frank said in a low voice. "Do you still want to go ahead with it? You don't have to, I'll understand. Believe me, your safety is my main concern."

He knew I had overheard his argument with Chuck, and although my first thought was that he was covering his ass, I knew better.

"I know, Frank. I'm fine, really. Let's just get on with it. I couldn't quit now, even if I wanted to."

"Earlier, when I was arguing with . . . I didn't mean to imply that the case was more important than you, your life. You know that, right? I was just heated and . . ."

I couldn't let him go on. "I know," I said. "Forget it. What else did the captain say?"

"He told me that, before Simon went into the water, he was shot . . . in the back of the head at close range, indicating that he was either with someone he trusted or that someone sneaked up and put a gun to his head without him knowing it. There were no signs of a struggle."

"Oh my God! Anything else?"

"Not so far. He said he would keep in touch."

"So what now?" I was almost afraid to ask.

"We need to go over some of our facts. I was going through my notes and I wanted to be sure we covered a few things. You were going to call some jewelers and find out about the initials on the inside of the watch. Did you get to that?"

I knew I should have made those calls but with the internet being so convenient, I decided to look there first.

Frank and I moved to his desk where he sat at his computer and brought up his file on the case.

"Where were we?" he asked

"The jewelers. I haven't exactly called them yet. But I did do some research on line and found out that it's unusual to place initials on the inside of a pocket watch. I also found some old pirate tale about the significance. It read that when initials were engraved on the inside, it signified a dissolving or vanishing. I took it to mean that someone just disappeared."

"No shit. Really?"

"Really, isn't that weird?"

"Is it some religious thing?"

"That's what I thought it could be, but so far I haven't found anything to indicate that in my research. But some of these religions change their rules daily so it could be tough to ever find out. I can keep looking though. I'm very curious about it, it's just too creepy."

"Do you have any other ideas on what it might mean?"

"I thought about superstitions. Magical stuff. That sort of thing. I've been spending some time researching those ideas too, but so far I haven't found anything there either."

"I'll put some thought into it and let you know if I have anything to add. What else?"

"You were going to have the watch and key dusted for prints, did you come up with anything there?" I asked.

"As a matter of fact, I did. The only prints found were of our friend, Ronald Gregory. I must admit, Sam, in the back of my mind I thought the lab would report..."

"My prints, right? You thought I touched the stuff with bare hands."

"Well, yeah."

"Gee, some people just have no faith!" I said, playfully.

"Good job, Sam. You did a good job."

"Thanks. Now we just have to find out what the key belongs to."

"Chuck asked if we'd had thought about a portable safe or jewelry box. I'm not sure why Ron would need a jewelry box but we should keep it in mind. I think we should focus on a safe or lock box, something like that, now that we know for sure they are his prints."

"I agree, I'll look around in the house next time I'm there."

"You're not going back in that house."

"Don't get overprotective on me, Frank. I'm just starting to feel better about it myself. I have to go and we both know it. How else can we check it out?"

Frank was silent. I was ordered to call him frequently, so he'd know I was okay. Although we both knew I could be in danger, we also knew that at this point, we had no other way to locate information. I had to take the chance. Frank gave me the ground rules and I was on my way.

I wanted to call Henry; I probably left him scared to death with me losing it like that at the news of Simon's death. It had been thoughtless of me not to have called him back earlier.

After I apologized and assured him that I was fine, I explained that I needed to meet with him and listen to the tape. He asked me to give him until tomorrow, adding that he would be seeing Christy and would have more for me then. I agreed, noting that I needed to make some calls and follow up on some research. For the moment, however, the first thing on my list was lunch. I threw together my own version of a chef salad, some ham, turkey, two types of cheese, and a few almonds, topped with a bit of Thousand Island dressing, served, of course, with unsweetened iced tea with a wedge of lemon. Yum, yum. I ate and read, something I do too often, due to the lack of a real social life.

Over the next few hours I had continued my research on the spiritual, mystical and the superstitious. Although I had reached the stage when I could probably have recited a few incantations and mix a couple of potions, that was as far as I had gotten. Anyway, it was very interesting stuff and I ended up with a new folder entitled *Magic* in my bookmarks before the search was through.

Switching gears, I searched through some sites on missing persons and came across a case where some of the evidence focused on newspaper articles. I immediately thought of the box of news clippings that were in Frank's office. I bolted out the door, keys in hand only to see Mrs. Bennett pull up out front in her ancient Audi. Pretending I didn't see her, I took off down the street, leaving her standing, waving after me as though there was a chance I would see her and throw my car in reverse. "Nice try," I said as I rode off. "Maybe next time."

"What's so important about these articles?" Frank asked when I told him what I wanted.

"I've come across something interesting," I said, taking the box and putting it under my arm.

"I don't mean to rush you off, Sam," Frank said. "But I have to go, important meeting."

"Another case?" I asked.

"Susan and I are going to a marriage counselor."

I bit my lip to keep from screaming. This couldn't be happening again. It seems like every time we got well into a case, something would come up with him and Susan. Sometimes I just wish they would get a divorce and be done with it. Now, when I wanted to tell him about the suspicions my review of the articles has generated, we were going to talk about his marriage. I wasn't thrilled with this idea but experience has taught me to be patient and listen. Frank Petulant was not a pretty sight.

I smiled at him. "Good, that's good, Frank. I'll talk to you later."

"Let me know what you find."

"Who say's I'll find anything?" I said.

I could see that Frank was preoccupied, possibly because he was nervous about his appointment with the marriage counselor, but I felt like he was dropping the ball on me. I had wanted his help and he wasn't going to be around to give it to me.

As I drove home, I thought of how glad I was that Frank wasn't giving up on his marriage. Then the slogan, "Three strikes and you're out," came to mind.

Mrs. Bennett's car was still there when I reached home. I peered around the side of the house toward the garden, which was her favorite hang out. She was talking to my friend and neighbor Kim, who tried to signal me to run for it while I had the chance. I decided I'd have to face her sooner or later so I approached her to find out what was aggravating her this week.

"Hi, Mrs. Bennett," I said, trying to sound as though I had been looking forward to talking to her for days.

When she turned and smiled at me, I thought, "Oh shit." I couldn't put my finger on it but there was something about her smile that sent chills down my spine. Probably because she reminded me of the bad witch from The Wizard of Oz. That movie scared the crap out of me when I was a kid.

"I wanted to ask you when it might be convenient for me to come and plant the garden," she said, happily.

"Plant the garden? Mrs. Bennett!" I exclaimed. "It's February."

"Miss Parker, this is the best time to plant for spring, didn't you know that?"

"Obviously not," I said sarcastically. I couldn't help it; she just brings out the best in me.

"Well?"

"Well, what?" I asked, still confused.

"The garden!" She was irritated with me. "Would it be okay with you if I begin planting?"

"Planting? The ground is like a rock! How are you going to plant anything in here?"

"I'll manage." She insisted.

"Suit yourself."

"When?"

"When what?"

"Miss Parker, the garden!"

"Oh, any day is fine, just not on Saturday or Sunday."

"Well then, I'll see you sometime next week."

"Okay," I said. "But can you plant something that won't attract bees? I hate bees."

She glared at me, exasperated.

"I was giving you the opportunity to run for cover," Kim said as soon as she left.

"Where have you been, anyway?" She eyed my shoe box.

"There is a lot going on. I'll tell you about it when I can." I hesitated, "Let's go out for a couple of drinks tonight."

"I wish I could, I made the mistake of accepting a dinner date after consuming my third glass of wine last night. I can barely remember what he looks like."

"Well, good luck and call me if you need rescuing," I offered, having done the same thing a time or two myself.

I went inside and contemplated what I would fix myself for dinner. Deciding that I wanted something good, I made sure I looked presentable and headed out. The Claim Jumper was busy as usual so I went into the bar and found a table snuggled in the back. I ordered a glass of chardonnay and a steak medium rare, and a Caesar salad. I have to admit, I felt like I stood out like a sore thumb. It seems everyone had a date but me. As I sipped my wine, I took inventory and lo and behold, across the bar, sitting in a booth, side by side, was Frank and...it wasn't Susan. Oh, shit.

CHAPTER 15

I woke early to a crisp morning. It was a little overcast but the sun was expected to shine, giving us a day the droves are moving here for, with temperatures supposed to be reaching about seventy-two degrees. I put on my socks and went immediately for my coffee. Having stayed up late reading, my eyes still burned and my mind was still racing. I had attempted to organize the articles under headings such as the type of death for which the mob was suspected of being responsible, such as gunshot, strangulation, drowning, accidental, etc. There were no accidents.

The piles were spread all over my floor and I avoided them, taking my coffee up to my bedroom. I needed to clear my mind and I found being near the information just drew me back in. Back in bed I tried to savor my coffee and enjoy the morning quiet, broken only by a couple of dogs who were apparently engaged in a barking contest. On the surface, life seemed the same. Coffee in bed. Mrs. Bennett lurking around outside. Frank ready with another tale of marital strife. But everything had changed and I was all too aware of it. A week ago I had had an overdraft at the bank. A week ago I hadn't know anyone who just disappeared. A week ago I had not been drawn to a mobster like a magnet to a pile of steel chips only to have been just as forcefully repelled when one of his friends had been found murdered. My life was not the same.

Today I would call Matt. Although he didn't call me as promised, and I know why, he doesn't know what I know. I'd have to come up with some excuse why I wanted to talk to him. No problem, I'd get creative. Then I'd head back to Coronado to meet with Henry and pick up the tape. I'd better make sure I've got some money in the account; I'd have to settle up with Henry. I think his mission is now complete.

Last night I had come across seven articles that involved a gunshot to the head before the victim ended up in the water. All of them made me cringe and brought me a new feeling of awareness. I no longer felt the distance I had when I had read about these people the first time, I now knew someone that had been silenced in the same way. Because that had to be the reason behind Simon's murder. He had somehow become too dangerous to be allowed to stay alive.

All of this horror had made me wonder about Simon. Had he known he was going to be shot? Had he, like Ron, suspected that he was in danger? I wondered if Ron had met the same fate and just had not surfaced yet. I had read that a body, once submerged in water, sinks to the bottom head down. Only when the body starts to decompose and gases begin to form does the body float to the surface. The colder the water, the longer it is supposed to take. It made me wonder about when this happened to Simon. It hadn't been that long since I had seen him.

I finished my coffee and decided I needed to get outside for a bike ride. I got myself cleaned up, put on my sweats and sneakers and was on my way. It felt good to be outside, the cold breeze was hitting my face and it made me feel so lucky to be alive.

As I rode down empty streets, admiring the trees, plants and some flowers still in bloom, not something you tend to see this time of year, I was drawn to the mountains. They held a slightly purple glow about them and I could see the faint twinkle of sunlight starting to show, and it gave me hope. Hope for a long life, and possibly more importantly, love.

Two hours later, I arrived home feeling as though a weight had been lifted from my shoulders. I had a sense of "letting go" and it felt good. I couldn't change what had happened to Simon, but I was ready to move forward and take down those responsible.

I showered, had a bowl of Lucky Charms and prepared myself for a call I had been dreading to make. It was a relief when his machine answered.

"Hi, Matt," I said. "This is Sam. I just wanted to call and see if you're okay. I heard about Simon. I'm so sorry. I'd like to see you. Give me a call. Bye."

I put a call in to Henry but he didn't pick up so I left him a message, as well. Then, because waiting is the worst, I thought I'd make myself useful. Getting out my cleaning supplies, I started in the kitchen and moved from room to room until the house smelled of Windex and the lemon scent of Pledge. I do love it when it's clean.

The first call that I received was from Henry. He was still hanging out with Christy and although the police had been searching the boats and had not allowed the owners near them, he thought they'd be allowed to return today. But Christy had told him she would not be going back there. Not ever.

"Why not? What's going on?"

"I don't know. She's been acting really paranoid. She's been on her cell an awful lot. First whispering and then a moment later she's yelling. She also keeps looking around like someone's following her. To tell you the truth, she's freaking me out. Is there anything I should be doing?"

"Oh no. Can you just stick with her? Stay close and listen to her and let me know if you run into anyone and pay close attention to how she communicates with them, you know, like if she seems nervous or hostile towards them."

"So, basically I'm baby-sitting."

"Yes, but you are being paid well for it and Christy is . . . well, she is a beautiful woman."

"I know, Sam. It could be a whole lot worse. Ha, Ha. Hey, am I in any danger? Should I have updated my will?" he said, only half joking.

"I think you're going to be fine. Have I told you lately how much I appreciate you?"

"Not nearly enough."

"Well, for the record, I appreciate you!"

"Okay. Sam. Enough kissing up. Are you planning to come down here today?"

"Yes, I just have to wait for a call. Will I be able to reach you on your cell?" I inquired.

"I'll be sure to keep it on."

"Thanks, I'll talk to you soon." I hung up, and immediately the ringer sounded again. I scooped up the phone.

"Hello?"

"Sam, he's been picked up for questioning."

"Frank?"

"Yeah, it's me. Did you hear what I said?"

"Yes, but who?"

"Our friend, Mr. Andrews."

"You're kidding? When did all this happen?"

"I just got a call from the captain. Apparently Matt was down at the Coronado marina asking about why he couldn't get to his boat. I understand that he made quite a fuss"

"Does the captain know about? . . ."

"No, he doesn't, and right now we should keep it that way."

"Let me ask you something, Frank. Why would Matt go down there? If he's responsible, wouldn't he want to be as far away from the scene as possible?"

I couldn't understand what would possess him to show up at the crime scene knowing how dangerous it would be for him. And what's worse, he makes a fuss to get on his boat.

"You'd think so."

"So what now?"

"The captain is on the inside of this, Coronado is his jurisdiction. He said he'd keep me posted. So, I guess we wait."

"Wait? Easy for you to say."

"I'll call you later, Sam."

"Bye."

I hung up the phone, and decided to head back to Coronado. Now that I knew Matt was not going to call me back I had no reason not to.

The coast is always a bit windy and colder than it is here, so I changed into my black jeans, white long-sleeved sweater and black boots. On my way out I grabbed my leather jacket and purse and headed for the car.

I phoned Henry from the car, to see where he would meet me and see how he was making out with Christy.

"Yeah?" Henry said in a low voice.

"Henry, it's Sam. Why are you whispering?"

"Can't talk now. Where are you?"

"I'm on my way. Where should we meet?"

"How about Keno's?"

"Fine. One hour."

"Good. See you then."

I wasn't crazy about going to Keno's but I guess there would be little chance of running into anyone I know there.

As I drove down the freeway, once again headed to this place where Simon had been found, I wondered why Matt would take a chance and show up there. Had he gotten word the job had been done? Did he go to stop it? No, he ordered a hit on someone he's known since childhood. He was a monster. I just didn't understand his motive. I wondered what Simon could have done to betray his trust. It must have been pretty serious to end up as he had.

Since the body had been found at the dock and Matt was not the only one with a boat moored there, I had to wonder if all the owners were being questioned or if they had evidence to take Matt in. After all, Simon had been his driver and that connection alone would be enough of a reason. It seemed that every question I asked myself had an answer I didn't want to hear. So in order to find an answer I did want to hear I had to ask some different questions. As I pondered what they would be, I found that before I knew it I was paying the toll and driving on the small streets of Coronado Island heading to Keno's.

Pulling into the lot, I wondered if Henry would be there. I hoped he would be as I was just not comfortable hanging out here by myself. Not really my type of crowd, I guess. But then, do I really have a crowd?

No need to worry about that, however, since the place was empty. It must be too early yet for the regulars. I looked in and was disappointed to see that Henry had not arrived. I was about to turn around and head for my car when I heard a voice from the direction of the bar.

"You're Miss Parker, aren't you?"

I turned and although Keno's was not dark, the sunlight was hitting my eyes in a way that caused a glare, preventing me to see inside.

"Yes, I am," I said, still not sure who it was that was asking.

"Come in, come in. It's nice to see you again."

Once inside I could see it was the man who owned the place, the man Henry had introduced me to the last time I had been here.

"Good to see you, too, Eddie," I said. "Has Henry been around here today?"

"Not yet. Are you expecting to meet him here?"

"Yes, that was the plan."

"Well, the plan may have changed. I saw the girl he's been spending time with get into a police car about a half hour ago. I didn't see him though, so maybe he'll be here."

"You saw her get into a police car?"

"Yeah, I own the boat docked near the *Lucky Man* and she spends a lot of time there. They asked her to go with them as she was heading to the boat."

"Did she go quietly? What I mean is . . . did she cooperate?"

"She seemed surprised to have even been asked, but she went along without making a fuss. To tell you the truth, I don't know why she was so shocked. The guy that was found the other morning? She knows him. I've seen him myself on several occasions. Wouldn't you expect to be questioned if you knew him? I understand she was the one who spotted him early that morning."

"Eddie, did the police question you?"

"They asked a couple questions and they searched my boat. I think they searched all of them."

"But they didn't ask to question you, formally?"

"Nope. I told them they could call me if they thought I'd be helpful, I told them where I work."

"Do you mind if I ask you another question?"

"Not at all. What's on your mind?"

"How long have you had your boat docked there? And do you know the owner of the *Lucky Man*?"

"That's two questions," he said, smiling at me.

"I know, but it would be really helpful to know."

"Are you a cop?"

"No, I'm a paralegal."

"Why so interested?"

"I'm working for someone who has disappeared. I think this death is related to my client."

"Good enough, I have had my boat there for eight years and yes, I know Mr. Andrews and Mr. Gregory."

"Mr. Andrews and Mr. Gregory, did you say?"

"Yes. I know them both, nice fellows but . . ."

"But what?"

"There has been some odd goings on."

"Like what kind of odd goings on?" I asked, not believing my luck.

"Every now and then they have a lot of company," he said raising an eyebrow suspiciously.

"What kind of company? Like parties with girls?"

"No, guys. Big guys who are not friendly. They wear black and look as though they were mixed up in something. I don't know what but something suspicious is going on. It's difficult to describe. They're just tough looking, I can't very well set the cops on them for that now, can I?"

"No, I suppose not. Have they threatened you in any way?"

"No. It's just that . . . well, you ever get the feeling about something that you can't shake?"

"Yes, I have."

"Well, that's what I get when they have these meetings. Just a bad feeling," he said, meeting in my eyes. "Maybe it's my imagination."

"No, no it isn't, Eddie. Can you tell me the last time they had one of their meetings?"

"Let me see, I'd have to say it's been about a month."

"Were Mr. Andrews and Mr. Gregory there?"

"You know, Mr. Gregory wasn't around at the time. I had seen the blonde kid who works for them bringing food and drinks aboard. I asked him if they were having a party, joking around, you know? He is usually pretty light hearted but that day he was very serious. I just ignored it and went on my way, but later that afternoon Mr. Andrews stopped by and asked me if they were disturbing me. Apparently, he wanted to be sure that they didn't. He seemed very concerned. I thought it was odd. We started talking and I asked where Mr. Gregory was, I told him I hadn't seen him around lately. He just said he was out of town for a while."

"So he went to your boat to ask you if they were disturbing you?"

"No, he came down here. I bought him a drink and told him they didn't disturb me at all. We talked a bit and then he said to please call him if there were any problems with his guests."

"He came here?"

"Yeah, odd huh?"

"Very. Have you had an opportunity to talk with him since then?"

"Haven't seen him around. He has a place up north where he likes to spend his time."

By now I had come to the conclusion that Henry had followed Christy to the police station. At least something was up since he hadn't shown up here. Of course, if Matt had come to check on things, there was the possibility that they had crossed paths, and that could be bad. No, Christy wouldn't let anything happen to Henry. At least that's what I told myself.

"So, Eddie, it looks as though I have been stood up. Would you mind terribly if I hang around here?"

"Can I get you a drink?" he asked smiling.

"I'd love one," I told him. Wishing it was cocktail hour. "How about an iced tea?"

"Coming right up."

He put the drink in front of me and poured a bowl of nuts. I took a sip and continued asking questions, knowing that one little tidbit of information could very well lead me to some significant clues.

"Have you ever socialized with Matt Andrews and Ronald Gregory?" I asked.

"Katie and I went to a club dinner one night, a barbecue, very casual, and we all sat together."

"Who was there?"

"Let me see," he said, frowning. "Matt Andrews, Ron Gregory and the girl."

"What girl?"

"The one that I saw today, I can't for the life of me remember her name."

"Christy?" I said in anticipation.

"Not Christy. Christina. She was very cozy with him, and he with her."

So Matt had been lying about her being his sister all along. I should have known. That look she had given him the night I had dinner on the boat had been the look of a woman scorned. It made me wonder, was she also part of the mob? Or just too involved in Matt to walk away? Why would he say she was his sister but she's giving another name? I had to hope Eddie would have some answers. The docks were, after all, his world.

"So Christina and Matt were a twosome?" I said innocently.

"No. Christina and Ron. They were head over heels for each other."

"Really?" Christina and Ron! I had though that things were complicated before but it seems that I had only scratched the surface. Because if Ron was the man she loved, why had Christina treated me the way she had, as though I were some sort of rival? And what about the so-called guest room in the house that Ron had listed as his address, the room which had obviously been lived in by a woman, the room where I found Ron's watch?

"I thought they might be getting married . . . well actually Katie had said something to that effect."

"Christina and Ron, huh?" That's strange. As I sat there I realized I had to get on that boat. If the key was in Ron's pocket watch, and he and Christina had something going, well . . . maybe she held the . . .

"Eddie, I have to go," I said. "If Henry comes in, please have him call me on my cell. I'll be around Coronado for a while." Before I started for the door leaned over the bar and gave him a big hug and a kiss on his cheek. "Thank you, you have no idea how much you have helped me."

As I headed for the door I heard him say, "Anytime Sam, anytime."

Once in my car I called Frank. "You're not going to believe this," I said, trying to temper my excitement with crisp professionalism and not succeeding.

"Now what?" he was not in a very good mood.

"First tell me what is wrong." I demanded. "You sound like shit."

"Will you explain something to me, Sam? What the hell is wrong with my wife?"

"I thought you and she were going to . . ."

"Yeah, I did too."

"What happened?" I said patiently. This was the way it always was with Frank. I couldn't count the number of times I had had to put something urgent on hold while he went on about his wife. He was a great investigator but his troubles with Susan always came first.

"She makes this big deal about going to see a marriage counselor, tells me I don't want to go because I'm afraid of the truth. I have issues with women because my first wife stuck it too me so bad I can't deal with it. Blah, blah, blah. So I agree to go. I tell her maybe she's right, maybe it will help to talk to someone, right?"

"Right," I said.

"Well, we go to our first session. Remember, you saw me on my way out? Anyway, this therapist, counselor, whatever they call themselves, starts asking each of us how we see our relationship. She goes first and rips me apart. I don't know how to communicate, I have intimacy problems, I live for the job, and so on. Then it's my turn to talk. First I have to tell Susan why I agree or disagree with her. You following how this works?"

"Yes, I understand. You're supposed to answer her in a sense, and explain how you see it." At least that's what I had to do when I was in counseling for anorexia; I assume it works basically the same. I always kept it short and sweet, unlike Frank!

"Right, so I start. I'm telling her why I don't agree about the sex issue and she stops the session. She says she can't deal with what I'm saying. The therapist- who's a woman by the way, tells her she needs to hear my side, that that's how we will come to an understanding of how the other person sees it. Well, that's when Susan starts crying and storms out. I'm left sitting there wondering what the hell just happened. The therapist just sat back and said, 'Will I see you next week?' Like nothing happened! Can you believe this shit?"

"I don't know what to say, no I can't believe it. Have you asked her what happened?"

"She's not talking to me. She acts like I dragged her there! Sammy, what is going on?"

"How would I know?"

"You're a woman!" he said- as if that proved anything. Why is it that just because I'm a woman I should know exactly why all other women act as they do.

"Frank," I said. "I hate to tell you this but I'm not like her. I don't know anymore about it than you do. And you know what else?"

"What, Sam?"

"I hate to shop!"

"Marry me, Sam."

"Can't, Frank. You're already married."

"Don't remind me!"

"So, do you want to know why I called?"

"Oh, yeah. What's going on?"

"I think I know where we can find the mate to the key," I said, confidently.

"Where? And how do you know?"

"On the *Lucky Man*, because I just found out that Ron and Christina are an item. At least they were a week or so ago, according to the owner of that joint called Keno's"

"No shit, really?"

"Really."

"So, what are you going to do? Or don't I want to know?"

"Can I just call you later? Time is a wasting and I have opportunity. I just wanted you to know where I was heading just in case."

"Stay out of trouble, Sam."

"Talk to you later." I hung up and drove directly to the marina, parked my car in the back of the lot and walked toward the dock. I didn't know what I would find. Maybe nothing. But I had to take the chance and look around. As I got closer, I found myself looking over my shoulder feeling much like a fugitive. I didn't want trouble, I just wanted answers. Oh yeah, and not having my face bashed in would be good too.

CHAPTER 16

As I approached the *Lucky Man,* I realized that my stomach was tied in knots. To say that I was nervous would be an understatement. With Matt and Christina both at the police station I felt it would be pretty safe for me to go on board and have a look around. I knew there was a possibility that I might encounter someone else there but I was completely willing to take my chances.

The dock was quite a different scene today. No cops. No crowds. No yellow tape. Everything seemed quiet, so I settled on the fact that I had to move on to the boat and hoped that the situation wouldn't change. I decided the first place I'd look would be in Christina's cabin. It was the most logical place to start, knowing as I did now, that she and Ron had a relationship. And, if by chance, I did encounter someone like a deckhand, I could simply say that I was a friend of Matt's and that he'd given me permission to look around. At least the first part of that was sort of true.

As I looked through Christina's belongings I came across the usual cosmetics; mascara, eyeliner and several shades of pink blush. She also had several expensive shampoos and a package of diet pills. In her dresser, there was some sexy red and black lingerie that was so sexy that it had to be from Victoria's Secret. As I searched the closet I found that she had a thing for antique dolls. I found it odd, these delicate dolls, possessed by a seemingly strong girl. But there on the shelf, a beautiful collection sat neatly in a line. Above her bed, there was a built in cabinet that held in it a collection of old books, mostly on the subjects of poetry and history. I removed a few of them only to find a compartment hidden in the wall. As I reached inside, I heard someone board the boat. I stood frozen, afraid to even breathe until I heard the footsteps move up to the top level. Thank God! If I was lucky, that would give me a chance to move to the galley and off the boat undetected. But unless I finished my search by looking in that compartment, I might never get another opportunity.

Leaning over the bed, I pulled open the door. Relieved to find it unlocked I reached inside. There was nothing but a cardboard box, small, about four by six. Knowing that I had taken one risk too many, I shoved it in my bag and slipped out into the galley, just in time to encounter Peter, who was coming up the stairs from the lower deck. His hair was disheveled and he looked as though he was rushing about.

"Sam, what are you doing here?"

My heart was beating hard. "Hi Pete, I called up but didn't get a response so I came aboard. Is Matt here?"

"Was he expecting you?" he asked, clearly alarmed by my presence.

"Not really," I confessed. "I was hoping to surprise him. He promised me dinner," I said, feeling uneasy, hoping he'd buy it.

"He's not here. I'm not sure where he is. Can I just have him call you?"

I got up, feeling relieved that I was going to get off this boat unharmed. "Sure," I said. "I've got my cell phone with me. I'm going to head to the yacht club for a soda. Then I have an appointment."

"When he gets here I'll have him call."

Was the suspicious look in his eyes just my imagination? What would Matt think when Pete told him? There was already the possibility that he realized I had more than just a passing interest in his affairs. Ron was missing and I had to face the fact that Matt might know that Ron was my client. If he thought for a second that Ron confided in me about his dealings, God only knows what it would mean for me...I told myself not to freak out.

"Thanks. See you later," I said as I departed.

Once safely off the dock I went directly to my car and opened the box. As I looked at what was inside, thoughts of my childhood came rushing back. It was a gift from my grandmother for my seventh birthday. All I wanted was to be a ballerina. I'll never forget how I felt when I opened the jewelry box and a tiny little ballerina began dancing, around and around. My grandmother put the shiny silver key in my hand and told me that I should keep it in a safe place, so I'd be able to keep all my dreams hidden away in that box.

Wiping a tear from my eye, I deposited the box in the trunk under some clothes I had been meaning to drop off at Goodwill. I then headed for the club and found a table by the window, ordered a diet Coke and breathed in deeply, feeling smug with myself for pulling that off.

I called Frank to let him know I had located a box and had possession of it. After delivering the newest version on the state of his marriage, he listened thoughtfully as I explained to him that I wasn't sure if it was "the box" and that I wouldn't know that until I had the key. I described it in detail, adding that I had gotten one just like it when I was seven. The keyhole on the front was small but from my memory of the size of the key, I thought it might fit. Thinking about it now, I had to wonder if I had made a mistake. Why would someone lock something in this? It didn't look very secure and I had the feeling that I had made a mistake and risked taking something that would not be worth the stress of having. And then there was the fact that somehow or other, in the course of this investigation, I had turned into a thief. I told Frank that I thought Pete was suspicious about my being on the boat. And then something else struck me. Why hadn't he mentioned the fact that Simon had been drowned? It would have been the natural thing to do. If he trusted me, that is.

Finishing my soda, I paid the check and got up to go. I hoped Henry would be around so I could get the tape and get back to check out the box. I went to my car and headed once again for Keno's. Eddie informed me that he had not been in so I went back to my car. As I got in, my phone rang. It was Henry, informing me he was at the police station with Christina but as of yet, doesn't know why she's been brought in. He would hang out for a while and see if he could find out and get back to me.

As I thought about it, I figured that since she knew the victim and was the first to see him floating in the water, it would make perfect sense for the police to want to talk to her. But in the back of my mind, I wondered if that was the only reason.

I sat in my car thinking about Christina and Ron and this whole mess that I have found myself in the midst of, when thankfully, my phone rang.

"Hello?" I said.

"Sam, you're not going to believe this." Frank told me. "Captain Wessler called me. He said a woman just showed up at the station. She said she knows who is responsible for the death of Simon."

"Really? Is the woman Christina?"

"No, her name is Tiffany, Tiffany Andrews."

"Tiffany Andrews? You're kidding!"

"She said she's Matt Andrews' younger sister. She told the cops that she knows who did it but she can't tell. She's afraid for her life."

180

"I don't think he mentioned a little sister."

"Well, that's what she said."

"I guess she could be. He did say he was from a large family. But how did she know about Simon?" I asked.

"I don't know. Maybe Matt called her." He said.

"Or maybe Christina did." I added.

"I guess she could have."

"So, this Tiffany, she knows who killed Simon?"

"That's what she told the captain."

"Well, if she knows than maybe Christina knows too."

"Sam, you're getting ahead of yourself. Let's wait to see her statement." He told me.

"So what do they do now?"

"Try to convince her to give them a name."

"How?" I asked, wondering what they could possibly say to her to have her risk her life.

"Offer her protection."

"Like? . . ."

"I'm not sure what they will offer her. There are a few things they could do. Police protection around the clock, that kind of thing."

"Do you think? . . ."

"I don't know. Hey, Sam?"

"What?"

"Do you know her, Tiffany?"

"No. Matt only said he had seven brothers and two sisters. He was sixth in line."

"That's a lot of kids."

"Yeah. How old is she, do you know?"

"No. I'll see what I can find out about her, I'll call you later."

"Wait!" I said, suddenly remembering something. "The letter to Ron, it was signed by T. Do you think it could be Tiffany?"

"We'll have to look into it," he said, remembering vaguely what I was referring to.

"Great. Call me if you find out anything on her," I said, eagerly.

I sat, not believing what I had just heard about Tiffany Andrews. I had never thought to ask Matt about his siblings and their names. I wondered if she could have written that note to Ron. What did it say? Think, think . . . something about making it work. What was it referring to? I'd have to see it again, there was something else. I know it.

I considered briefly going to the police station to find Henry but decided I'd better stay away. I didn't want to see Captain Wessler. I knew he wouldn't be happy about me butting into his case. But more importantly, I didn't think it would be a good idea to see Matt there. If he had a feeling I was involved in any way, me showing up would surely send up a red flag. That is not what I wanted to do.

This is when having a PI license would be especially helpful. As a PI, the police view you as an equal, or close anyway. Unfortunately for me, I'm not one, so the cops see me as a problem. End of story.

What I needed was more information about Matt. And now, with Simon gone, the only person I knew who might be able to provide it was Peter. Granted it was dangerous to encounter him again, this time asking questions. But danger seemed to be my middle name these days. If he knew something, there was only one way to find out. So I drove to the marina.

The anxiety I had felt earlier had returned, indicating to me that I was asking for trouble. I decided to go into the yacht club for a cocktail to get my nerve up.

I was sitting at the bar enjoying a chilled glass of wine when, hearing a familiar voice behind me, I turned to see

Eddie standing at a table, talking to some people who looked to be about the age to really be into the early bird specials.

"So, we meet again," he said, smiling.

"Why aren't you at your place?" I asked.

"I work all day; I have a younger gal that takes care of the bar at night."

"Good for you. Would you like to join me for a drink?" I asked.

"I would, thanks."

He sat down in the chair next to me and ordered a scotch and soda for himself and another glass of wine for yours truly.

"Ever find Henry?" he asked.

"Yes, he was at the station with Christina."

"What's he doing with her when he could be here with you?"

"He was doing it for me," I said.

"I don't get it. He's a nice guy but not too smart. He should be following you around."

"I think you've misunderstood our relationship. I asked him to stick with her. Really."

"Oh, that client, is she another connection?"

"I think so. He's been kind enough to help me out."

"Well, that's different. Is he meeting you here?"

"I'm not sure, I haven't heard from him recently."

"So then, what are you doing here all alone?"

"I'm not alone, I'm with you," I teased.

He laughed. "I guess you are."

"I have a favor to ask you, I was wondering . . ."

"What can I help you with?"

"I was going to go to Matt Andrews' boat to see if I can talk with Peter, you know, the blonde kid. I was wondering, will you just keep an eye out for me. I'm not sure if I'll be welcome and I'd like to know that someone knows where I am."

"I have an even better idea," Eddie said. "Why don't we plan to go out for a sail. That way I'll have a good reason to be looking for you."

We finished our drinks and walked down the dock together. As we got close to the *Lucky Man* I saw Peter washing down the sides.

"Hey Sam," He called out when he saw me. "Are you coming with us?"

"Where?"

"Fishing trip. Did Matt get a hold of you?"

"I haven't heard from him." I said. "But I'm not going to be able to join you. Will you please tell him that I had made other plans, but that I'm looking forward to seeing him?" Knowing what I know, there was no way in hell I was going to end up out in the middle of nowhere with Matt on a boat. I might do some crazy things but that wouldn't be one of them.

"Sure, he'll be disappointed but I'll let him know."

"Thanks."

"Bye, Sam."

My phone rang and I searched to retrieve it before the caller was forced to leave a message. Too late. It was a message from Henry telling me to call him ASAP. He had some information I might want to hear and where the hell was I anyway? I walked to Eddie's boat and told him I would be back; I had to call Henry. He told me to invite him too; we'd have a great time.

Henry picked up on the first ring. "Where have you been?" he said excitedly.

"I couldn't catch the phone in time. What's going on? Why all the whispering?"

"I was whispering so no one would hear me."

"Makes sense to me. So fill me in."

"Where do you want me to meet you?"

"Parking lot at the marina, I'm in the back corner."

"Be right there."

I went back to tell Eddie I'd be a little while longer, which didn't seem to bother him.

Henry got out of his car excited to tell me his news. He said, "Remember when I told you that Christina and I would be heading to her boat?" He said, as we walked to the bench sitting under a sprawling oak tree.

"Sure."

"Well, I stopped to grab a cup of coffee off the cart and she headed down the dock. As she was getting on the boat, a couple of cops came out of nowhere and started talking to her. Then they escorted her to their car and off they went."

"Did she say anything to you?"

"No, she walked right by me, looking very solemn. Didn't even give me a glance. It was really weird."

"So she didn't ask you to come to the station?"

"Not exactly. I didn't know what I should do, so I followed. When I had arrived she wasn't around but the cop at the desk said she had come in, so I waited. When she was released, she walked right by me again, didn't give me the time of day so I followed her outside."

"What did she say?"

"She told me to get lost."

"What?" I was shocked.

"You heard me. She told me to get lost."

"Like, get lost or I can't see you anymore."

"Just get lost."

"Why? What happened?"

"I have no idea. She just became so cold."

"So before she was brought in she was fine but after she had changed into super bitch."

He shook his head, still trying to figure out what had happened. "Yeah, I guess my charm wore off."

"Don't feel bad," I told him. "She was super bitch to me from the beginning. Oh, guess what?"

"What?"

"I think I found the box I was looking for in her cabin."

"That's great, Sam. But I hope I've completed my part in all this. I'm not really interested in pursuing her."

"You have really helped me out. I couldn't have done it without you."

"Done what?"

"Never mind, I will fill you in when it's all over, I promise."

"Okay, I'm out of here. I want to go home."

"Are you interested in going sailing with me and Eddie?"

"Not tonight, I just want to get back."

"Okay, but I have to settle up with you. Can we meet in a day or so, I didn't stop at the bank."

"No problem, I know where you live. Oh, the tape is back in my motel room, should I go get it now or can I deliver it when we meet?"

"Get it to me when we meet, okay?"

"Sounds good to me."

We hugged and he was off, happy to be heading back to Temecula. I was wishing I could go, too, but I couldn't, I was going sailing.

CHAPTER 17

Although it was quite cold, it was a beautiful night and sailing was a nice change from reality. Eddie was good company and a good cook. He made me dinner, chili and sourdough bread, and we ate out on the deck under the stars. Although I tried to forget about the case for just a little while, visions of Simon flashed in my mind as I gazed at the waves splashing furiously against the side of the boat.

We got back in after eleven and the docks were quiet. Some lights were on in the *Lucky Man* giving a dim orange glow to the upper deck. As I stood watching, I saw some movement and I wondered who was there. I was about to depart when Eddie informed me he was going to head home but invited me to stay on the boat if I'd like, seeing it was late and would be a long drive for me to get home. I agreed, and he showed me where I would find the small heater he kept on board and some extra blankets.

Once I was alone, I turned out the lights in the cabin, took some blankets and went up top where my view of the *Lucky Man* was fairly clear. I could hear voices carrying over the water and although the sound of my own heartbeat seemed extremely loud to me, I could still make out what was being said. As I listened, I thought I heard Matt's voice. It sounded strained. No, he was angry. In fact, the more he talked, the more upset he became. I heard him say something about someone opening his big mouth. I wasn't sure who he was talking to, but it was frightening to hear.

It was then that I realized that I had only seen the charming side of him. I don't know what was at the center of his rage, but the fact that he was capable of it made me wonder, would I ever experience it first hand?

And then I heard a woman's voice. It was Christina, apparently defending herself about what she had said at the police station. I heard the words "I wouldn't" and "worth any amount of money." Whatever it was, Matt obviously didn't approve and he kept calling her a stupid bitch. He said they had gone over it a million times, "Just shut up. Say nothing." He said, over and over again.

I felt afraid for her and realized that the face I had seen when she had looked at Matt that night in her quarters had been a face of contempt. She hated him. I wondered how long she had put up with this abuse. Now I understood why she was so cold. It was fear that had made her curl up inside herself. Complete and total fear.

Then I heard Pete's voice. He tried to calm Matt down without any luck because now Matt was so enraged that he was barely making any sense. I had heard enough and I was scared. If Matt stormed off the boat and saw me on the upper deck of Eddie's boat, what would he do? I didn't want to find out.

Once inside the safety of the cabin, I sat on one of the bunks, shaking violently; this time it wasn't just the cold, I was afraid. I was in this deep and I knew it could cost me my life.

The night became windy and I wished I had gone home. A storm was approaching and being there on a boat was frightening to say the least, even if it had been docked less than thirty feet from the yacht club. There had been no sound but the wind for at least an hour and I knew that it might be safe for me to go to my car and drive home. But "might" was the operative word. Whatever else happened, I didn't want to risk Matt seeing me. It didn't matter anyway, I knew I wasn't going to get any sleep. I couldn't shake the rage I had heard in Matt's voice tonight. It was what Frank and Chuck had warned me about.

It was about three in the morning when the rain came, pounding down on the boat so hard it sounded like nails hitting the fiberglass. Thunder was crackling in the distance and the lightning came in flashes, lighting up the sky so bright it was almost surreal. Because there was no sound from Matt's boat and no lights, I decided to put an end to my discomfort and go home. Gathering my belongings, I located my car keys and ran down the slippery dock.

As I ran through the lot, rain pounding down upon me, I thought I heard footsteps in the distance, moving in closer to me. Panic moved through my body as I tried to listen through the storm. The rain continued to pound down, drenching me in the process.

The lock didn't open easily and as I struggled with it I could feel the water soak into my shoes, leaving my feet soggy and cold. Looking over my shoulder, I saw a shadowy figure wearing what appeared to be a poncho with the hood up. It was coming towards me, across the dimly lit parking lot. My heart was pounding frantically as I struggled with the key and slid inside. I was about to step on the gas when I saw Eddie's face pressed against the window.

I took a deep breath and opened my window. "Get in," I said, giddy with relief. I unlocked the door.

"Sorry about all the water," he said, as he slid inside.

"Forget it." I told him. "What are you doing down here in this weather?"

"I woke up and when I realized how bad the storm was, I thought I'd better get down here and check on you." He said. "I'm glad you decided to leave. It's no fun rocking around in that tub when the waves get up."

"Really, I'm fine." I reassured him. "I just felt a little seasick from the boat moving around so much. I locked it up before I left."

"This storm wasn't supposed to come this far south. I would never have asked you to stay if . . ."

"Eddie, stop. I know," I said, trying to ease his mind. "Can I give you a lift?"

"I'm parked over there," he said, pointing to the area closest to the docks.

As I drove him over to his truck, he joked with me about going out for a sail again tomorrow, but I told him I'd have to take a rain check. When I left him, I realized that all my fears had abated. After all, what evidence did I have that I was in any real danger?

A red light gave me an opportunity to find a towel in the backseat, kept for use at the gym. Drying my face, I took off my soaked leather jacket and removed my shoes and socks, tossing them in the backseat. I turned up the heat and sat for a few moments, taking in the warmth. Glad to be safely off the boat, but wanting desperately to be at home, in my cozy bed.

The rain was still heavy and even with the wipers on high speed, I could not see clearly. When the light turned green, I slowly started on my way, driving carefully down the narrow roads. It was unsettling crossing the bridge but at this hour I didn't have to worry about other cars. The trip back to Temecula took much longer than usual, even though the roads were deserted.

Pulling into my driveway I had a sense of relief that I had made it unscathed. I was happy to get into my own bed and quickly fell into a deep sleep.

The next morning, I awoke with a pounding headache and an unsettling feeling in the pit of my stomach. Had all that really happened last night? Seeing someone I had thought to be so kind and gentle express so much rage had been disorienting. It scared me that I had been so easily manipulated into thinking Matt was someone I could care about, yet I knew I couldn't take it personally. He was a criminal. Deception was part of his role. The best I could hope for was that he didn't have a clue that I was mixed up in all this.

After some Advil and a shower, I was feeling better. It was still raining, although not as hard and I could imagine myself sitting in front of a fire reading a book. But that wasn't going to happen, not today. I had just finished making myself some coffee when Frank arrived. He followed me into the kitchen and I poured him a cup.

"So, where have you been?" he asked me. Last night, Chuck and I stopped over. We waited for a while but you never showed."

"I stayed down at the marina. I had an opportunity to spy on Matt."

"Are you kidding?"

"No. And you wouldn't believe what happened. Matt freaked out. Not at me, he didn't know I was watching, but he flipped at Christina."

"Why? What did he say?"

"I couldn't make it out clearly, but it scared the shit out of me." I told him.

"Well, I've got some news too. The girl, Tiffany. She's missing."

"Missing from where?"

"Captain Wessler released her yesterday. I guess she asked him to keep her locked up, she said she was afraid to leave the station, but he couldn't. He said if she didn't want to tell them who had whacked Simon he couldn't do anything about it and told her to go."

"Just like that?"

"He had her followed and she was seen checking into a hole in the wall down there. This morning when she didn't answer the door they had the super open it up. She was gone and there were signs of a forced entry."

"How could the cops not see that?"

"Whoever it was entered from the back window. It was broken."

"Any idea who got to her?" I asked.

"That's why I'm here. Were you watching Matt all night?"

"No. He and some of his guys went out on his boat to go fishing."

"Did you see them go out?"

I shook my head. "No. I was sailing with my friend and when we got back in they were already docked."

"Any idea what could have happened to her?" He asked.

"She probably took off, if he was my brother I would have." I said.

"Meaning?"

"He's got quite a temper. You should have heard him."

My guess was that Matt had gotten to Tiffany. He was so furious that Christina had said anything to the cops, and the fact that his baby sister was going to provide information to them willingly would have completely sent him over the edge.

The first thing I needed to do was to find out if they had gone out fishing, and I knew just who to ask. I told Frank I would make some calls and let him know. He told me that the cops had seen Tiffany go for coffee at 10 P.M. and that was the last time they had seen her.

Just then I remembered I had the box in my trunk. "I forgot to tell you, I found a box on Matt's boat. I was hoping we could see if the key fits."

"You mean this key?" He asked, taking out the envelope.

We examined the box, anxious to see if it was a match. Bingo, the key slid in and turned with ease. I opened it slowly, looking for the ballerina to pop up, but she wasn't there. Inside it was only a small piece of paper. The word *Weatherbee* was neatly written on it. Yes, it had to be . . . Dr. Everett Weatherbee.

Frank and I looked at each other, knowing we had found something important even though neither of us knew what it meant.

"Let's go to the office. I need to check something out," he said.

When we arrived, Frank flipped on his computer and put the box inside his safe.

"Look here." He said, returning with the manila envelope Ron left with me. "I think it's time we opened this. After all, he said you should if something happened to him."

"Why not?" I said. "So far, we have so much stuff to be baffled about that it may help to shed some light." I knew we probably should have opened it sooner, but frankly, I kept thinking he'd turn up.

Frank did the honors, placing the contents on his desk. There was a small envelope with a number on the outside of it and a tiny safety deposit box key inside, a videotape marked confidential and a stack of articles that seemed to have been copied from books, magazines and printed from the internet, which when I skimmed it, all had a common subject, various ways to disappear without a trace and the reasons for doing so.

As we read, we were both astonished at the diversity of the reasons why people want to disappear. Some of them included mental illness, wanting privacy, starting a new life, drug and alcohol addictions, running from someone, such as an ex-boyfriend or spouse, or maybe even a business partner or psycho. Yes, I am inferring that Ron could have simply decided to run and hide. The explanations were varied, and to put it simply, none of this brought us any closer to knowing anything. Did Ron disappear on purpose? Was he running from his, so called, friends? Or was it something else? What frustrated me the most was that if he did decide to just vanish, why not tell me? I was trying to figure out how to tie this all together but couldn't see it.

Frank invited me for lunch, rationalizing that a margarita would open our minds to see things from a fresh perspective. Happily I agreed.

The rain had stopped and the sun was peeking out from behind the clouds, creating a beautiful rainbow in the sky as Frank and I walked to our favorite watering hole, The Bank. We sat at the bar. Lunch consisted of chips and salsa, a sampler platter, and a pitcher of gold margaritas on the rocks. Just what the doctor ordered. We avoided talking about the case, Frank said the answers would come when you weren't paying attention, and soon our conversation turned to more personal matters.

"Did you and Susan make up?" I asked him, plunging into the deepest water I could find.

His look was ambivalent, to say the least. "I guess," he said.

"Oh Frank, your positive attitude is overwhelming," I told him. "What did she say about her flipping out at the counseling session?"

"Not a whole lot."

"You didn't press her to explain that?" I said, annoyed by the fact that he always backed down from his wife and ended up looking like a wimp. And he wasn't a wimp.

"What should I have done, Sam? Tackled her to the ground and made her say uncle?" He was pissed off at me for pressing him, but I didn't care.

"You seemed pretty upset about her behavior the other day," I remarked. "I would have thought that after all the shit she's been laying on you about going to counseling, you would have demanded to know what the hell happened."

"Well, I didn't."

"Why not?" I said, no longer able to hide my aggravation.

"Why do you care?"

"Because I do, Frank."

"Why, Sam?"

I wasn't about to let him push me. "Frank," I said. "You and I are friends, right? Friends care about each other. She's jerking you around and I'm curious to know why."

"So that's it . . . it's just because we are friends."

"Yeah."

"Sam, I don't believe you." he said, his voice down and a smile on his face, eyebrow raised.

"Believe it, Frank."

He moved in close to me. "I know the real reason."

"Oh, you do?"

"Yes." He was confident.

"Well then, why don't you explain it to me," I replied, guarded. This wasn't the way our conversations about his personal life usually went.

"Sammy, Sammy, Sammy. You want me."

"Oh, do I now?" I said, grinning, trying to keep things light. "Then why haven't I made a play for you?"

"You haven't made a play for me because I'm married."

"So," I uttered casually.

"So, you would never get involved with someone under those circumstances. You believe in honesty and brutal trust in your personal life. This . . ." he said motioning towards him and me, "would not happen because you could never do it to Susan, hurt her, even though you don't especially like her. That is why you have never made a play for me."

I stared into my glass, pondering his observation. "No, that's not it." I told him.

"Then what is it, Sam?"

"It's just too much fun flirting with you. If I ever got involved with you that would stop, it would get ugly."

"Why would it get ugly?" he asked, concerned.

"Because, you're a shitty husband." I was laughing and he started to laugh with me.

"Yeah, I know. Maybe I'm just not meant to be a husband at all."

By George, I think he's got it!

CHAPTER 18

My telephone was ringing as I entered the house and I ran to pick it up. Startled to hear Matt's voice on the other end, I had to sit down and gain my composure. His request was simple: "Come for dinner. I'm having some guests and I'd really like you to be there," he said, sounding as sweet as ever. I couldn't believe it, he never mentioned Simon's death. How could he be so cold hearted? I didn't know what to do. If he sensed my fear I knew it would put me in danger. I decided to accept, telling him I had an old friend in town and asked if I could bring him along.

I hung up and sat for a moment. Who could I bring? If I took Frank it could cause some tension between him and Susan. Our professional connection was one thing but asking him to accompany me to a social event might be something else, given the delicate state of his marriage at the moment. And since I didn't have anyone else to ask, I thought I'd just better go alone. Maybe Chuck would let me take that listening device we had used before. At least someone would be able to hear what was going on. I guess I would feel a tiny bit more secure.

I needed to find some way to ask Peter if they had gone fishing and thought he'd probably be at the party tonight, so I could ask him then. I wondered who else would be there. It could be interesting. I'd have to stay alert. I called Chuck and he agreed to set me up and stay nearby to be sure I stayed out of trouble. I would meet him at seven since the party was to start at eight. Plenty of time to prepare, I concluded. I was nervous but told myself that there was safety in numbers.

Trusting that I had to be getting somewhere in the case, I made more notes of the clues that we had discovered so far. The jewelry box and where I found it, the key that fit perfectly, the note in it that displayed only the word *Weatherbee* on it, and I made a note questioning whether it could mean Dr. Weatherbee. Also listed on my cards was the arrival of Tiffany and if she was in fact the T who signed the letter to Ron. Adding questions about where she came from, why she would risk her life by going to the cops, and anything else I could think of. I had to wonder, where did she fit into all of this? Then I added all of the information from the envelope. What bank had issued the safe deposit box key, and what was being stored there? And then there was the videotape and the articles explaining why and how one would disappear. I spent a good part of the afternoon on this activity and when I was finished I had added quite a few more cards to my growing collection.

I wondered if I would have an opportunity to check the drawer again but had to really think: if I could get to it unnoticed, should I risk taking a few of those letters? If I did, I'd need a bigger purse in which to stash them. Better to be prepared, I thought, going to scour my messy closet for something suitable.

Finding a nondescript black bag that I had bought at Kohls during a spring sale, I transferred my wallet, phone and some lipstick and had plenty of room left in which I could hide several letters. Satisfied with my choice, I put the pocketbook on my bed and I moved back into the closet to choose my attire for the evening. It was a gathering after all, and since my social life is quite sluggish, I do like to make the most of these events.

I decided on my black pants suit and white blouse; for my feet, black knee highs, very sexy I know, and low black pumps. I hated wearing shoes but I certainly didn't want to risk feeling out of place in my white Nike's. Then I added a simple silver necklace and the matching bracelet to finish off the look. My style would be categorized as dressy casual and that works for every occasion. And the fact that my black bag matched, well, you know, it is a must in the fashion world, from what I've observed.

With that out of the way, I was free to relax for a bit before it was time to get ready for the big charade. I was worried about how I would react to Matt's touch. I'm not a good enough actress to be able to melt in his arms the way I had before, so the alternative was not to be caught alone with him.

I decided to lie down on the couch in front of the TV for a while, hoping a distraction would help me to relax. As I watched re-runs of *Starsky and Hutch* I felt myself dozing. I didn't even try to fight it.

I was running through the house, Matt chasing me with a knife, and yelling about how I betrayed him. As I came upon a second-floor window he moved in slowly. His rage seemed to be focused solely on me and as he moved closer and closer to me I realized I had no choice.

Jolted, I awoke in darkness. I reached for the light and checked the time and realized I'd better hurry up and get a shower, dress and head over to meet Chuck. So much for relaxing.

Before going upstairs, I went to the kitchen and opened a beer, gulping half of it down standing at the counter. This was going to be a long night.

I arrived at Chuck's office ten minutes late to find him waiting impatiently, doodling on a pad at his desk, equipment out and ready to be tested. He was a stickler for punctuality and I again found myself at his mercy, apologizing profusely as he switched into lecture mode.

"Sam," he said. "Do you have a watch? Don't you realize when you are late it gives the impression you don't value the other person's time?"

"Look, I'm sorry, I fell asleep."

"Get a watch or clock or whatever it is you need to be on time. If you're late again I won't be here," he said, so smugly that, if it had been anyone else, I would have whacked him.

Once all listening equipment was in order and he went over the procedure I was to follow in an emergency situation, we were out the door. He followed me most of the way to Matt's and disappeared from my rearview mirror sometime before I arrived at my destination.

As I pulled up I saw several cars parked on either side of the road. This looked more like a full blown party than a small gathering of friends. I had to park my car down the street a bit and already my feet hurt from wearing heels. As I walked toward the house I spoke to Chuck about the situation.

"This looks like a big party," I told him. "There are about ten to fifteen cars parked on the street. I'll be milling about, listening for anything interesting. And if Pete's here, I'll ask about the fishing trip."

The house looked beautiful set off by two spotlights to produce dramatic effect. It also made me think of the spotlight cops put on prisoners, which was a bit unsettling. I heard oldies music playing somewhere and wondered if it was so loud that the bell couldn't be heard. I had waited long enough so I slowly pushed open the door.

The music was indeed very loud and sounded as though it were coming from outside. People were everywhere, young, old, some formally dressed and others not, all chatting in groups. Whatever else it looked like, it was certainly not a gathering of mobsters and their molls. In fact, everyone looked quite respectable.

I moved through the living room trying to see if I recognized anyone although why I thought I would was beyond me. In the sea of individuals I really only expected to know two, maybe three people. Matt, of course, and Peter and possibly Christina but that was it. Towards the back I could see a larger gathering and had to guess that the bar was located there. A professional bartender was manning the post and I ordered a glass of white wine.

"Are you looking for anyone in particular?" the bartender asked me as I sipped my drink and looked around the room. He had a full head of hair, bushy and very black, parted haphazardly. He wore the usual black and whites with a bow tie slightly tweaked to one side.

"Actually, yes," I said. "Have you seen Mr. Andrews lately?"

"I'm pretty sure he's in the back garden. There is a band out there and another bar."

"So how did you luck out to get to be inside on such a cold night?" I asked, somehow feeling a bit more relaxed.

"Oh, it's not cold out back; there are heaters and a tent. It's really a nice setup," he said, as he mixed a grey haired gentleman in a tweed jacket a scotch and water. "Have you ever been to one of Mr. Andrews parties?"

"No. This is my first one."

"Well, you have come to the right place. Mr. Andrews throws the best parties. Good food, lots of great wines and good music."

"So you've bartended for him before?"

"On several occasions. He really knows how to entertain."

"It looks that way."

As I looked at the crowd, I wished I had brought someone. Probably, I should have invited Chuck, but since our relationship was strained, I didn't think he'd accept anyway. Now I was regretting the fact that I didn't even bother to ask. I continued to scan the crowd for a familiar face and found myself wondering how Matt knew so many diversely different people. And then thought about how Simon should be here. I felt guilty and disrespectful because he wasn't, like we were dancing on his grave or something.

"Would you like another glass of wine?" the bartender asked.

"No thanks. I'm going to get going."

"Don't go. You will have a good time, I promise." His smile was infectious and his personality was just right for his profession. He was what I would call a people person. He made me feel as if I had a friend among all these strangers.

"Making promises already? We just met."

"Don't look now, but the man who has lured you here has just spotted you. I guess you can't escape now."

I turned around and saw Matt dressed in jeans, a white button down and a brown tweed jacket. He was making his way through the crowd, stopping briefly to chat on his way. As I watched him, I was taken back by the charm that almost oozed out of him. Then, I remembered that voice, the raving lunatic I had heard the night before coming from his sailboat. I remembered the way he had threatened Christina and...I was startled when someone tapped me on the shoulder. It was Pete, dressed in khakis and a navy polo shirt.

"I didn't mean to startle you. Are you okay?"

"I'm fine," I said, feeling my guard going up.

"It's nice to see you again."

"Thanks." I thought there was something different about him but I couldn't put my finger on what it was. "Hey, can I ask you a question?" I said, feeling rushed to ask before Matt got to us.

"Of course you can."

I thought maybe he had a few drinks in him, he seemed so relaxed and casual. "Did you guys go fishing the other night?"

"When?"

"Remember I saw you at the marina and you asked me if I would be going out fishing with you?"

"Oh, yeah sure," he said, uncertain.

"Did you go?"

"Yeah, we did," he said.

"When did you get back in?"

"I can't remember. Why?"

"It rained."

"We must have gotten back in before it started."

"That's good, I heard it was quite a storm." We stood silently for a moment. I was uncomfortable so I spoke. "This is some party."

"What can I get you to drink?"

Looking at him I held up my glass of wine. "I'm fine right now."

"Yes, you are," he replied.

Matt had finally made his way over to us. "Hi, Sam, I'm glad you made it. Did you bring your friend?" He was clearly in a festive mood.

"I'm sorry about Simon," I said, looking him straight in the eyes, wondering how I ever could have been attracted to anyone so obviously cold hearted.

Matt frowned. "Life goes on." He told me. "I don't really want to think about Simon right now."

I wanted to lash out at him, to accuse him of being monstrous in his disregard for a friend. I wanted to confront him with Ron's disappearance. But I controlled myself because – because it was my job to do so, like it or not.

I wanted to run out of there and scream. I was angry about Matt's apathy even after I brought up Simon and found it odd that it didn't even rattle him.

"So, where's your friend?" he asked.

"I decided to come alone." I said, irritated. "You said you were having a few friends over for dinner. I may be mistaken but this looks like more than a few."

Although I'm not a big lover of spending the night with a bunch of strangers, I did look at this as an opportunity to try to pin him down and find out why he was so at ease about his friend and maybe, just maybe he'd mention Ron.

"Yes, well the guest list got a bit out of hand," he said, looking around. "Come on out back. I've got a buffet set up and a chair with your name on it."

We walked through the busy kitchen and out the back door. The garden looked as though it had been transformed. To the left, a five-piece band belted out golden oldies while guests kicked up their heels on a wooden dance floor. There was a large white tent to the right lit with soft lavender spotlights where the six round tables were draped in white and lavender table clothes, each one holding about a dozen or so votive candles set on a circular mirror in the center. The effect was quite captivating. Two bars were set up, one on each side of the interior of the tent, and to the back sat a long buffet table.

Peter walked to the right, stopping at the bar. Matt escorted me to one of the tables where three people were already seated.

"Sam, this is Christina, whom you have already met," Matt said, "and this is Michael and Tiffany."

Christina frowned at me. She was wearing a sleek black dress and large dangling hoop earrings. Beside her sat a woman with a short floral skirt and white top and a man who had a flowing mustache and a black leather jacket over his white T-shirt.

Tiffany! Of all the places I might have expected to see her, this was not one of them. This was, after all, the woman who had been so frightened that she had appeared at the police station saying that she knew who had killed Simon. And yet, here she was, in what I had to assume was the most dangerous place she could be. Unless she had covered her tracks so well that neither Pete nor Matt or any of the others knew that she had nearly ratted on them. Because that was what I had assumed she was going to do.

"Nice to meet you," I said looking at them. "Christina, it's nice to see you again." I forced a smile.

I sat down next to Matt and across from the threesome. The air was thick and I felt as though I could cut the tension with a knife. I could see the resemblance between Christina and Tiffany right away. The only difference was about twelve or fifteen years and what seemed to be totally opposite personality types. While Christina seemed so serious, a woman who had to be in control, Tiffany gave off a feeling as being completely carefree, although now, it seemed like an almost hysterical sort of exuberance, or maybe she was just plowed. Christina's eyes blazed through me and I wondered if she had realized that her box was missing and whether she suspected me of taking it. It was hard to tell with her. She was so forceful, that she made me uncomfortable even without trying to. Whatever her problem was, it was obvious she didn't want me around. I didn't have a clue who this Michael person was but I thought that if I listened long enough some light would be shed on that little mystery.

Peter returned with a handful of champagne glasses as the bartender placed two bottles of Moet on the table and Matt filled our glasses.

"To your health," he said, his eyes intent on Christina and Tiffany. They looked back at him with cowardly expressions as Peter and Michael glanced away. It was difficult to watch as he seemed to humiliate them with his eyes, and it made me wonder how long they had been putting up with it. Too long, I concluded.

Feeling uncomfortable, I said I was going to find the ladies' room, and went into the house. Once inside the safety of the bathroom I called Chuck and quietly told him about Tiffany. He said he had heard everything, and told me I was to attempt to make contact with her. I would have to convince her that I could get her to safety, and then let him know where to pick her up. He also said that despite the fact that he wasn't happy about it, I'd have to keep Matt occupied so he could get her back to the police station without incident.

Making my way outside, I wondered how I would be able to convince Tiffany of anything. As far as she knew, I was her brother's girlfriend. Why would she trust me? Personally, I couldn't think of one reason but I'd have to persuade her somehow. Entering the tent, I saw that the table sat empty. "Great, now where did everyone go?" I asked myself.

I walked outside and stopped to watch the band. They were really good, and they dressed the part, too. Those poodle skirts were very sharp. I almost wished I had been born early enough to wear them, then quickly reconsidered. No, I never could have done it, I'm a jeans-and–T-shirt type of gal. It just wouldn't have worked for me.

I looked around hoping to find Tiffany. If I could just have a few minutes with her alone, maybe she'd listen to me. I needed another glass of wine so I headed back inside the tent to the bar and caught sight of Tiffany heading in my direction. She was alone.

She ordered a glass of wine and turned away from the bar and took in the sights of the crowd. "Having a good time?" she asked.

Not sure she was even talking to me, I glanced around to see if anyone was within earshot. She must be talking to me I concluded. "Sure. Are you?"

She gave me a shrug. "How did you meet my brother?"

I had thought about spinning a web of lies, but at the last minute, decided to play it straight. "It was an accident really. I was hired to look for Ronald Gregory." I said casually, as I watched her expression go from indifference to intrigue.

"You . . ."

"Look, I have to talk quickly. Your brother doesn't know anything about any of this. I met him because I thought Ron lived here. At least, this is the address he had given me when he hired me. When I came looking for him, Matt was here. I admit there was an instant attraction but I didn't know who he was at the time. I am now assisting in an investigation of his activities, as well. I was told that you know who killed Simon. Is that true?"

She nodded sadly, as she sipped her wine. "We're being watched you know," she said timidly.

"I know," I told her. "It comes with the territory. But I suppose you know that. Start laughing like I just told you something funny. Listen, I can get you back to the police station safely."

"If they see me leave they'll kill me," she said, as she brushed her long blonde hair away from her face.

"My friend, a private investigator, is nearby." I told her. "He can pick you up wherever you want."

"I can't risk it. If I leave he'll kill Christina. Look over there. He's seen us. He's crazy you know. Stay away from him."

"Come with me." I told her.

We quickly left the tent and headed for the house. Once inside, she went to freshen up and I headed back outside.

"There you are," Matt said, "I was hoping you hadn't gone home."

"When I came back from the bathroom the table was empty," I explained.

"I had to check the inventory at the bars and retrieve some more champagne. I didn't think I'd be gone so long, I'm sorry."

Only then did I notice that he seemed disoriented. His eyes were unfocused and he was swaying slightly.

"No problem," I told him. "I listened to the band for a while and came to get myself another glass of wine."

Despite the fact that he seemed to be in good spirits, his condition wasn't clear and it made me nervous. I certainly didn't want to piss him off. The issue I had to deal with though was that I didn't know him well enough to know what would do that. So, I decided that I'd just have to follow his lead.

"I saw you and Tiffany back here," he said, his eyes narrowing. "What were you two talking about?"

"I did most of the talking," I said with a shrug. "I just told her how much I enjoyed being here. It's a great party."

"What did she say?" he demanded, as he clenched his jaw and moved his face close to mine.

I stiffened. "She agreed," I said, not wanting to say too much. He'd probably be asking her the same thing later to see if I had been lying.

"You look cold. Would you like to go inside for a while?" he asked, taking my arm haphazardly.

"Yes, that would be great," I said, trying to stay calm as we started for the house. He held onto my arm too tightly, and I found myself wanting him to let me go. As he looked at me, his expressions seemed distorted and his behavior was aggressive.

The crowd had thinned significantly inside and my first thought was that it must be getting late. As I walked past the kitchen desk, now clear of envelopes, I realized now that Matt's suspicions had apparently been aroused. I knew it might be difficult for me to investigate inside this house and besides, I had to get Tiffany out of here. She was ready now and I didn't want her to cool off or have something happen to her.

When I went out on the front porch, Tiffany was standing there, lighting a cigarette.

"Christina will have to come with me," she said. "It's too dangerous to leave her here with him alone.

I couldn't have agreed more. If I had any doubts before, I was totally convinced now that Matt was dangerous. A sociopath probably. And it was up to me to see that Tiffany and Christina were kept safe – whether or not they gave me the information I needed, whether or not they could help me find Ron.

"Yes, of course," I told her. We'd like her to come."

"Where can your friend pick us up?"

"Anywhere you want," I said, as I looked around. I was feeling nervous about Matt coming out.

"When can we go?"

"Whenever you want."

"How about now?"

"Now? Okay." I said.

"Fine," she said, flicking her cigarette into the grass below. I remained sitting on the steps as she hurried back into the house, probably on her way to tell Christina the plan.

"Chuck," I said into the phone, "Did you hear that? We're going to..."

"Why didn't you just wait inside?" Matt's voice startled me so much that I almost screamed. "I said I'd be right back." I saw that Matt was scowling and my heart sank.

"I have a headache," I told him. "And needed some fresh air. Look, I've got to go."

"Come on back in. I want to talk to you." He said, grabbing my hand.

"No, I'm not feeling well." I said. "I really just want to go. I'll call you."

As I went down the steps and started across the lawn toward my car, uneasiness covered me like a wave crashing down, making it difficult to get air in my lungs. All at once I felt a pull on my arm and as I swung around I saw the look of evil in his eyes. I shook my arm free. "What are you doing?" I demanded. "Let me go!"

"Don't you ever turn your back on me, you bitch!"

I stood staring, not believing what I was seeing. "Who are you?" I said, pulling away from him. "What makes you think you can speak to me that way?"

"I am your future, so get used to it, honey!" Suddenly he seemed to have spun completely out of control. I screamed and dashed across the street just in time for Chuck's car to drive between us.

"Go, Sam!" I heard Chuck shout. "Just go!"

I jumped in my car and took off with Chuck behind me, leaving Matt staring after us. We joined up three blocks away. Locking my car, I left it in a deserted school parking lot and joined Chuck. Not until I was sitting beside him in the darkness did it really register with me that I had been in real danger. But there was no time to think about that now.

"We might have a problem." Chuck said. "We need to make contact with Tiffany and get her out of there. The question is, how do you want to go about it?"

"Me?" Why me?" I asked.

"Because, I need to watch your back," he informed me. "So…"

"I guess I go back." I said.

"They'll be taking a real chance, you know, particularly since you and I just made that get away. It's got to put him on alert."

"Maybe he'll be too busy thinking about me to worry about them," I told him. "For all we know, he's out looking for me right now. He's crazy, you know. I've never seen anyone act like that before."

"Look, Sam. I know you thought…"

"Forget it." I told him. "So, what's our plan?"

"We give him a little time to calm down and we head back." He said. "With any luck he'll be passed out."

"And if he's not?" I asked.

"Well, then you're going to have to come up with a reason why you had to go back. Tell him that you lost an earring or forgot something."

"Where are you going to be, you know, just in case?"

"Obviously, we should take your car," he said. "I'll park in the shadow beyond the driveway. You just try to get Tiffany and Christina out of there. I'll pick you up."

We drove back to the school parking lot and locating my keys, I handed them to Chuck. We got in the car and started back to Matt's. Adrenaline was pumping through me as I prepared for the worst.

We drove slowly approaching the house. As we got closer, we could see that the party was still in full swing. Cars lined the street and the music was audible, even from inside the car.

Chuck looked at me. "Are you ready?"

"Unhuh." I said, trying to convince myself that I was.

As I was about to open the door, a face moved into the window and I let out a scream. When I realized who it was I opened the back door and Christina and Tiffany got in, closed the door, and eagerly told us to, "go, go, go!"

Chuck drove down the street, turning on the lights as he sped up. We drove down some dark streets and within a few minutes were driving down Margarita Road. For a minute or two, no one said a word.

We turned on to Rancho California road and headed west.

"Where are we going?" Tiffany asked, in a low voice.

"To the police station," Chuck said. "I've got a friend of mine there that will be taking care of you."

"We can't go there tonight. That's the first place he will come looking for us. That's what happened last time. As soon as he realized he couldn't get a hold of me, he showed up. He has friends there. I'm sure someone tipped him off. Don't take me back there!" I could hear the fear in her voice as she spoke.

"That's not going to happen." Chuck said. "I'll take you through the back door, straight to the Captain's office. He won't let anything happen to either of you. I promise."

"Please, please...don't take me back there!" Tiffany pleaded.

"Well then, where do you suggest we go?" Chuck said, irritated. I could tell he did not want to deal with this situation.

I watched as Tiffany and Christina stared at each other, not sure where to go for safety.

"This is ludicrous! We can't get away from him. He'll find us, no matter where we go." Christina argued angrily. "Why did I let you talk me into this?" She demanded, eyeing Tiffany. "Do you realize how bad it's going to be for us now? How angry he will be over this stunt?"

"Calm down, Christina." I said. "It will be all right."

"You think so?" She barked. "He's not exactly happy with you either. After you took off, he was a raving lunatic. He almost came after you. We had to hold him down, for God's sake."

"What did he say?" I asked anxiously.

"He went on and on about..."

"Christina, stop!" Tiffany demanded.

"She should know. He's not going to let it go." Christina said, clenching her teeth.

"What? What did he say?" I asked again, afraid to hear it.

"He said that no woman walks out on him. Not now, not ever."

So, that was it. He was going to come after me no matter what. Now, here I am, not only responsible for getting Christina and Tiffany away from him, but I'm also the reason they are talking to the police. A lump formed in my throat. "I think I know where we could go for a little while," I said. Everyone's eyes were on me. "Let me make a quick call."

Within a few minutes we were driving to Harold and Carol's house. Upon our arrival, they greeted us with coffee as I filled them in on our situation.

"You'll be safe here," Carol said, trying to ease their minds.

"Don't worry about a thing," added Harold.

When Chuck excused himself, I was sure he was calling the captain and possibly someone at the Temecula department as well. I hoped he wasn't too angry about the change in plans, but I understood how the girls felt. I was now in danger as well.

Chuck returned, a smile on his face.

"What?" I asked.

"I talked to Captain Wessler, He wants us to head down south and meet him in one hour," he said. "At the station."

"But, what about Matt?" I asked. "He's probably out looking for us now."

Chuck picked up the phone. "Yes, can I talk to Matt?" he asked. "Where is he?" he said. "Oh, yeah, he was partying pretty hard. No, I'll call him tomorrow. Thanks."

"Well?" I said.

"We don't have to worry about Matt tonight. His buddy put him to bed. He's out like a light." He told me. "Now, let's get the girls down to the station, before Tiffany changes her mind."

CHAPTER 19

When we reached the station, I sighed with relief. It was some help that I knew more about the situation than I had before, thanks to what Christina and Tiffany had told me during the ride, including the fact that, when his parents had been killed in an automobile accident, he had been taken into custody for having been suspected of tampering with the brakes.

Once he had been let go for lack of evidence, his aunt and uncle, who had become his guardians, had become so disturbed by the fact that he had threatened to kill their baby daughter that they had not even reported him missing. After that, no one in the family had wanted to have anything to do with him.

Even years later, when he was an adult, they kept their distance because they felt certain that if they made contact they would risk his anger. His approach, it seemed was to accumulate damaging information about everyone he knew and threaten to use it if they did not cooperate with him. Ron had taken off because of that. Matt was, in a word, a frightening character.

Tiffany had also told me that she had not given the police this information because she was afraid that, if she did, he might hurt her or Christina. Christina, in particular, shared the most information about her brother's behavior. It seemed that being the eldest, she remembered the danger he posed to everyone he came in contact with, even as a small boy. One thing was very clear; the two women needed one another. And neither of them was ready to tell anyone everything.

They refused to talk about Simon and whether or not Matt had really killed him except to say that Peter was the one who had told them about Simon. And there was one more important detail. They had both heard Matt on the phone before that, saying that someone would have to be eliminated. That had been what took them to the police station in the first place. But then fear had kept them from telling the authorities what they needed to know before they could take action. I could only hope that now they would feel safe enough to cooperate.

"Hi, captain." Chuck said when we were ushered into Captain Wessler's office. "This is Tiffany Andrews and her sister Christina. And you've met Sam Parker."

"Nice to see you again." I said, shaking his hand.

"Likewise, Sam," he said smiling. "I hear you've been playing quite a roll in all this?"

I looked at Chuck, surprised.

"I had to fill him in, Sam," Chuck said.

"I'm glad you came down here," he said. "Have a seat."

"Tiffany and Christina didn't feel secure going to the Temecula station." I offered. "So we thought it would be safe to bring them here."

"It was a good idea. Mr. Andrews did, in fact, go to the station looking for his sisters and when the officer told him they weren't there he got a little upset. He's in jail now but we can't hold him long."

"The girls will be safe, right?" I asked, relieved he was locked up, even temporarily.

"Yes, they will be safe, as long as they cooperate," he said, firmly. "I'll have to get a formal statement."

"I know. They have been through a lot so go easy on them okay?"

"We will," he said gently.

Tiffany and Christina looked exhausted to say the least. My only hope was that they wouldn't lose their nerve. The captain must have felt the same way. He sure didn't waste any time starting with the inquiry. We sat quietly and listened as the captain questioned them. He was good, very good. He asked them about stuff that never crossed my mind and he did it nicely. He was kind and patient. I decided I liked him. I liked him very much.

During the two-hour dialogue, we had heard stories that were mind-boggling. It sounded like a "movie of the week" and I thought that, once this was over, it would be a good way for the girls to cash in on their experiences. Okay, maybe not. It might even be too unbelievable for television. Then the captain made arrangements for them to enter the witness protection program.

Once the girls were settled, Chuck and I headed back to Temecula. We needed to contact Frank and fill him in. But first, Chuck told me he would head over to the jail and check on Matt. He wanted them to find another reason not to release him and needed to get over there to see if they could. Chuck stopped off to get his car and took off. My mind was on other things.

I still had a lot of work to do. After a shower and something to eat I would feel refreshed and ready to go. Once showered, I decided to head over to Milano's for a much needed deli sandwich. Upon my timely return home, I checked my machine and found I had no messages. I decided to call Frank, hoping he was still around. No answer. I didn't want to leave a message so I tried his cell phone.

"Frank Meeker," he said, rushed.

"Hi, it's me, Sam."

"Where are you?"

"Home. Where are you?"

"Stake out. Unfortunately, there hasn't been any action."

"Has Chuck gotten a hold of you?"

"No."

"He hasn't called you?" I asked, alarmed.

"No. I haven't heard a thing from him," he said. "Why?"

"When he dropped me off, he was going to go to the station and then get in touch with you."

"Dropped you off where? What's going on?"

"We were on Coronado Island."

"You and Chuck?"

"Yeah, we picked up Tiffany and Christina and brought them to Coronado to meet with Captain Wessler. He interviewed them and then they met with the FBI so they could set them up in the witness protection program."

"I'm missing something, what the hell has been happening?"

"Let's meet somewhere and I'll fill you in. In the meantime, try to get in touch with Chuck, okay?"

"Okay. But I've got to stay put for a while, I'm about to wrap up this case."

"When would be a good time to get together?"

"I'll need a few hours. Why don't you come by the office?"

"Okay, I'll see you later." I said.

Hanging up, I found myself worried about Chuck. He was just not the type to blow off a plan.

While I waited until it was time to meet Frank, I kept busy tying up loose ends on a couple of my open files, relieved to have completed the research on a custody case and glad that my findings were in favor of the kid's dad, who, by the way, was not my client. It wouldn't sit well with the Mom but hey, facts are facts. Just as I finished my final report, I realized it was time to go.

The traffic was light as I headed into Old Town. As I pulled into the lot my phone rang.

"Hello?"

"Sam, there's been change in plans. Meet me at Texas Lil's. You know it?"

"Yeah. What's going on?" I asked.

"I had a lead. I had to stick with it. Gotta go."

Texas Lil's was just down the street so I decided to park in the office lot and walk. As I entered the darkened bar I caught sight of Frank, deep conversation with a striking redhead. I wondered if she was the important lead. She was tall and shapely in a black, backless jumpsuit. Her hair was full and wavy, falling down her back to her waist. She wore black spiked shoes and bright red lipstick that had a shine to it, even in the softness of the dimmed lighting. Frank was smiling and laughing in his blue jeans and light blue button-down. I stood watching them and hesitated to move in, not wanting to have to stand next to that woman. I am not glamorous in the least and just being in the same room with her made me feel inferior in a weird way.

Frank scanned the place quickly. I foolishly ducked down behind a group of people waiting for a table, not ready to deal with my awkwardness. Within a few moments I watched her walk daintily to the back of the bar. I quickly moved through the crowd and stood by Frank's side.

"Hi, I'm sorry I'm late," I said. "This place is pretty busy, do you want to go somewhere else?"

"Yeah, sure," he said, grudgingly.

"Are you sure?" I was annoyed at him.

"Sam, what's wrong?"

"Nothing. I just thought you wanted to hear what was going on. It's too loud in here to even hear myself think, much less fill you in."

"Okay, Sam, let's go."

We set out to go, as the redhead was heading back towards us. She eyed me as she positioned herself back on her bar stool. I eyed her back. Frank told her he enjoyed talking with her and we left, moving back through the crowd and out the door.

"What's going on here tonight? It's packed in there," I asked nonchalantly.

"I heard there's a Harley club event in town."

"Who told you that?" I asked, harassing him.

"It's obvious. There are Harleys all over town. But that's not why your panties are in a bunch, is it? For Gods sake Sam, I was just talking to the lady."

"Was she a lady? I thought she was for sale," I said, sarcastically.

He took a deep breath and shook his head.

"Sam, you are stressed to the max, you need a vacation or . . ."

"Or what?"

"Forget it."

We walked over to the office and headed upstairs. Frank unlocked the door and we went in.

"Did you get in touch with Chuck?"

"Sam, he didn't answer at the office, his cell phone or pager. I called the captain to ask if he might have heard from him. I'm waiting for him to get back to me."

"That's really strange. He told me he was going to call you."

As Frank looked for signs that Chuck had stopped in, I filled him in on all the details from the night of Matt's party on. He just listened, barely believing what I was telling him about the stories his sisters had told regarding his childhood antics as well as his latest behavioral aggressions. Periodically, he asked questions trying to piece it all together, but finally had to resign himself to the fact that he was a psychopath and had been all his life.

The call came as we were trying to think of where else to look for Chuck. The captain had called to say that Chuck had been found in pretty bad shape. He had been badly beaten and was in the hospital in Temecula. The captain had already called the station and had a policeman placed outside his door for protection.

"The captain said he's in bad shape."

"Shit. Did he see who it was?" I asked.

"He said he didn't see the guy, he was jumped from behind."

"Well, who would do something like this? I know Matt was in custody." I said, as I noticed Frank's expression change. "He was, wasn't he?"

Frank frowned. "He had been but they had to let him go. The captain wanted me to tell you to be careful, if it was Matt Andrews who got to Chuck he had to be pretty pissed. He said he could be looking for you next."

"Where are the girls? Are they safe?"

"Yeah, they're with the FBI sorting things out. They'll be fine."

"Okay." I said, relieved. "Let's go check on Chuck."

"No need to rush, he's in intensive care, we won't be able to see him." Frank said.

"God damn this guy. We have to nail his ass."

"We will but we have to locate him first."

"Where do you think he might be?"

"It's hard to say. But I'd bet he's around here somewhere."

I felt sick to my stomach and ran to the bathroom and threw up. This was taking its toll on me.

CHAPTER 20

A call from Captain Wessler prompted Frank and I to head down to Coronado Island. Since neither of us had eaten lunch, we decided to stop at a little diner in town. My stomach was still doing flip flops so I decided on some toast and 7-Up while Frank went for a burger and fries. The break gave us an opportunity to go over the newest information in the case and decide what our next step would be. The captain had thought Matt would have come back to Coronado and retreat to his boat, although he couldn't be absolutely sure, so he put an officer on watch anyway. Frank and I agreed, it would be a good place to start.

We stopped by Keno's to see if we could find Eddie, he had already gone for the day and I wondered if he might be on his boat. I suggested we check the marina bar before walking down to the dock. It turned out to be a good call. Eddie was sitting there, drinking a scotch on the rocks.

"Hi Eddie, fancy meeting you here," I said.

"What are you up to this fine afternoon?"

"Well, I was hoping you could help us with something."

"What is it?"

I introduced them and explained that Frank was a private investigator assisting me on a case. Frank explained as much as he thought necessary to Eddie and asked if we could borrow his boat to use for our stakeout. Eddie happily agreed, and gave us the combination and some other instructions for use. We exchanged cell phone numbers and told him we'd be in touch. He said he was glad to be able to help and to let him know if we needed anything else.

As Frank and I headed out to the dock, I informed him that we would have to pass Matt's boat in order to get to Eddie's, so we'd have to be careful. Although we didn't see any movement on the *Lucky Man,* we moved past it quickly. Being back on Eddie's boat brought back memories of the stormy night when I heard Matt's heated voice, berating Christy in front of Peter and whomever else was there. Now that I knew that he was a sociopath, I felt frightened once again. I shivered and Frank put a protective arm around me.

"Don't worry now, Sam," he said. "Just keep telling yourself that nothing will go wrong as long as I'm with you."

I tried to smile as though he had succeeded in reassuring me but all I could think of was Chuck falling to the ground, blood running down the side of his face.

I found the binoculars that Eddie had told us about, and some blankets as well, while Frank put in a call to the captain to let him know where we were and what we were doing. The captain told him he had a cop watching the boat as well. Christy was to be escorted onto the vessel to get a few personal items out of her cabin, before she had to disappear. Frank told him we would keep an eye on things as well, and let him know if we saw anything.

The night was clear with scattered clouds, bright stars and a moon that looked so big I thought I could touch it. There was a slight breeze that sent a chill through me as I sat with a blanket wrapped around me on a spot on the upper deck just beside the control panel, which gave me a perfect view of Matt's boat. Frank and I took turns with the binoculars, as he explained the most vital part of a stakeout, which basically consisted of the importance of staying awake.

"I have to tell you, Sam, you're really hanging in there with this. You could have bailed on numerous occasions but you didn't. I've worked with cops that didn't have the guts you've got."

"Yeah," I told him, "but I may regret my decision if Matt beats me to a pulp."

"He won't, Sam."

"How do you know that?"

"I know it because I'm not leaving your side until we get this guy."

I smiled at him, hoping he meant it.

"Are you afraid?" he asked thoughtfully.

"Yes, I am. I can't believe that I was . . . that I thought I was . . ."

"Hey, Sam, don't be so hard on yourself. It happens more than you think."

"You warned me and I didn't believe you." Suddenly, I was on the verge of tears, and then I was in his arms, holding him tight, feeling his warmth against my body. Then he looked into my eyes as he slowly kissed me on the lips.

"Frank . . ."

"I know, Sam."

But what did he know? That he was moved? That I had no right letting him kiss me? That his relationship with Susan wasn't already in enough trouble? But all that didn't seem to matter now. We were on this case together and if there was danger, he would protect me.

I awoke to a beautiful sunrise. The sky painted in shades of pink and purple with a touch of orange on the horizon where the sun was shimmering on the water. The day would be cool and clear. I sat feeling the cold against my cheeks and acutely aware of calmness within myself.

"Good morning," Frank said, "Coffee?"

"Oh yes. I definitely want coffee."

I was getting real tired of not having a toothbrush and fresh underwear. I would have to remember to keep some extras in my bag. I excused myself and went down to use the head. Gazing in the mirror I was horrified that Frank was seeing me looking like this.

I cleaned myself up as well as I could, thankful that I had some lip gloss.

I wasn't sure how I felt about Frank, but I knew that I didn't want him to see me at my worst. I ran my fingers through my hair and went back on deck. This was as good as it gets.

Frank took a look at me, then a second glance.

"What?" I said, defensively.

"You look good, really good."

"Oh, please!"

"You do. In just minutes you have transformed yourself."

"Meaning?"

"Meaning, never mind. I can see your sense of humor is failing you."

"No, it's not."

"Sam, trust me, it is."

"Look, I'm tired and stressed out. A little more sleep and I'll be back to normal, my sparkling personality intact."

"Promise?"

"Yes, I promise."

We sat drinking coffee, watching for Matt. Neither one of us mentioned the kiss despite the fact that it was obvious that we were both thinking about it.

"Thanks." I said.

"For what?"

"You know, for comforting me last night. It was nice."

"It sure was." He said, smiling.

It was just about seven when Frank called the hospital to check on Chuck. The doctor said he was going to be okay, but would need to get a lot of rest. He would continue to keep him comfortable with medication. Frank asked him to tell Chuck we would be there as soon as we could, and that he had notified his family. They should be visiting some time today.

The next call was to the captain. Frank told him there was no activity on the boat and we were leaving to go grab some breakfast. He was told that Christina and Tiffany were fine. They would be out this morning with an officer to go through their stuff.

We headed out, looking for some place out of the way to have a bite to eat and stumbled upon a cute little place near the water. It had a dock attached to it which I thought was pretty cool, so we went in. Even though it was busy it didn't take long for us to be seated. I was starving since my dinner had consisted of toast, and I had eaten like a bird. I'm not much of a breakfast person so I ordered a BLT on rye toast. Frank, feeling embarrassed, apologized to the waitress, explaining that I could be difficult. She shrugged it off, and said it was no big deal.

"Where is Matt's sidekick these days?" he asked me.

"Pete? I haven't seen him since the other night at the party. You know what is odd? He seems different to me, I said, thinking about him.

"How?"

"I don't know, I can't put my finger on it. The last few times I've seen him I've just had a weird sensation, like he reminds me of someone."

"Sam, these situations make it pretty easy to let your imagination get the best of you."

"Yeah, I know."

Our breakfast was served and we both concentrated on the task at hand, eating. It felt good to have a decent meal, my stomach was full and I was feeling more energetic. We drove back to the marina with plans to clean up the boat, get back to Temecula, and over to visit Chuck. As we pulled into the parking lot, we saw a police car parked up front and a young man in uniform standing guard in front of the *Lucky Man.* Apparently Christina was on board. I wondered if Tiffany had come with her or stayed safely with the police.

Once on Eddie's boat we took our places on deck and again observed the activity on the *Lucky Man.* Frank had the binoculars and said he saw some movement. One person on deck, a female. He wasn't sure who it was so he handed me the binoculars. It was Christina, wearing a white blouse and faded blue jeans. I watched for Tiffany, thinking she may be with her, realizing that she was not an occupant as Christina had been.

I wondered what she was doing walking around in plain sight. Here she was about to disappear; change everything in her life as she knew it and yet she seemed so unaffected.

I didn't see anyone else but I continued to watch and wondered what she was up to. I had thought she was supposed to be gathering her things but it didn't look as though she was doing that. Her cabin was in another area and I thought it was strange that she was taking her time. Something was wrong. I could feel it.

"Frank, isn't she supposed to be getting her stuff off the boat?"

"Yeah, it seems to be taking her a long time. Let's go check it out."

We walked over to the cop and Frank flashed his PI License as he began asking questions.

"Have you been here very long?"

"Sir?" asked the gentle voice.

"I'm curious to know how long you have been here. I understand from Captain Wessler that this was supposed to be a quick trip."

"Yes, sir. The lady asked me to give her more time; she said she was having a difficult time finding some of her personal belongings. I asked her to be quick about it, but it does seem to be taking her a long time."

"This is Miss Parker, my assistant. She knows Miss Andrews and would like to offer her help packing her things. Would you mind if she went aboard and asked Miss Andrews if she would like her assistance?"

"Well . . . I'm not supposed to allow anyone on board," he said, unsure.

"Would you like me to call the captain?" Frank asked, forcefully.

The young officer stood there, unsure of what to do. He looked up at Frank. "Yes, sir. I think you should. My orders are not to allow anyone on board."

I felt relieved that he had not caved in under pressure and I smiled at him. He shot me back a slight smile, satisfied with himself. Frank called the captain and put the officer on the phone. Within a minute I was boarding the boat.

I moved slowly up the stairs to the upper deck, the only sound was the squawking of the seagulls flying overhead. I peeked around the corner and saw Christina sitting with her back to me, at the small table. She appeared to be fiddling with something. I almost said her name when a small object dropped to the floor. It was a capsule. I stayed quiet, watching her as she picked it up. She took a bottle and dropped several pills in it one by one; I listened to the clinking sound they made as they dropped into the plastic bottle. I took a deep breath and walked in.

"Hi, Christina," I said.

"What the hell are you doing?" she demanded.

"I was just coming to see if you needed some help." I told her.

"Why did you come up here?"

"I'm trying to help you," I said, wondering why she was being so aggressive.

"Well, I'm fine." she said, casually.

"What are you doing?"

"Oh, I'm . . . I'm getting my vitamins," she told me, her eyes averting mine.

"Can I help you pack?"

"No, I'm not taking much, my bag is downstairs. Meet me outside. I have to get one more thing."

"Let me help . . ."

"If I had needed some help I would have asked for it," she told me. She was wearing faded blue jeans that sat low and tight on her hips and a white blouse, and despite the strained look on her face, was as beautiful as ever. I wondered why, hating Matt as she had, she had agreed to stay on this boat as captain. Had that been part of the blackmail? There were so many questions to be answered and it seemed clear that Christina, no matter how much she had talked the night before, was in no mood to answer them now.

"Why don't you wait on the dock if you feel the need to baby sit," she told me, slipping a few more capsules into the bottle. "I can't stand being watched, okay? Is that too much to ask?"

I had no choice but to leave, although I wondered where she had piled the things she had come here to get and if she had looked in the compartment by her bunk and found the box missing. But I realized that the best I could do was to wait for her to leave the boat and keep my eyes open to see what she was carrying.

"No, it's not. I'll wait outside," I said solemnly. I turned and descended the stairs; my gut telling me that something was not right.

I shot Frank a look as I got off the boat.

"She okay up there?" he asked.

"Fine, she'll be right down."

Frank immediately told the officer we would be right back. We walked a little ways down the dock.

"What's up?" he asked.

"I'm not sure. When I went up on deck she was filling a pill bottle. I didn't think anything of it so I made my presence known and offered to help her finish up. She's wound up pretty tight. She just about bit my head off for offering."

"What kind of pills?"

"She said they were vitamins."

"Vitamins?"

"Yes. That's what she said."

"So what you're telling me is that you are suspicious of her because she's stressed out?"

I thought about that for a moment. "Yeah, I guess so."

"Sam, let me ask you something. Wouldn't you be stressed out if you were in her situation?"

I nodded.

"You need to chill out, Sam. She's got to be on the edge. Don't toss her over."

I took a deep breath, still not convinced that there wasn't something else going on. I just couldn't put my finger on what it was at the moment.

"Okay, Frank. I'll chill."

"Good."

We walked back and waited for Christina. She appeared with a black duffle bag and the officer escorted her to the car. She ignored me as she past by, giving me a knowing smile as she got into the car. A chill ran down my back.

The car pulled away and Frank started for the lot. "Ready to get back home?"

"You go ahead, I have to take care of something. I'll see you later."

"Sam, what are you doing? The cops have everything under control. Let them do their job."

"I'm going to visit a friend," I told him. "Do you mind?"

"Just stay out of trouble," he responded, clearly annoyed. And I suppose I couldn't blame him. Still, given what had happened, I thought he'd give me a little more credit.

Getting into my car I had a weird sensation that I couldn't shake.

Why was Christina so paranoid about having me help her? Last night she seemed so fearful but today she seemed almost defiant. I could understand being stressed out and afraid but this was different. And what the hell was that weird smile she shot me? It was the type of look you'd give to someone who cut you off on the freeway, not someone who has helped you to escape a dangerous situation. For God's sake, I had helped her to get away from Matt.

There was more to this, I knew it. All I had to do was find out what it was. I also knew Matt was out there somewhere and that I was probably in danger. I wondered if he would be on Coronado or may have headed back to Temecula. Deciding I had to know, I called his house in Temecula and expected to get the machine. The voice that answered was Peter's.

"Thank God it's you," I said, reassured.

"Sam? Are you okay?"

"Yes, I'm fine. Is Matt around?"

"No, I haven't seen him."

This felt odd to me. He was Matt's right hand man and yet, apparently, he didn't have any idea what was going on? He knew something; I could feel it. I didn't want to give him any information so I wrapped up the call.

"If you talk to Matt will you tell him I called?"

"Sure. Where can he reach you?"

"I'm home," I said, glad that I wasn't.

I didn't know how much Christina had shared with Peter about her relationship with Matt but it would be strange, if Matt was violent as often as Christina had said he was, if Peter had not seen many demonstrations of his bizarre behavior. I do know he was on the boat that night, and saw Matt freak out, yet he ignored it. I wanted to know why. Maybe that was their game. But this was more than a game, it was about a group of criminals, it was about murder and it had to end.

As questions swirled in my head, I walked down the dock until I came to the *Lucky Man.* I didn't want to think about what I was doing as I hoisted myself on deck. I only knew that I had to find out if there was any information on board that might clear this up. I knew the cops were in the picture now and that I should butt out and go home but I couldn't. This had become an obsession for me. It's all I could think about, and although it was dangerous, I couldn't rest until I had some answers.

I started up top and worked my way through the vessel, searching for anything that might give me a clue about Ron's disappearance. I was looking around one of the cabins when I heard a motor grow louder and louder and then finally, stop. I heard voices, laughter and then felt a slight jolt that nearly made me lose my balance. I wanted to take a look but found the cabin window faced the parking lot. Then the sway of the boat told me someone had boarded.

I felt my heart rise into my throat as panic set in and I looked around for a place to hide. The head was my only option so I slid inside, locking the door. That was when I heard the rumble of a motor again, this time growing fainter and fainter. And then there was no sound at all and I realized that whoever had boarded the boat must have left. Had it been the police, I wondered, coming back to retrieve more of Christina's belongings? Unlocking the door, I passed through the cabin and went down the corridor to the galley where, peeking around the corner, I saw Matt, wiping down fishing gear.

Pressing myself into a corner, I was trying to figure out what to do next when I heard him greet someone who, for a single horrifying second, I thought might be me. And then I saw Christina come in and give him a big hug.

What the hell is going on? I thought. They talked like nothing had happened. What was she doing here? She was supposed to be off preparing for a new life.

"Look, Christina," I heard Matt tell her, "I'm feeling great. A little time out fishing will fix any kind of a disagreement."

It was a Jekyll and Hyde moment. Could this be the same man I had last seen shaking his fist at me in rage as I ran to get away from him? He was casually dressed in jeans, a white polo shirt and boat shoes and from where I stood, seemed so relaxed and carefree as he spoke to Christina. She, on the other hand was visibly angry, and as their conversation continued, her stance stiffened.

"You need to take your medication to keep your mood in check," she said. "You know what can happen if you ignore that. We've been through this before."

"When I'm on the medicine I don't feel like myself," he protested, throwing down his tackle and pacing as he rubbed his temples. Clearly he was becoming agitated. "It's making me feel sick, and I'm losing time. Sometimes a few hours and sometimes I can't remember days at a time. Did you know that I don't even remember the end of my party? And there have been other times, too. You have me taking this shit and then before I know what is happening, I'm feeling dizzy and black out."

He continued to pace as his anger grew.

"The doctor told you there would be side effects."

"I'm going to get back to the doctor," he barked, "but until then I'm not taking anymore pills."

"You're going to take them, Matt," she insisted, putting her hands firmly on her hips. "I'm not going to argue with you about it. I'm the one who has been following you around all your life cleaning up your mess. This is the least you can do for me. Here take it."

I heard the pill hit the floor.

"God damn you!"

"I said no," he said, irately. "What are you doing? Put the gun away."

"Are you going to take your meds or not?" she demanded. "I told you that sometime you'd push me too far, and now you have. Make up your mind, Matt. Either way you lose."

"Christina, please put that down. You wouldn't . . ."

"Don't fuck with me. It's my turn now."

I moved to the left and saw Christina standing over Matt, gun straight down by her side. Edging back around the corner I got to my feet. The sirens were moving in and as I held my breath I thought there might be hope. If I could only delay the moment when she would pull the trigger.

"You're not alone," I said, coming out of my corner, standing in the doorway, arms at my side. "You can't afford to do this, Christina. I don't know how you even began to think you could get away with it. Hear those sirens? The police are already here.

234

And in that moment when I had caught her unaware, Matt moved forward to take the gun. The explosion deafened me, and I could see his lifeless body slump to the floor.

CHAPTER 21

Frank had heard that I had been on the boat during the shooting and he was definitely not happy.

"Damn it, Sam," he said. "I told you to stay out of trouble!"

I was silent on the other end of the phone, knowing I had screwed up. After hearing the lecture from Captain Neil Wessler, who had come in from home to berate me personally, I was numb to any more expletives directed my way.

"Are you finished?" I asked quietly.

"For now," he said, clearly still pissed off at me.

"How's Chuck feeling?"

"He's going to be fine. He won't be too pretty for a while, but he's up and around."

"Did you have a chance to ask him about who he thinks it was? Who beat him up?"

"He says he didn't see but he's betting on your pal, Matt."

"Please tell him I'm sorry. I'm coming home as soon as they are done with me at the station."

"Good, then I can keep an eye on you!" and then, his voice mellowing, "Are you okay? For God's sake, go home and get some rest. I'll call you later and check up on you."

I have to admit, I was wiped out. I was still trying to figure out what had just happened. All I knew now was that Christina had made me look like a big fool and I didn't know why. She had gone on and on about Matt and how crazy he was, and just when she was safe with a new life to look forward to, she shows up on the boat, hugs Matt and then proceeds to shoot him. I still didn't know what happened to Ron and found myself feeling like I was running in circles trying to figure it all out.

Before I left the station, Captain Wessler told me that Matt had made it. He was in bad shape but he was still alive. The hospital would keep him posted on any developments. Then he told me again how I had interfered, and made it perfectly clear to me that I almost got myself killed in the process. He told me to go home, and said he didn't want to see me on the island again, not until this was wrapped up. I was taken back to my car and escorted by the police as far as the bridge. Obviously, they didn't trust me when I promised I'd go home.

The ride was relaxing and I was glad, in an odd way, that Matt had made it. That conversation between him and Christina had me feeling uneasy. Although I had believed that Matt was the dangerous one, what I had heard seemed to tell a different story. I had the feeling that Christina was the one running the show, and I couldn't for the life of me figure out why she would come back if she was so afraid of him. Of course, then I had to wonder about Tiffany. Was she lying too? I thought about it the whole way home, still not any clearer about what had transpired.

The security of my house was like a warm blanket. I was so happy to be home and alive. Although I tried not to think about it, I couldn't forget that moment when Christina had held a gun on me. At any time she could have blown me away. Captain Wessler and Frank were right. I had been a fool to face her unarmed, but what they don't realize is that I didn't go looking for her. I shook the thought from my head and went to take a hot shower.

Once cleaned up and fed I sat in front of the television watching movies through the night, finally going to bed around two.

I called Frank as soon as I woke up at eleven. I had slept a long time and felt rested, but uneasy about what had taken place over the last few days. I had to face the fact that it was my fault that Chuck had been beaten to a pulp, and possibly the reason that Christina had shot Matt as well. I didn't like being responsible for all this. It weighed hard on my mind and I was feeling like I might break down and cry and never stop.

We met at Milano's on Rt. 79 south. After ordering iced tea and sandwiches with fries Frank began firing questions at me. I went through the sequence of events that had led up to the shooting and then told him that I was sure that the fight between them had to be about more than his medication. Why would she shoot him over that? He agreed that it sounded like something else but added that if Matt has been abusing her for long she may have just had enough. That was true, I suppose, but it still didn't sit right.

We headed back to the office to look through the case file and Frank put a call into the hospital so I could talk to Chuck. He said he'd be fine and not to worry. He would be out of there in no time. I felt really bad but he didn't seem to blame me; that was nice because he could have.

"Frank, I've been thinking about something," I said when we hung up. "Chuck thinks it was Matt but doesn't know for sure, right? Could it have been someone else?" I asked.

"Oh man, Sam. We know he has a temper, we know he had been in custody, and we know he was pissed off at his sisters. Chuck was there just after he was released. Matt waited for him and beat the crap out of him."

"How did he know that Chuck was involved? He only saw him once, when he was in a rage as I left the party."

"That's right. That's how he knew Chuck was helping you out."

"But when he and Christina were arguing about the medication, he said he didn't want to take it because it made him feel sick and have blackouts. He told her he didn't even remember the end of that night because she had made him take it during the party."

"You believe that?"

"He didn't know I was there. Who would he be trying to snow by saying it? Christina has been in control of his medication and it was making him sick and that's why he refused to take it. That is what he was telling her."

"So what?"

"She didn't seem to care. She didn't ask about his blackouts or anything. She just held him at gunpoint and demanded that he take it. Does that sound like someone who is afraid?"

"So what are you saying?"

"I think she's lying."

"You're kidding, right?"

"No, I'm not kidding."

"You're losing it, Sam. I'm sorry but you are."

"Why would you say that?" I demanded. "Think about it for a minute. Does that behavior sound logical to you?"

"Sam, go home and get some rest. Go see a movie or meet with some friends or whatever else you like to do for fun. Take a break from this. I'll call you in a few days."

"What are you going to be doing?"

"I've got to go to Vegas. I have another case I need to follow up on. I'll call you."

"Okay. Hey are you taking Susan?"

"Go home and mind your own business for a change."

I took that as a no and wondered if he was telling me the truth or just wanted to get rid of me. Probably, he was telling the truth. After all, he wasn't the one obsessed with this.

I needed some questions answered so I headed straight to the hospital to see Chuck. He had some visitors so I waited in the lounge. I hate hospitals. I have never been a patient in one and I hoped it would stay that way. The smell made me woozy and I couldn't get past that, although I do have the utmost respect for those who work in the medical field. They save lives, for God's sake. But knowing this didn't make me feel any more comfortable.

After about fifteen minutes a heavyset nurse came and told me it would be okay to go in. I was nervous to say the least and I held on to the guilt for getting him involved and ultimately beat up.

When I walked into Chuck's room, I was startled to see how battered up he was. His left eye was bruised and swollen and he had what looked like a very deep cut over his lip. His right arm was in a sling, due to a dislocated shoulder, but he was sitting up, a smile on his face.

"Hi, Sam," he said, grinning. "I'm glad you finally got around to visiting."

"You look awful," I told him. "Does it hurt?"

"Your charm is devastating. But it's okay. To answer your question, I'm a little sore but I look worse than I feel. As a matter of fact I'll be getting out of here in the next day or so."

"Chuck, I'm really sorry for getting you involved in this. I didn't think anything like this would happen. I don't even know how I got myself into this."

"This isn't your fault, Sam," he assured me. "Get that through your head. I wouldn't have helped you out at all if I hadn't wanted to. You stumbled on to something big here. I know it, Frank knows it and now the cops know it. You should let them take care of things now. You were hired to find out who was after Ronald Gregory, and ended up into something much more than you can handle. Let it go."

"I know. It's just hard to drop it after all I've been through. I feel like it's not over and I have this thing about not finishing something I've started."

He shifted in his bed and I noticed his right hand was bandaged. Whoever had attacked him clearly meant business. He was probably lucky to be alive.

"I talked to Frank," he told me. "We are going to stay with it but we both think it's time for you to let it go. We'll continue to keep you informed. We don't need you getting hurt too."

"I know," I said. "Probably, you're right. I'm sure there is someone out there who is getting divorced or needs a will."

"Don't be disappointed," he said, coaxing me. And I realized how different his attitude toward me was now. Maybe I had actually done something to impress him, although, I couldn't even guess what it could have been. "You have done a great job," he said. "You should be proud of yourself."

"Since you think so, would you mind if I ask you a question? Frank said you didn't see the person who did this to you. Is that right?"

"I didn't even have a chance. I was hit from behind and was knocked out."

"So, you don't know for sure that it was Matt,"

"It had to be Matt," Chuck told me, frowning. "He'd just been released and he must have seen me in the car when I cut him off the night you left the party. We had been face to face. Besides, who else would have done it?"

"I'm not sure. I'm just not convinced it was him. It could have been anyone."

"Sam, stop trying to save this guy."

"I'm not trying to save him. The fact is, you didn't see who it was, so how can you be so sure it was him?" I inquired, suddenly annoyed. He of all people should know that you can't assume it was him just because he could have been there. Why couldn't he accept it?

"Okay, I don't know, but I had three hundred bucks on me in cash and it wasn't taken. As a result, I don't believe it was a random attack. It was someone who wanted to get to me for some other reason. The only one I know that may have wanted to do this to me is Matt Andrews."

I left wondering if he was right. Perhaps it would be good for me to get out of town. I needed to distance myself from all this, to let it go. Hopefully, I'd be able to look at it all with new eyes. Plus, I have to admit, I was scared. There was a very real possibility that I was in danger. Matt and now Christina were behaving rather unpredictably and I had the feeling that it could have been me beaten to a pulp instead of Chuck. Yes, I would get myself out of town. I would sleep and read. I love the beach this time of year so I packed a bag and headed south. As I drove down the freeway I gazed at the long stretch of road in front of me, and the mountains that went on as far as the eye could see. Though they were brown this time of year, the shadows added a beautiful shade of lavender when the sun hit them at this time of day. The promise of the beach with its cold air and rousing surf took me back to a time when I was a carefree teen. That was a time when the beach cured everything. A broken heart? Hit the beach. Flunk a class? Hit the beach. And so on.

Exiting the freeway, I moved on to Del Dios Highway, a narrow two-lane road that curved and swerved above a small lake. The further I drove, the better I felt.

The coast is lined with beautiful small towns but I decided to head to Carlsbad, my favorite, because of its unpretentious nature.

From Del Dios, I hopped on the 5 Freeway and within a few minutes found myself heading down 101, otherwise known as the Coast Highway. I didn't yet know where I would spend the night but was confident that, this time of year, reservations weren't necessary. At Pompo beach, I parked the car. No one was around except for a handful of surfers, all enjoying the robust waves that made them rise before the sun and spend their evenings in water so cold they would freeze without the aid of the thick wetsuits that kept them so well insulated.

Removing my sneakers, I rolled up my blue jeans. The seagulls were out in full force, snatching up fish and trying to hold on to them, as other seagulls waited patiently for one to drop, diving to catch it in midair. This was a group that didn't like to share. The loud baulking sounds made that clear.

It felt good to have my toes in the cold sand, and as I stood watching the sunset, I felt like a weight had been lifted from my shoulders. The beach could still cure all.

I decided to spend the night at a cute little bed and breakfast on the beach, only because the rates were low out of season. I was in the mood for something comforting for dinner so I went to a little Italian place and sat at a window table in order to watch the people walking by. I ordered lasagna and a glass of red wine and ate slowly, enjoying the ambiance and listening in on the conversations around me. Later, completely relaxed, I fell asleep to the sound of the ocean.

CHAPTER 22

After two days of peace and quiet, I was eager to find out what was happening in the real world. It had been good for me to get away; I could see that now. I felt I would be able to view things more rationally now. The traffic was heavy most of the way home but it didn't bother me in the least.

It was just before four o'clock, and although it was Sunday, I decided to see if Frank was in his office before I headed home. His truck was in the lot so I headed up.

"Well, it looks to have done you some good," he said, when I had told him where I had been. "You look much better."

"Thanks, I feel pretty rested. Is anything new?"

"As a matter of fact there is. I have been leaving messages for you at home. Don't you check them?"

"I haven't even been home yet, what's going on?"

"Well," he said, sitting beside me on the small leather couch, "the other day I met with the captain and a few of the guys working on this case. The captain had one of his officers conduct a full investigation of Matt Andrews' habits over the past several years. They've discovered that he hasn't been involved in any criminal activities, as far as they can tell. He's gone totally legitimate except for the fact that he's still in contact with some of the guys in the ring. From what they tell me, he has a few enemies because he has gotten out. Don't get me wrong. He did his share, and he's become very wealthy because of the businesses he's set up along the way, probably using illegal money I might add. And he has some psychological problems."

"I know," I said. "His sister told me he spent some time in hospitals."

"Yeah, well I guess he's gotten progressively worse and has been on some medication to keep him from going over the edge. Anyway, we don't think he killed Simon or anyone else for that matter. At least not lately."

"Do they know if he had someone else do it?"

"That's not likely. He took care of his burial and paid all his debt so that his family wouldn't be burdened."

"You're serious." I was stunned. The picture of Matt that I had drawn in my mind didn't allow for this kind of philanthropic activity.

"Yes, I am. Now what the captain wants is to come up and see what we, or should I say, what you have put together on this. I'm supposed to call him as soon as I hear from you."

"That's fine. Give him a call now."

According to Captain Wessler, he was going to gather up his files and meet us at Frank's office tomorrow morning at nine sharp. I was to bring everything I have.

The next morning, I woke at six and went to the gym. It felt good to sweat and my energy level was once again in high gear. Home and showered, I had a quick bowl of cereal, drank some coffee and headed out. Upon my arrival, about fifteen minutes early, the office was dark. Sitting on the steps, I thought about what might happen today and found myself eager to see if the police had found anything else of interest.

Next to arrive was the captain. As he was locking his car, Frank pulled in and they walked up together. We said our good mornings, Frank put on some coffee and we got down to business.

We were told that, at the last minute, Christina had decided she wasn't going to have any part of the witness protection program, saying that she didn't want a new life. She said that, although Matt was crazy, he needed her. This had apparently come as a surprise to Tiffany, who had said that Christina had been calling her for months, reminding her of how cruel Matt had been when they were children. Christina had also said that Matt was presently involved in some type of criminal activity, something really bad, but had never told her exactly what she meant. The problem was that she always broke down, crying hysterically, before she could reveal precisely what she was talking about.

Tiffany claims that she came here to help Christina and discovered her brother's strange behavior to be quite unsettling, that sometimes Matt seemed to be perfectly normal, and that at other times he would go berserk, although when asked about it, he denied that there was anything unusual about his behavior and acted as though it never happened. Tiffany thought that her brother needed help but Christina wouldn't let her call a doctor, saying he was on medication to control it, and she had been put in charge of making sure he got it. Tiffany was getting so many mixed messages that she wasn't sure what to do, so she just took Christina's word for it. When Christina decided to leave the station, Tiffany told us she, too, had been acting strange but just thought it was stress related. Tiffany had admitted that she hasn't been around her siblings for a while and hadn't heard anything about any of this until, several months ago, when she had started getting calls from Christina telling her that Matt was after her. She said she wasn't sure what to believe anymore and just wanted to go back home.

Again I went over the conversation I had heard between Christina and Matt on the boat before she shot him. I told the captain that I thought it was odd and asked if he had checked the boat for medication of any kind.

"It's at the lab as we speak." He said. "We should be hearing from them anytime."

I gave the captain copies of all my notes on the case and looking over them, we all agreed, we were missing something.

"What I don't understand is what happened to Simon? Why was he killed?"

"Simon was with us," the captain said.

"What do you mean by that?" I asked curiously.

"He was an informant for the FBI."

"What?"

"I just found out myself," Captain Wessler said. "Apparently he went to them and offered to be an informant. He knew Andrews was out of the mob but said that he could still get some stuff on him and the others, a couple of big fish, as he called them. We think one of these guys knocked him off."

"So Matt Andrews really isn't active anymore?"

"Not recently, but someone wants us to think he still is."

"What about Peter Manning, the guy that is his sidekick?" I queried.

"We're checking it out. He would seem to be the most likely suspect but we can't rule anyone out."

Frank went to the safe and turned everything he had over to the captain. He was going to take it back to the station and check it out and see if it brought us any closer to finding out what was really going on.

Once Captain Wessler had left, Frank and I went to get a bite to eat. It was two o'clock and I was starving. After a turkey sandwich, I headed for home, leaving Frank to catch up on his reports. Upon returning home, I added all I had learned today to my own notes. As I re-read them, I realized that some of the gaps were beginning to close although not everything made sense.

As I stared at the index cards, I put myself through a free-thinking exercise that I had been taught by my criminal law instructor who believed that solving crime was about using all available sciences as well as some intuition and common sense. The exercise itself consists of allowing all things to be possible as long as the facts could be supported. Even the most ludicrous ideas were allowed. I love this because it allows me to completely open my mind to any and all possibilities and sometimes that's all I needed in order to read between the lines.

My thoughts were flowing and when an idea came to mind I created a flow chart of the activities that had occurred. It was a little off but the possibilities were there. Against my better judgment I decided I had to check it out.

Once again, I found myself traveling the back roads of Temecula in search of the truth. I had come up with a theory that might hold up but it was a long shot. I was willing to gamble on it.

The day was bright and warm, and people were out washing their cars and working in their yards, a clear sign that spring was on the way. With the news that Tiffany would be at Matt's I decided to head over and have a chat with her. Walking up the path to the door, I remembered how sweet Matt had been to me when I had sprained my ankle running to get out of the rain. It all seemed like it was so long ago.

I knocked on the door and within moments, Tiffany opened it. She was dressed casually in navy slacks and a crisp white blouse. Her hair was tied back in a sleek ponytail. She looked tired and older somehow. She was surprised to see me and cautiously invited me in.

"Hi Tiffany," I said. "How are you holding up?"

"I'm not sure. My sister just shot my brother and I don't know how it all happened. I guess I'm not doing too well. What are you doing here?"

"I'm trying to piece this together and I thought you might be able to fill me in on a few things."

"I really don't know how I'll be of any help."

"I won't take up too much of your time," I assured her. "I just have a few questions."

"Okay. Do you want anything?" she asked as she led me into the living room.

"No thanks."

"Have a seat."

We both sat down on the couch at opposite ends. I noticed the sun was shimmering through the window, forming a brilliant shadow on the wall. Bringing my attention back to the task at hand I got right to the questions, not wanting to give her time to change her mind.

"The other night you had said that Christina was filling you in on what Matt had done to you as kids. Do you remember that?"

"Yes."

"What did she tell you about that?"

"I was the baby, and apparently I don't remember a whole lot about being a kid. She told me that Matt had done some mean things to me but I don't recall that. I honestly can't recall him being anything but wonderful. I looked up to him. But she tells me that I have blocked it out."

"What about all the stuff you had said the other night?"

"I basically repeated just what she had told me to say."

"So, Christina told you to say all those things about Matt? Why did you do it?"

"She said I don't remember because it was so horrible. She told me it was a defense mechanism and said that I had

had to forget the things he did to me or I would have gone crazy or something."

"Do you have any idea why she would insist you lie to us about your recollection of Matt?"

"No, but whenever I told her that my memories of Matt were pleasant, she got upset and said I was wrong. Christina has always been high strung, but I've never seen her like this."

"And you really don't recall any bad behavior from Matt."

"No. He was a lot of fun. He took good care of me."

"How about since you have been here. Have you noticed anything odd about the way he's acted?"

"Most of the time he is just as I remember him. He's fun and smart and really nice. But occasionally he did become irate and very volatile. And then he's not like himself."

"Is there any pattern to it?" I asked her. "I mean, is there any particular kind of event that triggers his change in mood?"

"No," she admitted. "But now that you mention it, it usually happens in the evening, just after he takes his medicine."

We were getting somewhere. I knew it!

"I had heard that Christina gave him his medication. Is that true?"

"Yes. She was very insistent on him taking it, even after he had told her it was making him feel terrible."

"Did he say that?"

"Sure, it wasn't any secret. He had even complained to me that Christina was too involved in his life. He said she acted like his mother."

"Why did he put up with it? He's a grown man."

"He said he felt sorry for her. You see, she had lost her husband a while back and had a difficult time getting over it. That was when he offered her a job as the captain of his boat. He thought that she might meet some friends that way. You know how involved that marina scene is. He wanted her to start a new life, and eventually move on."

"But you said that you and Christina were afraid for your lives." I reminded her. "Why didn't you just leave?"

"Christina convinced me that Matt was dangerous. She spent a lot of time here, I though she knew what was going on. She said she didn't leave because he begged her to stay and take care of him; she couldn't just walk out when he'd been so generous, getting her on her feet and all. He is generous. Even Christina never said he wasn't that. Anyway, she thought that I should come and see him and then together we could convince him to check himself into a psych hospital."

"So what happened?"

"Most of the time he seemed fine, so I told her I couldn't go along with it, but she wouldn't listen to me. She said that it's what he needed. Then when I saw him enraged one night, I had to believe Christina was telling me the truth."

"And now?"

"I don't know. I figure she must have been afraid of him, otherwise why would she have shot him?"

"That's what I'm trying to find out." I said, and then changing the subject, "do you know what kind of medication he's on?"

"It's called Librium."

"Isn't that to relieve symptoms of anxiety?"

"I don't know."

"Does Matt suffer from anxiety?"

"Christina says he's manic depressive, borderline psychotic."

"Why would he be taking medication for anxiety if he's manic depressive?"

"I don't know. Maybe we should call his doctor?" Clearly my questions were frustrating her.

"Look, I'm sorry," I told her. "But I'm just trying to figure this out. It wouldn't make any sense to be taking medication to treat something else."

"So, let's call his doctor," she said, pressing.

"He probably wouldn't tell us. That kind of thing is confidential," I told her. "But we could . . ."

"What?"

"We could look in his room," I said, hoping she would agree.

"I don't know . . ."

"Why not? At least we'd know the truth." Matt's room was impeccably clean and held the faint scent of men's cologne.

"No." I told her. "We won't find anything in here. We need to check Christina's room."

"You're right." She said, moving down the hallway. "Well, are you coming?"

We opened the medicine cabinet and found several prescription bottles. One by one we read them out loud and discovered that they were in fact, all anti-anxiety drugs. The buffet of pills included Xanax, Valium, and Ativan, as well as Librium. With so many different prescriptions I could only guess that there was a possibility that maybe he could have a problem. But then a thought came to mind. The bottles all held quite a few pills, yet none were nearly empty. Also, why would he have to be forced to take them if he was addicted to them? It wasn't adding up. I also had to consider the fact that after he took his medication he became violent. These drugs wouldn't have that effect. Just the opposite. Why was he becoming violent after being given anti-anxiety medication? I wondered if it could be an allergic reaction or something like that.

"Are there more of these pills around the house?" I asked.

"I don't think so," she said. "I'm pretty sure they're all kept up here," she said.

I thought about whether I should . . . of course I should. I put the bottles in my purse and we headed back downstairs.

"Is there anything else?" She asked, moving to the door.

"Just one more thing, I said. "Has Christina mentioned anything about having Matt sign over property or bank accounts or anything like that?"

"Oh my God!" Tiffany exclaimed. "That's it."

I left Tiffany and headed straight to Frank's office, explaining to him that I needed to know how to get some pills checked through the lab at the police department. We put in a call to captain Wessler and he made arrangements to get it handled, adding that he had the results of the pills from the boat and was going over them.

Finally, I felt like we were really on to something. I was sure of it now.

CHAPTER 23

It hit me while sweating on the stair master. I had a gut feeling and had to follow through. I put in a call to Frank and told him to meet me at Matt's in one hour. Arriving early, I knocked on the door. Tiffany opened it just enough to peek through.

"This isn't a good time." She told me, closing the door.

I stuck my foot in. "I need to talk to you."

"I've said enough," she said.

"Talk to me, Tiffany. It can't matter now."

"But it does," she said.

"I'm not leaving until you let me in."

She looked back and reluctantly pulled the door open. I stepped inside. There on the couch was Christina dressed in a black dress pants and a coral blouse.

Surprised I said, "Hi Christina."

"What are you doing here?" she asked, angrily.

"I have a few questions."

She reached for her purse and slowly pulled out a .38, eased the safety off and pointed it at me. "Ask away."

Staring down the barrel, I tried to remember why I was there. I glanced at Tiffany, who sidestepped away from me toward the chair across from the couch where Christina sat.

"You've got two minutes," she said.

"Why are you lying about Matt?"

"I'm not lying. He's an animal. You've seen him."

"I know you've been drugging him. I just want to know why," I told her.

Tiffany seemed to shrink in her chair.

"I'm not drugging him. He's on medication so he doesn't harm anyone, including himself," she said, eyeing Tiffany.

"He's on anti-anxiety medication," I reminded her. "I'm not sure how familiar you are with them, but they make you mellow, not flip out. What are you really giving him?"

"That's enough questions," she said, looking tense.

"Put the gun down." I told her.

"I'm the one giving orders." She said getting to her feet. She circled around and stood in front of the large bay window that overlooked the front yard. "Now, why don't you move over there and have a seat on the couch," she said, motioning with the gun. "You should have left it alone."

As I moved toward the couch I had a clear view out the front window to the street and caught sight of Frank's car passing by. I kept my eyes on the gun, hoping he wouldn't be too late. Then I heard a door open from down the hall, and a familiar voice.

"T," he called. "We need some grub. It's been seven hours since we fed our friend and we need him alive."

I looked at Tiffany in shock. It was her!

She stared at me, motionless, as Peter walked in and gave Christina a kiss.

"I didn't know we had company. Why didn't you tell me T?" he said, looking at Christina.

I swallowed hard. "You're T?" I asked her.

"It's my nickname for her." Pete said. "Nice to see you again, Sam."

He looked just like Peter but the voice...where did I know that voice from?

"Oh my God!" I said.

He moved close to me and smiled. "You're smarter than I gave you credit for, Miss Parker."

"Why, Ronald?"

"It's complicated."

"Tell me anyway," I said.

"I don't think you'd understand."

"Try me."

"T...Christina wanted to settle down, have a normal life. You know the routine, nice house, a couple of kids. She was getting tired of all my business deals failing and came up with an idea to get what she wanted."

"This was your idea?" I asked her.

"I saw how things always came so easy for Matt and to be honest, it pissed me off. I tried to convince him to bring Ronald on as an equal partner but he wouldn't do it, so I had to make him realize that he couldn't continue to handle the businesses himself."

"So, you thought drugging him would do the trick?"

Apparently Christina wasn't ready to admit the truth, even now.

"Go ahead and tell her. We're going to kill her anyway." Ron demanded.

She took a deep breath. "He had to feel himself loosing control," she said, glancing at Tiffany, who had not moved.

"And you were happy to make sure he did just that?"

"Someone had to," she said, admiring her manicure.

Rapidly I sorted through everything I had learned. I stared at Tiffany. "You knew all along, didn't you?"

"I..." she glanced at Christina and Ron.

"She didn't know about any of it." Ron told me. "After reviewing Matt's will, we discovered that Christina had not been the benefactor as he had told her. We needed Matt to sign over all assets to T, and since he wasn't cooperating, we decided to bring in Tiffany to help him make the decision to do so."

"So, you're home free," I said.

They glanced at each other. "Not exactly," Ron told me.

"He didn't sign?"

"No."

"Is that why you became Peter?"

"Right again, Sam."

"Nice work. Who did it?"

"Why? Are you planning on getting something done?" he asked.

"Maybe."

"It was Dr. Everett Weatherbee."

"He's good," I told him.

"Yeah, I thought so too," Ron said, smiling.

"Where's Peter? Did you kill him too?"

"Too?"

"You wasted Simon didn't you?"

He rubbed his forehead. "We had to. He was causing some problems for us."

Christina was visibly irritated. "Okay, that's enough!" she shouted, lifting the gun a little higher, now pointing it at my chest.

"No!" Tiffany begged. "Don't do it."

I stiffened, taking in a shallow breath. So, this is it? This bitch is going to blow me away. I knew I shouldn't have trusted her. For some strange reason I felt very aware, and I wondered if that's what happens when you're about to die. Where the hell was Frank anyway?

All at once Frank burst in behind Christina and held a gun to her head. "Freeze or I'll blow you away!" he commanded. "Drop it."

Ron bolted towards the kitchen, attempting to escape through the back door. The gun fell to the floor as cops moved into the house, dragging him back in to join us.

Peter had been found in the basement of the house. He was gagged, bound and drugged, a prisoner, being held by none other than Christina and the man who literally stole his identity.

When questioned about why I was chosen to participate in his scheme, Ron was delighted to expound upon the fact that I would get in the way of any "real" investigation by tainting evidence and throwing the cops off balance. He had cleverly fed me information along the way, to keep me from losing interest, counting on my amateur status to get him off. He severely underestimated me.

Due to the quick thinking and bravery I had demonstrated during this ordeal, Chuck and Frank have decided to take me on as a PI trainee. My first official case will be assigned to me next week, when I get my badge.

THE END

EPILOGUE

The call came as I was about to head out to the gym. Frank told me that the police had raided several of the locations where the businessmen mobsters had lived and worked, and had located millions in stolen goods and jewels as well as a variety of illegal drugs and weapons.

The base of operation was the construction company that Ron had told me he had owned. He did not own it and never had. It was a company that was owned by Matt Andrews and managed by Jon James.

Ronald and Christina had fallen in love. Ronald had been a career criminal but grew tired of that life. He was jealous of Matt, his longtime friend and a millionaire, and came up with a scheme that would allow him to retire a wealthy man. Christina was hesitant, but greedy. They began to frame Matt for crimes committed by Ron and his cronies, one of them going as far as calling on Dr. Weatherbee to change his identity to mirror Matt's. Then they began to slowly poison Matt, lacing his anxiety medication with PCP, which explains the violent behavior that was witnessed by so many.

They had planned to kill him but couldn't actually do it until he had signed over all assets to his loving sister, Christina, also known as Tina, at least to Ron. Clearing up the mystery of the note signed by T.

The videotape and the safety deposit box were found to have information that pointed to Christina as the person responsible for the whole operation. Ron was planning to frame her and take everything. He had another appointment set with the good doctor to have his identity changed again. He wouldn't be keeping it.

Matt recovered from the gunshot wound inflicted by his sister and was cleared of all criminal charges. He continues to run his businesses successfully and is dating none other than yours truly.

AUTHOR BIOGRAPHY

Maria Pease is a copywriter originally from Long Island, N.Y. She lives in Temecula, California with her husband, Scott, and her children, Steven and Alexandra. This is the first of the Samantha Parker Mystery Series.

CPSIA information can be obtained at www.ICGtesting.com
Printed in the USA
LVOW101034050513

332322LV00001B/45/A